A YACHT TO DIE FOR

A Maggie Bloom Mystery

A YACHT TO DIE FOR

LINDA S CLAYTON

iUniverse, Inc.
New York Lincoln Shanghai

A YACHT TO DIE FOR

iUniverse, Inc.

For information address:
iUniverse, Inc.
2021 Pine Lake Road, Suite 100
Lincoln, NE 68512
www.iuniverse.com

This is a work of fiction. Names, characters and places are used fictitiously, and any resemblance to persons living or dead is unintentional.

ISBN: 0-595-28101-X

Printed in the United States of America

For Paul, the best husband I've ever had

Acknowledgements

I am grateful to Rachel Sowers for giving me a job in her shop in Harbour Town. All the time she thought I was working, I was really in the back room writing.

Since my experience with boats is limited to gorging myself on cruise ships, I am indebted to Charlotte and Ray Faust and Suzanne Mousseau for all the nautical information they provided.

I am also indebted to Susan Vitek, who got sandy, wet and sunburned helping me think up ideas for the cover.

A huge thanks to Carolyn Clayton-Luce, who made my computer and manuscript behave after I badly botched both. This book would not be in print without her help.

And great big hugs to all my children: Paul, Alicia, Carolyn, Tim and Dan for believing that I could do something other than prepare fantastic meals. There is no longer any need to put *Here Lies A Good Cook* on my tombstone.

INTRODUCTION

▼

The figure wore a wet suit. Like a shadow, it crept through the dimly lit salon, slid silently past the galley and moved up the stairs to the wheelhouse. Here, it lingered in front of the electronic equipment filling the dash. A gloved hand rested briefly, almost tenderly, on the teak instrument panel.

Minutes later, the shadowy figure slipped overboard and swam underwater to the mouth of the harbor. At the retaining wall, it surfaced once to search for the narrow opening between the wall and the banks of the shore.

Finding the break, the figure swam through and reached solid ground below the eighteenth green of the Harbour Town Golf Links. There it up-righted a yellow kayak, pushed it into the water and paddled away, unseen by anyone but Mrs. Gloria Goldstein, who was looking out the third floor window of her son's Cutter Court villa.

Mrs. Goldstein never told anyone about the lone figure in the kayak because later that day she and her daughter-in-law had a disagreement about child rearing, and she returned earlier than expected to her Teaneck, New Jersey home.

CHAPTER 1

▼

The explosion rocked the golfers on the eighteenth hole of the Harbour Town Golf Links, making Stanley (Chip) Wuchinich of Medina, Ohio the first person in the course's history to drive a golf ball through the window of a Ketch Court villa using a putter.

Passengers on the ferry to Daufuskie watched in horror as a cloud of acrid black smoke obscured the famed lighthouse and blotted out the sun. Another deafening blast, this time from deep in the bowels of the ship, reduced the forty-five ton, $1.3 million luxury yacht to an airborne pile of fiberglass and aluminum.

I had just settled my neck onto the shampoo basin at the Harbour Town beauty shop. The explosion scared me so badly, I sat straight up, banging into the ample chest of Lydia, the proprietor, who was applying Medium Ash Brown and Honey Blonde to my roots.

"I'm so sorry," I said as I flung a clump of wet hair out of my eyes, "but what in the world was that?"

"Dunno, Maggie." Lydia scrambled to catch a bottle of peroxide before it smashed into the sink. "But something bad. That's for sure."

I didn't stick around to chat with her. I hoisted the gray, beauty shop smock around my waist, pounded out the door and followed the smoke to the burning harbor.

Panicked tourists clogged the crushed oyster shell path that rimmed the yacht basin. Security men tried to keep them back as police wrapped yellow tape around a large portion of the harbor. Fire burned from an oil slick in one of the slips. I picked my way through scattered debris and tried to see which boat had blown up.

"Maggie! Maggie Bloom!" A hand grabbed my arm and held on for dear life. "Where's Joey? Have you seen him?"

I looked into the terrified eyes of Tiffany Archer.

"He hasn't come back to the boat. I fixed lunch for him and everything, but he didn't come." Her eyes searched the harbor as she talked. "Oh, my God, Maggie, that's near the *Second Chance*." She pointed to a cloud of black smoke and burning fuel. "Joey was working on Andrew Roop's boat this morning. Come on."

She still had my arm in a death grip, so I had no choice but to trot along after her. I longed to ask why her present husband was working on her ex-husband's boat but figured this probably wasn't the time for in-depth questioning.

Ignoring cries of "you're going the wrong way, lady," Tiffany pushed through the crowd of people trying to get away from the harbor. As we approached the scene of the explosion, a soot-covered fireman held out his hands and said, "You can't go any further, ladies. Please get back."

"I have to." Tiffany scanned the harbor. "My husband is there somewhere. He's working on…"

Andrew Roop's boat, the *Second Chance,* was gone. In its place was a carpet of blazing oil.

A groan went up from the knot of people watching the police activities. About twenty feet from the burning boat slip, rescue workers lifted a body from the water and placed it on a stretcher.

Absolute terror made Tiffany shake off the cop who tried to grab her arm. Since we were still attached, she pulled me under the police tape, and together we ran to the ambulance. We reached the van just as the body was being loaded.

The corpse didn't resemble any human shape I had ever seen. Covered by a sheet, it looked like a large lump with no distinguishable body parts. Only the foot, which dangled off the stretcher, indicated there was a human being, or what was left of one, under the cloth. The foot wore a sandal: a brown scuffed sandal, with one of the straps torn.

Tiffany dropped my arm and let out a yelp. Prepared to catch her if she sank to the ground, I was startled to see her clap her hands and do a little dance. She kicked up her heels a few times, shouted a few hallelujahs, then composed herself and said, "We can go now."

People around us backed away as if they were in the presence of an un-medicated crazy lady. At that moment, I wasn't so sure myself. I put my arm around her shoulder.

"Are you okay? If you're not having some kind of seizure, maybe you should tone it down a bit."

Pure joy radiated from her face. "Don't you see? It isn't Joey."

I shook my head. "We don't know that, Tif. All we can see is a foot."

"Just to be sure I'll look again, but I'm positive. I don't even need to see the face. Joey doesn't wear sandals. In fact, he doesn't own any." She pointed to a very dirty foot and to the dark hair on the deeply tanned leg and ankle. "For sure it isn't Joey. He has red hair and peach colored fuzz on his legs."

She thought for a minute and then said, "And it isn't Andrew either." His legs are white, and they don't have hair." She shuddered. "I never liked his legs."

*   *   *   *

Tiffany waited while I ducked into the beauty shop to get the dye washed out of my hair. Lydia wasn't there so I stuck my head into the sink, turned on the faucet and let the water run until it was clear. I toweled it dry and combed it with my fingers.

Unwilling to go home, Tiffany and I went to the general store, bought ice teas and carried then to a bench in front of Fashion Court, one of the snazzy boutiques in Harbour Town. I was pleased to see that my friend had calmed down and was able to speak without giggling and dancing.

"So tell me," I said as soon as we had settled ourselves, "what on earth was Joey doing on the *Second Chance*?"

Tiffany took a sip of her ice tea and leaned back against the bench. "I know it sounds strange. Anne Roop called Joey yesterday and said one of the engines on the boat was heating up. She couldn't find their regular mechanic so she begged him to take a look at it. She said otherwise Andrew was gonna fix it himself. When Joey heard that, he said he didn't mind doing them a favor. You know how he feels about amateurs fiddling with boats." Her eyes clouded. "I just can't figure out why she didn't call someone else. I mean it's kind of funny after everything with Andrew." Her voice trailed off. "Anyway, I guess *Second Chance* meant his life with Anne. He bought it after we were divorced. Remember? One day he came sailing into the harbor with a brand new boat and a brand new wife."

How could I forget. It had been such a salacious scandal that every single resident of our community knew every single sordid detail. We had heaved a collective sigh of relief when Andrew Roop finally stopped obsessing about his ex-wife. Most of us had been embarrassed when he talked about her; saying no other man was ever going to touch her "perfect ass" and "magnificent tits." Not that anyone thought his description of Tiffany was inaccurate. In fact, he could have added a few remarks about her velvet, tanned to perfection skin, huge green eyes and silky blond hair that never needed the help of a Clairol product.

We also thought he was obsessed to the point of stalking her. Tiffy told me Andrew followed her at night when she went home from her waitressing job to her North Forest Beach apartment. When she started dating Joey Archer, we all held our breath, waiting for something horrible to happen, like Tiffy finding some hapless animal cooking in her stew pot, but Andrew left Hilton Head and when he came back with Anne, he seemed to have forgotten all about his ex-wife.

"Joey even turned down a charter this morning," Tiffany said as she fished a lemon wedge out of her drink. "He said in the long run it would pay off." She frowned. "I don't really know what that was supposed to mean, but I'm sure it was something good." Her face brightened. "He's taking me out to supper tonight. He told me to wear something sexy."

We were interrupted by the clang of heavy gold bracelets banging together. The overpowering scent of Chanel perfume mixed with the heavy aroma of blooming Confederate Jasmine made my eyes water. My best friend, Lucy Rotblumen, plopped down on the bench and smoothed her scarlet caftan around her legs. In the bright daylight, her orange hair flamed like the sun. She peered at us through huge, round sunglasses.

"I swear, that blast scared me so badly, I nearly swallowed my tongue." She poked the aforementioned organ with her finger to make sure it was still attached. "It's a good thing this didn't happen yesterday, or I'd be toast. Anne hosted a little luncheon on the *Second Chance*. Some sort of fundraiser. I'm not exactly sure which charity got my $5000."

A tiny frown tugged at her lower lip, then quickly disappeared. "It doesn't really matter. Julius's accountant will write it off on our income tax."

Julius was Lucy's much older husband. According to Fortune magazine, he was worth many, many millions. He'd made his money buying distressed real estate—first in New Jersey and eventually all over the country—and turning run-down buildings that no one wanted into desirable properties.

In case anyone thinks Lucy was born to the world of wealth and privilege, let me hasten to say that her family manse in Bluffton, SC consisted of a sagging, gray clapboard house, a chicken coop, a rusted Chevy on blocks in the dirt front yard, and a yellow dog named Bud.

Even though she is as tall and sturdy as a pine tree and would be suited for work as a lumberjack, she spent five years of her young adult life working as an exotic dancer at the Purple Pelican on Hwy 170. The folks who owned the club weren't picky about their dancers. As long as the girls were willing to wrap their legs around a pole and roll their eyes in ecstasy, the bosses were happy. Her stage name was Flame.

One night when she was dancing, Julius Rotblumen, who was wasting time waiting for his Ferrari to be repaired in Savannah, wandered into the club and sat at a table close to the action. When he suddenly grabbed his throat and turned bright blue, Lucy jumped off the stage, grabbed the significantly shorter Julius around the waist and skillfully applied the Heimlich maneuver until a piece of pretzel flew out of his mouth and across the room.

After that, they fell in love. Honestly. They really did. Julius was so short, the top of his forehead rested on Lucy's sensational chest. She was tall enough to step on him, should the urge arise. But they adored each other. He showered her with extremely ostentatious jewelry and houses. I always held my ears when she tried to tell me what she gave him in return.

She and I became best buddies in the third grade, after she told Martin Warner that if he tried to take my lunch cookies one more time, she would squash him into beetle juice. For emphasis, she showed him a large, reddish brown stain on her hand, which was really a combination of indelible ink and chocolate brownies, but to Martin's terrified eyes looked like the spattered remains of one of his friends. Lucy has always had a flare for the dramatic.

She poked me on the arm. "Have you heard the news?

I shook my head. I was nearly blinded by the glare coming from hoop earrings big enough to hold a shower curtain.

"They think they know who was on the *Second Chance* when it blew up. I just had a phone call from Harriet Sloan, the Roops' neighbor.

She said the word is that Nathan was on board. Apparently he had gone there to fix something on the boat and had decided to take a nap."

I heard Tiffany gasp. Instinctively, I took her hand. Nathan was Nathan Roop, Andrew's twin brother. No matter what Tiffany felt about her ex-husband, this had to be a bad shock for her.

"Since there's not much of a body to bury, I understand, if it is Nathan, there will be a service immediately." Lucy glanced at Tiffany, who was hunched over in misery. "I'm so sorry, dear. I suppose I could have phrased that more delicately."

Tiffany brushed tears out of her eyes. "That's okay. Nathan was a nice man. He always treated me good. I feel bad for him."

Not half as bad as he must feel, I almost said, but I kept that thought to myself.

CHAPTER 2

▼

At 4:30 the next afternoon I squeezed into my one good black dress, discarded a pair of black, strappy sandals as too frivolous for the occasion and stuck my feet into a pair of old, black pumps that were a size too big. By curling my toes, I could manage a kind of forward shuffle that would have to do. For the hundredth time, I wished I paid more attention to my wardrobe. But, since my life revolved around dogs, paint and vegetable gardening, I didn't have much need for fancy duds. Now I didn't have time to buy anything new.

I drove as fast as the speed limit allowed to South Forest Beach Drive. The Roops provided valet parking, so I left my Jeep Cherokee in the hands of a teenager, who looked distinctly disappointed at my non-Mercedes vehicle, and minced my way up the front walk to Roop's spectacular ocean-front home.

Anne Roop stood at the door welcoming people who had come to pay their respects. As I waited, I noticed she had twisted her sleek, dark hair into an elaborate braid. She wore a simple but I'd be willing to bet, extremely expensive black dress which ended a good six inches above her knees. I also noticed that on her feet were strappy black sandals.

When it was my turn, she offered a slender, limp hand and acknowledged my offerings of sympathy with a wan smile. As I turned to go into the house, I could have sworn I saw her impatiently check her watch; a diamond encrusted Rolex.

Uncertain what to do once I was inside, I pretended to search for a friend while I secretly admired the house. There was a magnificent needlepoint rug in front of the fireplace: delicate magnolias and sprigs of laurel and jasmine carefully stitched on a background of royal blues and soft greens. I had to admit it added the finishing touch to the luxurious ivory brocade couch and wing chairs. I closed my eyes and inhaled deeply, smelling the rich furniture oil on the gleaming Louis XIV desk.

Beyond the living room was a lovely sunroom, with white wicker furniture covered in the palest shades of pink, yellow, blue and green glazed chintz. And beyond that was a perfectly manicured lawn, kidney shaped swimming pool and the sparkling Atlantic Ocean.

As I wandered around the house, I listened to snatches of conversation. The main subject was, obviously, Nathan.

"My dear, did you hear? His body was so burned it was almost unidentifiable, but the corpse was wearing that Rado watch Nathan bought in Singapore. Also his gold herringbone chain. That's how they were able to identify him."

"I can't believe Nathan is dead. I just saw him; it can't have been more than a day ago. Such a good-looking man. They certainly didn't act like twins, did they? Nathan was so debonair."

At a buffet table laden with enough food to feed all of South Carolina, I loaded up on shrimp, some kind of bite-size puff pastry, a wonderful smelling paté and, since I was watching my diet, stalks of tender, crisp celery. I showed extreme restraint by dipping only one stalk into a creamy lemon vinaigrette.

Although the house was full of people, I didn't see anyone I could sidle up to and dish the dirt with. I spoke to a few people I knew from the tennis club, but that was about it. I decided I'd adequately fulfilled my social obligations, and it was time to go home.

As I made my way through the crowd, I saw that Anne had left her post at the door and was milling around the room, talking to those who were anxious to hear the gory details. I recognized Walter Dowling, a tall, dignified man with white hair and an impressive tan. He was a local lawyer.

Andrew Roop blocked my exit. He stood in the entrance to the room, signs of the recent tragedy evident on his face. His eyes were lackluster and red rimmed, and his face had an alarmingly white pallor. Water dripped from the cuffs of his navy trousers, and there was a big black smudge on his pale blue, Brooks Brothers shirt. He certainly wasn't dressed for mourning.

"Dowling, I'm glad you're here," he said.

Anne rushed to his side. "Darling, I'm so happy to see you. Would you like to freshen up?"

He looked more like he needed a transfusion. Oblivious to the fifty or so people crowding his living room, Andrew strode past her to the mirrored bar and selected one of the Waterford decanters. His hand shook as he splashed a large amount of vodka into a crystal highball glass. After he downed the contents, he spoke to Walter.

"Nathan shouldn't have been on the boat. I can't understand it." Andrew ran his hand through his curly dark hair. "He was supposed to be on his way to Miami. The last thing he told me was he had a meeting scheduled with the Gantner brothers. Phil Lincoln was going to fly him down in the Cessna."

As he reached for the decanter, Anne put her hand gently over his. "Please don't, Andrew. This isn't a good time for that."

Fifty people moved closer, unwillingly to miss a single second of this startling scene. Embarrassed to be witnessing what was should have been a private conversation, I pressed against an enormous, built-in fish tank, hoping I was invisible. A large orange and blue fish with spiny red gills and bulging eyes swam over and blew bubbles at me. It sucked at the glass as if it were trying to bite my shoulder.

Andrew swayed on his feet, the combination of alcohol and shock about to deliver a one-two punch. "Dammit, don't tell me what to do. When, according to your perfect standards, would it be a good time to drink? My brother just died. Does that qualify?" He stared at her out of owl eyes. "Just leave me alone."

The crowd gasped.

Like a mother dealing with a difficult child, Anne tried to lead him to a sofa. He cursed as his shin banged against the trunk of a porcelain, jade green elephant with a blooming amaryllis on its back.

"Why don't you sit down, darling? Or better yet, go upstairs and take a rest. I can have Freedom fix a hot bath for you."

"I can fix my own damn bath," he snarled. He shook himself free. "I have things to do."

"Of course you do," Anne said soothingly. "If you'd prefer to stay here, I'll ring for some hot coffee."

This was awful. I wished someone would grab Andrew by the neck and haul him out of the room before he said anymore.

Andrew, however, obviously didn't care who heard him. He ignored his wife and appealed to Walter. "How could this have happened? The police are stupid incompetents. They have no idea what caused the explosion." His eyes narrowed craftily. "But you don't have to be a rocket scientist to figure it out."

"What do you mean by that?" The lawyer looked uncomfortable.

"That son of a bitch Archer was working on the boat yesterday morning." He pointed an unsteady finger at his wife. "Why did you call him? There aren't enough other mechanics in the harbor, you had to go and call that particular one? I told you I never wanted to see that son of a bitch again."

Behind his back, Anne spread her hands helplessly to the assembled guests and shook her head. To Andrew she said, "I think you're a bit confused right now, darling. And I hope you're not accusing that boy. This has been a terrible shock. It's no wonder you're distraught."

Andrew poured himself another drink. "Don't talk to me about the boat. Or Nathan. I don't want to hear."

Anne moved from behind the couch and spoke to Walter Dowling in a low voice. Within seconds we were all politely but firmly escorted to the front door and bid a hasty goodbye.

CHAPTER 3

▼

The island was so abuzz with the news of Nathan's death that I had trouble getting any work done. I'd already had four phone calls from folks wanting to talk about the *Second Chance,* and it was only nine thirty in the morning.

When the phone rang for the fifth time, I grabbed the receiver and said, "Speak."

It was my ex-husband, Peter, and he was very excited. Knowing he had a habit of talking for at least a half hour every time he called, I tucked the cordless phone into the crook of my neck, so both of my hands would be free to work on my painting. As he droned on about his new partnership in a Boston law firm, I only half listened. This picture of a Bernese mountain dog was driving me nuts.

Mrs. Jordan had insisted the dog had the temperament of an angel, and she wanted it to be evident in the painting. That might be true, but the dog also had a distressing habit of putting his paws on my shoulders, knocking me to the ground and rummaging in my crotch with his nose. Try as I might, I just couldn't find the angelic quality Mrs. Jordan was talking about.

I squirted more Payne's Gray onto my palette and absentmindedly wiped my fingers on my shirt. No one should have a Bernese mountain dog on Hilton Head, I decided. These dogs needed snow and a keg of cognac around their necks, not sweltering heat and sand fleas.

Mrs. Jordan had once brought the dog to my house, "so he can become accustomed to you and your environment." Wally and Willow, my English cocker spaniels, had fled in terror when he zoomed through the living room, knocked a Murano glass pelican off the coffee table and taken a drink out of the toilet.

Peter's enthusiastic voice jerked my concentration back to the phone conversation.

"I just wanted to run this by you to see what your reaction would be. What would you say if I brought my new boat to Hilton Head? It would be a real kick to sail down the Intracoastal. Hell, I might even go on to Florida. Maybe sail to the Keys."

He sounded young and enthusiastic. I longed to ask him why he kept calling to tell me about his life when it was his fault that I wasn't in Boston sharing it with him. Instead I said, "It's up to you, Peter." Then, because I simply couldn't help myself, I added, "Will you be coming alone?"

"What difference does that make?"

I recognized his crisp lawyer tone. I sighed, realizing that even though he was apparently interested in seeing me again, he still wasn't going to share all the details of his private life. After a few more minutes we hung up, agreeing that he would sail to Hilton Head and I would meet him in Harbour Town for a drink.

Talking to Peter broke my creative mood. The painting temporarily forgotten, I stood at my sunroom window and looked out at the marsh. A snowy egret posed like a porcelain statue on a piece of driftwood. Beyond it, a warm, afternoon sun sparkled on Broad Creek and on the white sailboats on the Intracoastal Waterway.

As I always did after I talked to my ex-husband, I wondered what my life would be like if I'd forgiven Peter for his midlife crisis. Against my will, an image of Christine, the blond home wrecker, flashed through my mind. It still galled me that Peter had gone for the vapid, vacant type: someone whose head served mainly to hold bleached hair. Without thinking, my hand flew to my tangled mess of chestnut hair that always looked like birds had made it their home. I also glanced down at my chest. It was respectable, but certainly couldn't compete with the perfect, surgically produced twin peaks that Peter's bimbo sported.

The bimbo had made an all out effort to seduce Peter, and it had worked. The divorce had been messy. I tried not to think about the days of roaming the empty house in Sudbury, Massachusetts, assessing myself critically in the full-length mirror and existing on diet Coke, Ben and Jerry's Chubby Hubby and buckets of Xanax.

When I finally couldn't take it any longer, I ran away to Germany for an extended stay near my oldest childhood friend. That hadn't worked out very well either, because I'd been accused of murder. But that's another story.

So, it was extremely puzzling and a bit distressing that Peter was calling again and acting as if nothing unpleasant had ever happened between us. He's even had the gall to call me his "Blooming Meadow of Magnolias," which had been his special way of teasing me about my name when we were married. As a child, my name was Magnolia Meadows. When I married Peter Bloom, well, I'm sure it's obvious. Say all three names together and I guarantee no one in the room will keep a straight face.

So here I was, a divorced, forty three year old woman living on Hilton Head with two dogs and supporting myself by painting furniture, flower pots, coat hangers, glasses or pictures. I slapped color on any material that would accept paint.

This artistic career certainly hadn't been a deliberate decision. When I moved here, I'd had this dream of opening a business called Maggie's Munchies. I planned to bake delicious goodies and sell them to cafes and stores. The only problem was, I only had one munchie recipe, and that was for double fudge chocolate chip cookies. When folks wanted me to vary the product, I was finished. I don't cook very well.

My plunge into painting was accidental. I decorated some planters for my front porch with pansies and tulips and other flowers. A friend thought they were pretty and asked if she could buy them. After that, the whole thing snowballed. It amazed me to see what price people would pay for some daubs of paint on the handle of a toilet plunger.

It isn't what you'd call serious art, but it pays the mortgage. And it sure isn't what I was trained to do. I have a Fine Arts degree from the University of South Carolina, but there isn't much demand on Hilton Head for an expert in 17th century Flemish art.

But, all in all, I couldn't complain, and I was proud of myself that I could now talk to Peter without wanting to cut off an essential part of his anatomy, which had been my fervent desire in the Xanax days of yore.

I was so lost in reverie, it took Wally and Willow's frenzied barking to make me realize the doorbell was ringing. I wiped my hands on my jeans and followed them to the front door, scooping up a pair of panties and a bra that Willow had retrieved from the laundry hamper.

A weeping Tiffany Archer stood on the porch with my copy of the *Island Packet* under her arm. Dismayed, I led her into my studio and sat her down in one of the yellow wicker chairs.

"I guess we should skip the pleasantries. What's wrong, Tiffy? You look like you've lost your best friend."

Tiffany fished a crumpled Kleenex out of her pocket and wiped her eyes. "I don't know where else to go. Or what to do." She wadded the tissue into a wet ball and searched for another.

"Here, use this." I offered her a fairly clean painting rag and waited for her to collect herself.

"It's about Joey." Tears spilled down her face, making her green eyes look like pools of ocean water. "Joey's gone missing. He's disappeared. I haven't heard from him since the day before yesterday."

Relieved, I smiled and said, "I thought it was something terrible. Did you guys have a fight? That's not unusual, Tif." I geared myself up for a pep talk; lovers have quarrels—God knows I knew enough about that—and they patch things up. "He might be working on a boat somewhere," I said. "Or maybe he's out on a run with tourists and had some kind of mechanical trouble. There are a million possible explanations."

"No, you don't understand. His boat is still at the pier." This time the tears cascaded down her face. "He would never leave the *Moon-dancer*. You know how he feels about that boat. He says I'm his first love and she's his second. I just know something awful has happened to him." She honked loudly into the rag. "And that's not all. Sheriff Griffey says he's a suspect."

"A suspect in what?" I asked, trying to make sense out of what Tiffany was saying.

"In the murder of Andrew's brother. He says Joey could have had a motive." The words tumbled out of her mouth so fast I had a hard time following her. "The sheriff questioned me for a long time this morning about how I must know where Joey was and how I could be an accomplice. He says it was murder—not an accident. They found some gizmo—I don't know what you call it—in the mess of stuff after the explosion. Someone deliberately blew up the *Second Chance,* and the police think it was Joey."

I laughed out loud. "What a ridiculous idea! This is Hilton Head, not Miami. We don't have murders here, Tiffy. We're nice people. Surely you misunderstood. I mean, let's face it. Everybody on the island is talking about Nathan's death, and everybody has a theory about it. But honestly, I've never heard a word about murder. "Besides," I continued, "even if there is some evidence of a crime, why pick on Joey? He didn't have any ax to grind with Nathan. I thought they didn't even know each other very well."

Tiffany gulped and blew her nose again. "Because Nathan looked so much like Andrew, them being twins and all. The sheriff says Joey confused them and thought he was blowing up Andrew."

"I still don't understand, Tiffy. That's all ancient history with you and Andrew. Joey knows you love him. And he's never been jealous of Andrew."

Tiffany suddenly got very busy playing with the painting rag, folding it over and over into neat pleats.

"What? Is there something you're not telling me?" I massaged my temples with my fingertips. The beginning of a fierce headache lurked behind my eyes. First Peter's news about coming to Hilton Head and now this.

Tiffany's red-rimmed eyes looked straight into mine. "A while ago me and Joey went out with some of his buddies. He never drinks, but I guess that night he had some beer. Someone mentioned Andrew's boat, and Joey said Andrew didn't deserve a boat like that since he only used it to 'troll for chicks'." She winced. "And then Joey said someone should do Harbour Town a favor and blow both of them out of the water. Somehow, Andrew found out what Joey said, and he told the police. But Joey wouldn't do anything like that, Maggie. He had too much respect for boats to blow them up."

"But not too much respect for Andrew." It was out of my mouth before I could stop myself.

"That's a mean thing to say. Joey doesn't like him very much but it's kind of a, you know, distant dislike. Not personal. Mostly because Andrew wasn't nice to me." She looked down at her hands. "Joey knows I love him more than anything."

I tapped my teeth with the end of a paintbrush while I studied Tiffany. The girl's shoulders sagged in misery, and the sad look on her pale face was enough to break my heart. The story had all the attributes of a good B movie, I decided, but I didn't believe Tiffy had the imagination to make it up. I had to admit she was genuinely distraught. She also spoke the absolute truth when she said Joey loved boats. Everyone in the harbor knew he treated them as if they were holy objects. And there was no doubt he loved Tiffany. To my knowledge, he had never displayed even the slightest bit of animosity towards Andrew. He was as open and guileless as his wife. I wished, though, that Tiffany had a few more concrete facts, such as exactly what device the sheriff found that led him to the conclusion of murder.

"How do you know all this? I have to tell you, it sounds crazy."

Tiffany unfolded the *Island Packet* and pointed to an article. "If you don't believe me, look at this. I nearly died when I read it this morning, and then the sheriff came to ask me all those questions." Tears streamed down her face. "I just can't stand this."

I took the newspaper and scanned the headlines. Sure enough, there it was in bold, black print.

"LOCAL MAN SOUGHT IN BOAT EXPLOSION"

"A spokesperson for the sheriff's department has confirmed that Wednesday's explosion in Harbour Town was the result of foul play. Investigators have found the remains of an explosive device among the wreckage of the 45-ton yacht, Second Chance.

The spokesperson said the sheriff's department is actively seeking Joseph H. Archer, 31, a fishing boat captain.

When contacted for a statement, Andrew Roop, 43, the owner of the Second Chance, said there had been problems in the past with Mr. Archer. He further stated Mr. Archer had threatened him with bodily harm, and he had intended to ask the sheriff for a restraining order against Archer. He also said reports that Archer had been hired to work on the Second Chance the morning of the blast were false. "I would never have let that person anywhere near my boat," he stated.

Anyone with information regarding the whereabouts of Joseph Archer is asked to call the sheriff's department."

Tiffany tore the paper out of my hands and hurled it across the room. "That is such a lie. Joey never threatened Andrew. How could he say such a thing?"

Her ponytail swinging behind her, Tiffany paced the length of the sunroom. "I swear I've never been madder in my life. That is a wicked lie, what Andrew said about Joey being at the *Second Chance*. He knows perfectly well his wife called and asked Joey to fix something. Remember? I told you about it the other day."

I nodded in agreement.

Tiffy stopped her pacing and knelt down to throw her arms around Wally. The dog responded by energetically licking her face. Without looking up she said, "Will you help me, Maggie?"

"I don't know what I can do," I began. Out of the corner of my eye I caught a glimpse of my dog painting in progress. I had to have it finished in two weeks. Mrs. Jordan wanted it framed and hung for a dinner party she was giving.

Straightening up, Tiffany planted herself firmly in front of me. "The sheriff thinks he did it and I know he didn't. Please, Maggie. Joey is in trouble somewhere. I just know he is. Please. You're so smart and clever and can think up what we can do. If you don't help, I don't know what I'll do."

I looked at her eager face and felt my heart sink. There was no doubt in my mind that Joey Archer was in trouble. I prayed that for Tiffy's sake, he also wasn't up to his baby blue eyes in murder.

CHAPTER 4

▼

Even to my untrained eye, I easily spotted the deputy assigned to watch the *Moondancer*. He lounged against the railing of the pier, pretending to study the parasailers above Calibogue Sound. As an added touch, he had a pair of binoculars slung around his neck. When I jumped aboard the boat, he turned slightly, his eyes sweeping over Tiffany and me.

"He's been here since this morning. They're hoping Joey will come back so they can catch him." Tears welled up in Tiffany's eyes. "I just can't stop crying. This seems so impossible. And I couldn't find anyone who's seen Joey. Everyone just keeps saying 'no' and giving me funny looks."

The bright morning sun made Tiffany's hair shimmer like a cloud of golden cobwebs. Dressed in pink shorts and a mint green halter-top, her legs and arms tanned a healthy, pale copper color, Tiffany looked like everyone's idea of the perfect girl next door: not like someone who could be an accomplice in a murder plot.

I glanced around the *Moondancer*. The deck was well polished, the boat smelled faintly of fresh paint and the small galley and main cabin were neat and tidy. It was obvious that a loving hand tended her regularly.

"I don't know what you think you can find here," Tiffany said. "I know every inch of this place. Besides, there's not much room to hide anything. See?" She waved her hand around the small cabin. "We have a couple of storage bins but nothing more."

I tossed my Vera Bradley tote bag onto a bench in the cabin and pushed my sunglasses up on my head. "I'm not thinking that something is hidden. If we assume Joey is innocent, then we can also assume he wouldn't have hidden anything. But there might be something that you never noticed before, some ordinary thing that would help us now."

"Like what?"

"I don't know," I admitted. "But we have to start somewhere. We'll search this place thoroughly, and then we'll figure out how to tackle Anne and Andrew."

I squeezed past Tiffany to inspect three small cupboards above the sink. Ceramic dishes with a tiny, pink heart pattern were neatly stacked on a top shelf. Glasses of various sizes lined the bottom. Two plastic mugs with "Joey" and "Tif" printed in red letters stood on the spotless sink. I opened drawers and peered into the cabinet under the sink.

"I think this stuff about Joey wanting to harm Andrew is a lot of nonsense," I told Tiffany. "You had completely severed ties with Andrew; no alimony or anything to keep you two in touch with one another. Right?" I peered into a blue and white flour canister in the shape of a cat.

"Right. Andrew was so nasty when I told him I wanted to leave, I just left. He kept telling me I was a little fortune hunter. I told Buddy Simpson, you know, Arnold's brother—well, he was my lawyer—I told him to tell Andrew's lawyer that I didn't want anything. And I'm glad I didn't." Tiffany rubbed at a spot on the sink with her thumb. "I never did like the stuff that was so important to Andrew. All those fancy cars and that house."

I straightened up and wiped my hands on my shorts. "Andrew must have had some good points or you wouldn't have married him."

"Oh, he did." Tiffany blushed. "In the beginning he was so sweet, and I thought he was such a good looking man. He told me he liked to walk on the beach and fish. Things like that. But that only lasted for a few months. Then he began to drink so much and drinking made him act funny. I really didn't like him when he was drinking. That was before you and I knew each other."

I nodded, thinking about the first time I'd seen Tiffany. It was at the Harbour Town swimming pool, and she had been teaching a bunch of local kids how to do the backstroke. I'd watched as Tiffany, a strong swimmer, cut effortlessly through the water, and the kids eagerly tried to copy her motions. After the lesson, we'd struck up a conversation, and I'd instantly liked her positive, bubbly personality and her genuine enthusiasm for life. It was great to have a friend who wasn't heavily into bridge, luncheons and golf. Under Tiffany's vigilant tutelage, I'd also learned new skills: like how to catch shrimp and clean a sea bass.

"I don't much like to talk about it," Tiffany continued. "He acted like, you know, he owned me; always asking where I was going and following me, even when I went to my Mom's. And, "there were other things he wanted to do that were…"" She hesitated, and judging from the scarlet flush that spread across her face, I figured she was thinking about other unattractive aspects of Andrew's personality. Tiffany searched for the right word. "They were evil. I thought they were evil." She shook her head as if to rid herself of bad memories.

I didn't ask any questions, but I longed to bop Andrew Roop over the head. In my humble opinion, he was spoiled and weak. Even his body language spelled 'loser'. He moved with his shoulders hunched slightly forward in a shuffling, diffident walk, as if he didn't have the energy or motivation to pick up his feet. But, I could see how his curly black hair and smooth baby face had probably appealed to Tiffany.

He certainly wasn't my type. I liked tall, muscular men with good teeth and thick hair. Or at least I had in my last life. The next time around, I was going to insist on high moral character, even if the man looked like Bugs Bunny.

"It was a good thing his daddy had a pile of money," I said to Tiffany. "That's about all Andrew has going for him."

Tiffany nodded. "Andrew used to talk about his daddy. Sometimes I thought he wasn't very proud of him. You know, wishing he'd had some important job in a fancy office instead of running a fish company."

I laughed at my friend. "Tiffy, Roop Enterprises trades on the New York Stock Exchange. It's not exactly a fish company. They've diversified into all kinds of things."

"I know. But I used to like it when Andrew told how his daddy started out selling shrimp that he'd caught himself from the back of his pickup truck and then making and selling that Lowcountry stew because he thought all the tourists would like it."

I knew the story well since it was a Lowcountry legend. At the age of twenty-three, with only one small boat and a huge ambition, Andrew's father, Paul, started what was to become Roop Enterprises. Born in a small wooden house in Bluffton, he attended school sporadically, much preferring to spend the warm days shrimping and fishing on the May River and the waters around Hilton Head. An enterprising boy, he opened a roadside stand on Hwy 278, and sold fresh shrimp and Georgia peaches.

When the northern visitors bought all his shrimp and peaches, he added Vidalia onions and homegrown tomatoes to his stand. Soon there was too much work for one person. He built a bigger stand, this time with a special bin for ice, and hired Buck, another high school dropout, to help him.

One day a tourist from Cincinnati asked about a local dish containing shrimp, corn, sausage and potatoes. On the very next day, Paul hung a sign on his stand offering "Lowcountry Stew, cooked with authentic Lowcountry spices." You had to give him credit. He was no dummy. He bought a huge steel pot and a hot plate and let the tantalizing aroma of boiling shrimp and spices waft over Hwy 278.

Business boomed. Restaurants ordered his shrimp, and tourists paid good money for the stew. He bought a bigger boat, then another. With the proceeds from the shrimp, he opened small restaurants in Savannah and Charleston.

One afternoon, during the lunch shift in his Savannah restaurant, he met Marjorie Cutliff of Beaufort, who was lunching with her mother. She had wispy brown hair covered by a daisy-encrusted hat, myopic blue eyes, which looked unblinkingly through wire rimmed glasses, bright red lips and a lantern jaw. Paul, who had spent most of his life among the fish and shrimp, thought she was the most beautiful woman he had ever seen. They were married seven months later, with Mr. and Mrs. Cutliffs' grateful blessings.

Eight months after the wedding, twin boys, Andrew and Nathan were born.

Paul changed the name of his company to Roop Fish and Shrimp Co. Inc. By the time the boys were twelve, Roop Fish and Shrimp delivered seafood to one hundred and forty seven cities in the United States. Marjorie, who had a quick head for figures, invested the profits in the stock market and urged Paul to diversify. He bought some real estate in Florida and North Carolina and a hunting lodge in Pennsylvania, where natural gas was discovered. On the boys' first day at Choate Academy, Roop Enterprises began trading on the New York Stock Exchange.

In spite of his amazing financial success, Paul never bothered to polish his behavior or his language. He liked to sit on the porch of his comfortable home on the May River in Bluffton, swig Jim Beam from a jelly glass, clean his fingernails with his pocketknife and dream about the day his boys would take over the company. Fortunately, he didn't live to see the results.

The old Mr. Roop would have approved of Tiffany, I mused, as I shook out the contents of an old duffel bag. He'd have called her down-to-earth with none of them phony airs. And he would probably also have thought she was too good for his son.

Tiffy and I searched every inch of the galley and tiny cabin, but found nothing. In the forward cabin there was a double bed, neatly made up with a yellow quilt. There was also a closet and two storage compartments.

When I opened the closet to look at Joey's clothes, Tiffany swallowed hard. "I miss him so much. I pray all the time that he's safe and comes home soon."

I gave her an encouraging pat on the shoulder. "I do too, Tiffy. I do too."

On Joey's side of the closet were blue jeans neatly arranged on hangars, a green windbreaker, two pairs of canvas shoes, a pair of brown moccasins and a pair of tan Docker slacks. A stack of folded T-shirts and underwear filled the top shelf.

"What was Joey wearing the day he..." I didn't want to say disappeared, so I said, "worked on Andrew's boat?"

"I know perfectly. He wore the grease stained jeans he kept for when he had to make repairs, an Atlanta Braves T-shirt with a red plaid, long sleeve shirt over it, you know, like a jacket. And his old tennis shoes."

"Are any clothes missing?"

Tiffany shook her head. "Everything is here. Even his wallet. Look." She picked up a battered, black billfold from the top shelf. "He never takes it when he goes on a job. He's afraid he'll drop it when he squeezes into those cramped spaces."

Tiffany looked inside. There was $11.00, a South Carolina driver's license, expiration date 4/14/04, a picture of a smiling Tiffany holding Peanuts, the cat, and another of the *Moondancer,* with Tiffany posed on the bow.

There was also a receipt from a grocery store with a phone number scrawled on the back. Tiffany showed it to me.

"If this was important enough for Joey to save, it might mean something," I said. "Do you recognize the number?"

Tiffany furrowed her brow and chewed on a fingernail as she studied the digits. Finally she looked up. "I can't be a hundred percent sure, but I think it's Andrew's unlisted number. I used to know it by heart. It's the one he always told me to use. His good friends were supposed to use it also."

"Well, there's only one way to find out. Call the number, and if Andrew answers, hang up."

Tiffany dialed the number, listened briefly and hung up, shaking her head. "They say it's no longer in service. Maybe I was wrong about it having been Andrew's.

I tucked the piece of paper into my pocket and picked up my bag. Swinging it over my shoulder, I said, "Don't worry, Tif. We've only begun to hunt for Joey. I wish I could stay longer, but I've got a ton of things to do, and I've got to find something to wear to the Biederman's party tonight." I gave her a hug. "I'll call tomorrow. In the meantime, think about Joey's friends. Maybe make a list of them. We can check them out and see if they can help us."

As I stepped off the *Moondancer*, the man assigned to watch the boat casually pulled a notebook out of his pocket and wrote something in it. Then he swung around and intently studied two pelicans sitting on the pier railing. He didn't fool me. I knew he'd written my name, time of arrival and time of departure in his little black book.

*   *   *   *

By the time I arrived at the Biederman's, the party was in full swing. Since the hosts of this gathering were good friends of Roops, I wondered about the propriety of celebrating so soon after Nathan had been blown to bits, but I suppose, once you have hired the caterer and florist, there is a momentum that not even death can halt.

I hated these affairs, but sometimes they brought new customers, so I couldn't afford to turn down the invitations. You never knew who was suddenly going to pop up between the smoked salmon and the crème bruleé and order a complete set of hand painted pitchers and matching, long stem glasses.

The heels of my shoes made little clicking noises as I walked across the marble floor of the cavernous entry hall. I resisted the urge to test for echoes. I put on my happy face and stepped down into the sunken living room where at least seventy people milled about laughing and chatting. Two tuxedoed waiters passed trays of drinks and canapés. I took a glass of champagne and, while I got my bearings, wandered over to the wall of windows at the end of the room. A lone sailboat with a red and yellow spinnaker bobbed gently in the ocean.

"Quite a sight, isn't it, my dear? I'm so glad to see you here. Did you get my phone messages? You really should be more diligent about returning calls."

"Nice to see you, Winifred," I lied. As I always did when cornered by Winifred Burmeister, I looked for a way to escape. Finding none I stepped back, hoping Winifred would at least respect my personal space. "I've been meaning to call you, but I've been so busy with painting."

"I see." Winifred moved forward. "I hope you haven't forgotten about chairing the Pooch Promenade. It's such a vital fund raising activity for our group."

How in the world did you "chair" a Pooch Promenade? A bunch of dog owners pledged a certain amount of money for every lap their pets dragged them through the Forest Preserve. It seemed simple enough. But, since I agreed with the attempt to raise money for the animal shelter, I had also agreed to organize the event.

"I have everything under control," I said, making a mental note to start calling people tomorrow morning.

"Good. There was something else I wanted to talk to you about." Winifred's voice slid into cozy confidentiality. "You know Tiffany Archer so well. I was wondering, my dear, has she told you any tidbits? I mean, I wouldn't want to pry, but it's such a terrible thing about Nathan Roop." She looked around the room, a sly smile on her face. "Although I dare say there are a few ladies here who aren't sorry to see Nathan dead."

I drew away. "What on earth are you talking about? No, don't tell me." This woman made my skin crawl. "I'm sorry, Winifred, but I really don't want to hear."

Winifred put a plump hand on my arm. "Don't be silly. Of course you do. For instance, there's Stephanie Miller." She pointed to a sleek blond in a figure hugging black dress and enough jewelry to pay the national debt of a third world country. "Did you know, my dear, that she and Nathan had a little *techtel mechtel* a while ago?"

"No, I didn't know that. I also know I'm going to regret asking this, but what, exactly, is a little *techtel mechtel*? It sounds like a disease."

"My dear, you know—an affair. Her husband Buzz was away doing that golf thing in Scotland, and Stephanie was bored. It started out as a harmless way to get rid of *ennui* but Stephanie became, shall we say, enamored and wanted him all to herself." Her lips disappeared into a disapproving line. "That, of course, wasn't possible. Nathan liked variety."

"I have to go now, Winifred."

"And then there's Harry Kirn. I understand he backed Nathan in a business deal; something about a chain of fruit drink stores. It folded and Nathan couldn't repay the loan."

I shook my head. "Where in the world do you get your information?"

Winifred, however, was on a roll and began ticking off names on her fingers. "Nancy Solomon's husband caught her in the cabana with Nathan. Meredith, I can't think of her last name but you know her, my dear, that lumpy little brunette who is always throwing French words into her conversation. She and Nathan took a boat out on the Intracoastal and didn't come home for two days. I only know this because they went aground on a sandbar in front of Malovitch's house, and I just happened to be walking on the beach at the time."

I felt a twinge of sympathy for the unlucky Meredith.

Winifred patted her thin salt and pepper hair. "Of course, I wasn't foolish enough to fall for his glib talk. I have far too much respect for myself."

I knew I'd hate myself in the morning, but what the heck.

"Are you saying he made a pass at you?"

Winifred's cheeks flushed a delicate pink. "I'm just saying, my dear, that I had no intention of becoming one of his floosies—a notch on his headboard, so to speak."

My eyes swept over the woman in front of me. Winifred was short and nearly square, with a round face and close-set, pea size, brown eyes. Tonight she was dressed in a lime green full skirt, sprinkled with appliqué daisies and a matching, frilly, puffed sleeve blouse. As added decoration, she'd tucked a daisy behind each ear. I thought she looked like some sort of toxic shrub. It was hard to believe Nathan would have been interested in her. Apparently satisfied that I now realized she was a sexual force to be reckoned with, she prepared to leave.

"Ta ta, darling. Must be mingling now. It does give you food for thought, doesn't it? So many people had a reason to want Nathan dead. It could have been a rejected lover or a furious husband." She stepped back into my personal space and whispered, "Although I do think Joey Archer did it. That type of person is prone to violence, don't you think?"

She disappeared before I could stick out my foot and trip her.

CHAPTER 5

▼

The next morning I did some sleuthing; partly because I had promised Tiffany that I would help her find her husband, and partly because I was curious myself about Joey's whereabouts. My feet squished in my soaked Nike running shoes as I slogged my way through the steady rain in Harbour Town. A few brave tourists huddled under the awning of the Crazy Crab restaurant but, otherwise, the normally bustling marina was empty. The rain blew off the Sound, stinging my bare legs and making it impossible to keep my head up.

At Andrew's slip, I stopped and looked down. Even though the area had been thoroughly searched after the explosion, I could still see reminders of what had once been a beautiful yacht. A coffee cup with small pink roses had somehow survived intact and bobbed on the water's surface; a scorched cushion, probably from a deck chair, lay on the dock.

Whoever blew this boat up had a pretty good knowledge of explosives, and as far as I knew, Joey had none. There hadn't been a trace of anything even remotely resembling bomb parts on the *Moondancer*, and Tiffany swore he wouldn't have known how to make one.

As I lingered, I searched my memory for information about Joey. Born and raised in Bluffton, Tiffy had told me. Loved boats all his life and had spent boyhood summers crewing on a fishing boat. Bought the *Moondancer* a year ago and started his own charter fishing business. Tiffy either didn't know or hadn't wanted to supply any information about his education. Not that it mattered. All the education in the world wouldn't help him now—not if he had something to do with the demise of Nathan Roop.

From my own observations I could add that Joey was friendly, open, not overly ambitious, fond of fishing and not particularly bright. He reminded me of a happy, enthusiastic puppy, which is not the profile of a killer. Even my creative imagination couldn't conjure up an image of Joey actually planning and carrying out such a vicious crime. Still, I reminded myself, if he isn't guilty, where is he? There were only two possibilities; he blew up the *Second Chance* and ran, or something else, something uglier than I wanted to contemplate, had happened to him.

A tiny object wedged in a crack in the pier caught my attention. Ignoring the gusts of rain that threatened to sweep me into the harbor, I got down on my hands and knees and pried the thing loose. It was a slim screwdriver, about two inches long with a brass handle. Cupping it in my hand, I walked toward the shops, the metal cold against my skin. At the Fashion Court, Susan Lowerby, the owner, stood at the door waving an umbrella.

"You look like a drowned rat, Maggie. Let me give you this. You can return it anytime. Or come in and get dried off."

As Susan stepped aside, I smelled the combination of fragrant sachets and expensive body lotions. The shop sold a bit of everything: lingerie, baby clothes, handbags, jewelry and delightful odds and ends, such as hand painted china and whimsical pillows. Susan smiled cheerfully as she handed me a roll of paper towel.

"It must be important to drag you out in this mess."

I swiped at my hair and face, mindful of the water I was dripping on the carpet.

"It is. I'm trying to find someone who saw Joey Archer the morning of the explosion." I looked at my friend. "You know the sheriff suspects him of murder."

Susan straightened a selection of Vera Bradley bags on a display case. "I heard. Frankly, I think it's a dumb assumption. We all feel terrible for Tiffany. But why doesn't he come back?"

"Good question. I wish I had the answer." As I spoke, I juggled the little screwdriver in the palm of my hand.

Susan noticed and said, "I see you have some of our merchandise."

I must have looked at her blankly because she continued, "That thing in your hand. It's part of a gimmicky little set. But look here. There's a little blob of red on this one." She scraped the spot with her fingernail. "It won't come off. Must be nail polish or something. Anyway, let me show you." From the counter, she picked up a white hammer, hand painted with yellow and purple pansies. "See this? If you unscrew the handle, you'll find a screwdriver inside, and if you twiddle this thing off the end, there are three more screwdrivers in decreasing sizes. The one you have is next to the smallest. This item is a big seller. For $27.00 a customer can take a unique gift to someone back home. And they really do work."

I laughed. "You don't have to sell me. I found this in the debris in Andrew's slip. I don't know why I picked it up." Suddenly remembering what had caused the piece of metal to be in the water, I rammed it into my pocket, wishing I had thrown it out.

The bell on the door tinkled. Anne Roop propped her umbrella by the front door and walked briskly to Susan.

"If you're not terribly busy, I'd like to see some nightgowns, Susan. I'm in a bit of a hurry." Anne adjusted a pale cream, peach and mint silk scarf over her white cardigan. "Nice to see you again, Maggie," she said with the warmth of someone greeting an IRS auditor. She stared with distaste at my neon orange running shorts and soaked Salty Dog T-shirt.

I wasn't really surprised at her attitude. At the time of Andrew's divorce and remarriage, the local residents had chosen sides. All those who felt Andrew was well rid of an uneducated little gold digger were firmly behind Anne. I belonged to a small contingent of folks who cheered for Tiffany. Apparently satisfied that she had fulfilled her social obligations, Anne ignored me and turned to Susan.

"I have a busy schedule so if you could show me some gowns, I'd appreciate it."

"Just a minute, Anne," I said. I smiled inwardly to see the displeasure creep into her eyes. "I've been meaning to call you. There's something I'd really like to talk to you about."

"What is it? This isn't a good time." Susan's presence kept her from adding, "And I can't imagine we have anything to say to each other."

"Just a quick question. Do you remember what time of day it was when you called Joey Archer and asked him to repair your boat?"

Anne scowled; tiny frown lines working around her eyes. "What do you mean, 'called Joey Archer'? I did no such thing."

"You didn't mention that Andrew was going to fix the engine himself if Joey wouldn't help?"

Anne shook her perfectly coifed head. "Absolutely not. Why would I ever call Joey Archer for anything? Since you are so friendly with his little wife, I'd think you would know that. After what she put Andrew through, I want nothing to do with those people."

Her mouth pursed as if she had bitten into something rotten. I couldn't wait to pursue the point.

"So let me get this straight. You didn't call Joey, and neither you nor Andrew had any contact with him. Right?"

"I don't feel I owe you any kind of an explanation about anything, Maggie. Now if you'll excuse me..." She inspected a gown that Susan held up for her consideration. "No, the fabric is too stiff. I want a soft silk."

"But Mrs. Roop, this IS silk."

"It feels like rayon or polyester. Show me a sheer silk."

Anne Roop was so busy giving Susan a hard time that neither lady saw me leave the store.

*   *   *   *

The harbormaster's office was a room squeezed between the Quarterdeck and the Café Europa. Although small, it allowed Allan Delon, the harbormaster, a view of all boats entering and leaving the marina.

"Sorry to keep you waiting," Allan said as he hung up the phone. "We've got all kinds of people requesting space in the marina and there just isn't any." He flipped through some papers on his desk. "I've got a request for a berth from the captain of the *White Sands*, a one hundred twenty five foot baby from the Caymans." He waved his hand toward the water. "They're out there somewhere, waiting for me to free up something."

Mindful that the harbormaster was a busy man, I talked fast. "I guess I'd like to know if you saw Joey Archer on the day of the explosion, or if you saw anything out of the ordinary—like maybe a boat that didn't belong or something." My voice trailed off. I was tired and wet and I longed to go home and forget about Joey Archer for a few hours.

Allan stretched out his long legs and cocked his feet on the desk. Well over six feet tall with wild blonde hair and posture like a Marine drill sergeant, his presence alone usually assured order in the harbor.

"Didn't see Archer. Feel really bad about him. But funny you should mention a boat. Some idiot did enter the harbor without contacting me first. We get a lot of novices, but nearly all of them know enough to arrange for slippage before they come in. This boat was in and out before I could do anything about it. It was particularly annoying because the harbor was closed while we got the debris from the explosion cleaned up." He looked embarrassed. "I guess that's why I missed it. Figured it was some damn ghoul wanting a first hand look at the disaster."

I felt my heart beat faster. "Who actually saw the boat in the marina?"

"Dave. He was at the fuel dock. But there was so much confusion he didn't pay much attention either." When he saw my disappointment, he added, "There's no point in asking him. He really didn't see anything."

"I understand. I just feel sorry for Tiffany, and I'd do anything to help her. No one in his right mind could believe Joey is a murderer."

Suddenly tense, Allan glanced around the small office as if making sure no one could overhear what he was about to say. Then he looked me straight in the eyes.

"How well do you know Tiffany?"

"I'd say very well. Even though there's a few years difference in our ages, we've always had fun together. She's a sweet girl, and I can't stand seeing her unhappy. That's why I'm trying to help her."

Allan's shoulders relaxed. He doodled on a piece of paper in front of him before he spoke. "I had to make sure you felt like the rest of us here in the harbor." He glared at me. "We feel pretty protective of both of them."

"And I do, too." Afraid of sounding overly sincere, but anxious to know what was on Allan's mind, I decided I had said enough.

"I didn't tell this to the police," he began, "because I like Joey and can't believe he had anything to do with the *Second Chance* business. But something odd did happen." He brushed a clump of unruly hair off his forehead while I held my breath. "About three days before the explosion, Joey came in all upset. He paced up and down, really agitated. Not like the laid back Joey we know, but really mad. I'd say he was furious. When I finally got him to tell me what was wrong, he said, 'that son of a bitch has the title to my boat.'"

I knew I sounded as shocked as I felt. "The title to the *Moondancer*? But that boat is Joey's pride and joy. He would never give it up. Did Joey sell it?"

Allan shook his head. "I don't think so. He just kept saying over and over, 'that son of a bitch has the title to my boat' and when I asked him what son of a bitch, he said, 'there is only one on this island'."

Allan's and my eyes locked in mutual misery. I spoke the two words we both were thinking. "Andrew Roop."

The harbormaster agreed. "Who else could it be? And there's something else. I don't know if you know this, but Roop has tried hard to put Joey out of business. He's been lurking around the dock, bad mouthing Joey to potential customers, saying his boat isn't seaworthy and crap like that."

Stunned, I sank back in my chair. "But surely Joey is making a decent living. I've heard Tiffy talk about how busy he is."

Again Allan shook his head. "Business hasn't been that good. I know because he spends a lot of time hanging around my office. I'd guess he's having a hard time making ends meet. The *Moondancer* wasn't cheap, and Joey doesn't have any extra money."

This news really upset me. I'd always assumed Tiffy and Joey were financially okay. Sure, they probably didn't have any extra money, but the *Moondancer* was well cared for, and I'd always thought Joey had steady work.

"But Tiffany never mentioned there was any trouble with charters. They both seemed so upbeat and happy. I'm glad you didn't tell anyone. I must admit..."

"You don't have to say it. It doesn't look good for Joey."

I stood up and extended my hand to the helpful harbormaster. I noticed my shorts had left a wet mark on the plastic chair. "Thank you for telling me all this. And please, keep believing in Joey. We'll get everything straightened out."

But I had also read enough mystery novels to know that motive, means and opportunity usually added up to guilt. Joey had the opportunity, and if what Allan said was true, he also had a motive. If I found out Joey also knew how to make explosives, I would probably have to go back on Xanax. Or take up smoking. I'd start with the patch and work my way up to a pack or so a day.

CHAPTER 6

▼

"That is just the meanest thing I've ever heard of. And it's not true." Crimson blotches stained both of Tiffany's cheeks as she strode along the pier. I had to break into a jog to keep up with her. "I'm gonna find Andrew Roop and wring the truth out of his scrawny little neck. Joey would never give him the title to the *Moondancer*. If Andrew has it, he probably stole it."

"Hang on a minute, will you, Tiffany? And for heaven's sake, slow down. We're attracting a bit of attention." A group of Japanese tourists had stopped to stare appreciatively at the leggy blonde hurrying through the harbor.

"I don't want to slow down," Tiffany called over her shoulder. "I want to find Andrew. You don't have to worry about me, Maggie. I know how to deal with my ex-husband."

"That's exactly what I'm afraid of."

I managed to grab her by the arm and plop her down into one of the rocking chairs in front of the Harbour Town Craft store.

"Listen to me. You can't go barging in on Andrew all wild eyed and furious, because you'll just give him more ammunition to feed to the sheriff. We have to think logically." Seeing I had Tiffany's attention I said, "Now, take a deep breath and tell me if you can think of any reason, however remote, as to why Andrew might have the title to the

Moondancer. Financial problems, maybe? Was Joey having trouble making the payments on the boat?"

"No! Andrew is a spiteful, mean man who wants to stir up trouble between Joey and me. I hate him. I wish I'd never heard the name Andrew Roop."

Tiffany tried to explode out of the chair, but I was quicker. I pushed the younger woman back and waited for her to calm down. I had never seen Tiffany so angry, and I didn't know which I preferred; the meek Tiffany sobbing into a handkerchief or this wild woman acting like a loose cannon.

"Tiffy, you've got to lower your voice and stop yelling Andrew's name all over the place. See that couple?" I jerked my head in the direction of a man and a woman openly listening to the conversation. "There has been something about the Roops in the *Island Packet* every day since the explosion. Don't give them anything else to write about."

Her shoulders slumped. "Then help me, Maggie. Help me get the title back. That is, if he has it, and I don't believe for one minute that he does. Joey would never give it up."

"And how would you suggest we go about doing that? I don't think Andrew's in any mood to talk to us."

Both of us glanced at the harbor as a ship's horn signaled its departure. We watched as a pretty woman dressed in white shorts and a blue and white striped T-shirt caught the bow line and secured it to the deck of a good sized trawler.

"See that, Maggie? I used to do that with Joey. I'd crew for him and keep the *Moondancer* nice and clean. And we were so happy." Her voice was a whisper. "I just know he'll come home soon, and I can't let anything happen to his boat." A soft hand slid into mine. "Please. I can't go to Andrew's house. But you can. Just go and have a look, and see if you can find the title."

"What?" I jerked her hand away and stood up, facing my friend, who seemed to have lost her mind. "You want me to break into

Andrew's house and look for the title?" I shook my head. "Don't go wacky on me, Tiffany. We don't need any idiotic ideas."

"I could tell you exactly where to look," she pleaded. "Andrew always keeps his important stuff in one of two places. And it wouldn't exactly be breaking in. The title doesn't belong to Andrew. And I used to live there. That sort of counts, doesn't it?"

I started toward the parking lot. "I'm going now. We'll talk tomorrow when you're a bit more rational."

Tiffany followed me like an eager puppy. As I fumbled with the combination lock on my bike, Tiffany said, "I swear I'm gonna scream just as loud as I can and attract all kinds of attention and yell Andrew's name all over the place if you won't help me. Just ten minutes in the house, Maggie, and if you can't find it, that'll be okay too."

"No!"

Tiffany opened her mouth and shrieked as if her pants were on fire. The Japanese tourist swung his camera to his eyes.

"Will you help me now?"

"Still no."

I didn't believe she would have the nerve to scream again. But I was wrong. She took a deep breath and opened her mouth.

"All right. I must be the stupidest person on earth to agree to this. But we have to have a plan, and you have to do as I say. And, no more than ten minutes in the house. If I don't find it, I'm out of there and we never mention this again."

Tiffany clapped her hands together. "I knew you would. You're so clever. And you know Andrew doesn't deserve to get away with this."

I pedaled slowly in the direction of Lighthouse Road. "Don't press your luck," I yelled back to Tiffany. "Now leave me alone so I can think about what an idiot I am."

On the way home, I stopped to see why a crowd had gathered at the edge of a lagoon. Fearing there had been an accident, I pulled my cell phone out of my pocket so I could call for help in a hurry. As I approached, a magnificent, blond haired, fair skinned hunk of a man broke out of the crowd and ran up to me. I poised my finger over the dial on the phone.

"Ja, please, can you tell me if those alligators are real? My friend over there says they are robots, like the ones at Animal Kingdom in Disney World."

His friend was female, blond and built like Peter's bimbo. She stood at the water's edge, watching a ten-foot alligator rapidly make its way to where she was standing. I could understand the alligator's haste. He was anticipating an extremely tasty first course.

"I think you'd better get your friend out of there."

Without waiting for him to take action, I yelled, "Hey! You! Step away from the alligator," at the top of my lungs.

When that didn't work, I raced to the water, grabbed the stupid girl by the hand and dragged her to safety. I could feel reptilian eyes glaring at me.

"These are not plastic toys designed to amuse tourists," I shakily informed the blond god. "They are real, live 'gators. Only an idiot would deliberately try to get close to one."

He shook his head. "It is not good to have these things here. Much better if they were robots."

I considered telling him that they were indigenous to the Lowcountry, and that we were actually encroaching on their habitat, but decided against it. As far as I was concerned, anyone dumb enough to think Hilton Head would stock its lagoons with plastic amphibians was free to stick his toes in the water. Maybe even do a little fishing.

I got on my bike and pedaled home. For a few minutes, at least, my mind had stopped worrying about Joey and Tiffany.

*   *   *   *

That night, Tiffy and I concocted a plan while we talked on the phone. It wasn't a very brilliant plan, but it was the only one I could come up with on short notice. We knew that Anne Roop had a hair appointment the following day and would be out of the house. What we had to do was devise a scheme to get Andrew away long enough for me to hunt for the deed.

We decided to use Tiffany as bait. Actually I decided. Tiffany objected vigorously. Going on the assumption that Andrew's passion for his ex-wife hadn't been completely extinguished, I would send Tiffy, dressed in the skimpiest bikini we could find, to the beach in front of Andrew's house. She would strut back and forth until Andrew saw her. I predicted the sight of his ex-wife practically undressed and alone on the beach would send him racing out of his house. Tiffany found several things wrong with our plan.

"I don't ever wear skimpy bikinis. You can't swim in those things. And I don't want Andrew panting all over me. I told you, I can't stand that man."

"I know, but let's remember this was your idea to hunt for the deed. I would certainly rather not break into his house."

"Maybe there's another way."

"And what would that be?"

"I don't know. But you can't have any idea how horrible that man can be. I don't want to be alone with him."

"That's fine with me. We'll forget about finding the deed."

There was silence on the other end of the phone. Finally she said, "All right. I'll do it. For Joey."

"Just make sure you keep Andrew there long enough for me to get in, hunt for a few minutes and get back out. I don't want to get caught."

I could just imagine what the grapevine would say if it heard Maggie Bloom had been caught pilfering Andrew Roop's papers. I'd have to move again.

*   *   *   *

The next morning I drove to South Beach, parked my car in the marina and walked to Roops' house. Like a cat burglar casing the joint, I looked left and right before I plunged into a clump of palmetto fronds. After twenty minutes, my legs ached from crouching in an awkward position, and my eyes hurt from staring intently at the house. For the thousandth time I checked my watch. Anne Roop should have left five minutes ago for Harbour Town. Lydia at the Harbour Town beauty shop had assured me that Mrs. Roop never canceled her 10:00 hair appointment.

I looked across the dunes at the beach. Tiffany was there, arranging and rearranging a red beach towel. She wore a very teeny red and white polka dot bikini, a wide brimmed straw hat and dark glasses. She looked sensational. As I watched, Tiffy arranged herself sexily on the towel and slowly rubbed lotion on her tan legs. Andrew would have to be a eunuch not to respond to her.

I struggled to control my own ragged breathing. Let me hasten to add it wasn't the sight of the ravishing Tiffany that had me gasping like a beached flounder. I am one hundred percent heterosexual, thank you. My airway was constricted because it was clogged with fear. I hated it when I put myself into situations where the outcome might land me in jail. And, unfortunately, this wasn't the first time I'd done something that one might consider slightly illegal. But in Germany, I'd been saving my own skin, so breaking a few laws—well, actually, quite a few—seemed perfectly okay. This was different. Tiffy was a great friend, but I really didn't think I was ready to land in the slammer for her. I decided to give Anne Roop ten more minutes. If she didn't come out, I'd go to the beach, throw a robe around Tiffy and call it a day. We'd have to think of something else.

In exactly four minutes and twenty seconds the garage door opened and a green BMW backed slowly out, gathered speed around the circular drive and disappeared in the direction of Harbour Town. I peeked out from my hiding place long enough to see Anne Roop behind the wheel. I wiped my sweating palms on my shorts. Now all we needed was Andrew. What if he didn't see Tiffany and never came out of the house? For all I knew, he could be holed up in his bedroom with a bottle of vodka.

I knew he was home because Tiffy and I had called him from the South Beach Marina before we came to the house. When Anne answered, I had identified myself as the secretary to a boat dealer in Charleston, and I'd hung up when she went to summon Andrew.

Freedom Lavender was also gone. At precisely 9:30, just as Tiffany had predicted, the housekeeper drove away in an old Honda Civic to do the weekly marketing.

Come on, Andrew, I mentally urged. *Look out the window.* After what seemed like an eternity but in reality had only been a few minutes, I saw the sunroom door open and a man stride across the lawn towards the beach. It was Andrew, and he strutted like a preening peacock in front of Tiffany. Next, he stood awkwardly in front of her, obviously unsure of what to do. Tiffy crooked a finger at him and patted the towel invitingly. Andrew didn't need a second invitation. He sank to the towel with an attitude of familiar intimacy, which made me feel sorry for Tiffy.

With Andrew out of the way, I felt safe enough to sprint to the patio from my hiding place behind the guesthouse. Seeing no one, I slunk along the periphery of the garden to the main house. At the sliding glass door of the sunroom, I hesitated. No use getting weak kneed now. And I couldn't stand there debating forever the wisdom of breaking into Roops' house. Time's a wastin'. Short of actually copulating on the sand, which I was sure Andrew wouldn't object to, Tiffany wouldn't be able to keep him there forever.

I pushed the door open and slid inside. The sunroom was cool. The rose colored, Italian marble tile floor smelled faintly of Pine Sol, as if someone had scrubbed it recently. Three ceiling fans whirred noise-lessly in perfect unison.

I felt chagrinned about tromping over the beautiful red and blue Kashan rug in the living room. I checked the soles of my tennis shoes to make sure I wasn't dragging hunks of debris across the floor.

The house looked different without hordes of people in it. When I'd been there for Nathan's wake, I hadn't noticed the mass of photos on the polished grand piano, or the spectacular jade collection in a cabinet against the wall. Bouquets of fresh white roses, tulips and daisies, accented with sprays of baby's breath and green ferns spilled out of Chinese fish pots.

I was aware that I was wasting precious time, but I couldn't resist lingering in front of the most spectacular art collection I had ever seen in a private home. There was a large Miro, a Chagall and a Picasso from his blue period, not to mention a small but exquisite Renoir and an impressionist painting of a cathedral at dusk, which I knew was a Monet.

A portrait of Anne, dressed in a white chiffon gown and holding a rose, hung over the fireplace. I'll admit it had been a long time since I'd sat in Professor Bernstein's classroom and listened to the theory of composition, but there was something wrong with this painting. It struck a jarring note in the otherwise perfectly appointed room. The portrait was stiff: not only in the fixed smile on Anne's face but also in the wooden handling of her arms and torso. There was no graceful flow of her hand into her lap, no delicate brushstrokes or subtlety of shad-ing.

What surprised me the most was that Andrew, who was so obviously aware of great art and had the means to purchase it, would settle for this very mediocre painting of his wife. But, there was no accounting for people's taste. Maybe he was so besotted with Anne that he thought this portrait was wonderful.

Another, more likely thought occurred to me. Perhaps Andrew didn't have much to do with the commissioning of this painting. I had a feeling Anne Roop got what she wanted, and I could imagine she would find this stiff, artificial portrait appealing.

I finally remembered what I was supposed to be doing. Checking my watch, I realized I had spent a precious four minutes looking at the paintings. I hurried into the hall and tried to remember what Tiffany had told me. Andrew had a desk in the library. There was also a small room on the second floor where he kept all kinds of papers and junk. "He's a pack rat," Tiffy had said. "Maybe Anne has changed him, but when we were married he saved all kinds of things: old newspapers, strange souvenirs from trips he had taken, even old 78 phonograph records." I decided to try the library first, then the second floor, if I still had time.

The library reminded me of a very expensive lawyer's office. The walls were mahogany paneled. Leather bound books that looked like they had never been opened filled two walls of bookcases. I stood in front of the mahogany desk trying to make my hand pick up the papers scattered all over the top. Never before in my life had I snooped in anyone's private papers or read anyone's mail. Not even Peter's, which may have been a mistake, now that I looked back on it. I'd have found hotel receipts for the nights he spent with his bimbo and would have known what was going on before he got his chance to tell me.

Remembering my ex-husband's devious behavior made me square my shoulders and pick up some papers. Maybe if I had snooped a bit more, Peter wouldn't have taken me so off guard, casually mentioning between the *insalata mista* and the *tiramisu* at our favorite Italian restaurant that he had fallen in love with someone else.

I whistled softly as I glanced at the first three papers in my hand. They were bills: $7,000 for a Sarouk rug, $4,281.97 for an Escada cocktail gown, $623 for Egyptian cotton king size bed sheets. I put the stack back on the desk, wondering what it would feel like to sleep on $623 sheets. There were other letters from creditors asking for immediate settlement of outstanding accounts. Interesting, but not what I was looking for.

In the top drawer of the desk was a checkbook from First Union Bank showing a negative balance of $2,012.56. A savings account statement showed that Andrew Roop possessed the grand sum of $1,427.30. This sure didn't jibe with the furnishings of the house and the life style they maintained. I guess I'd expected six digit totals in his bankbooks. Clearly, he seemed to be in a bit of a financial predicament.

The receipts for his paintings were in a plastic folder. Each painting was documented and authenticated. They had been purchased over a period of eleven years, and the price Andrew had paid for these masterpieces was staggering. There was no doubt that each painting was the real thing. Andrew had made several trips to galleries and museums in Europe, and each seller had provided a thoroughly genuine history of the pictures.

I put the receipts back where I found them and quickly searched the rest of the desk. Finding nothing, I looked around the room for another hiding place for the title, but there was none.

A burgundy leather couch and armchair with footstool, a burled rosewood coffee table and floor to ceiling bookcases were the only other furnishings in the room. I briefly considered looking through the books, in case Andrew had hidden the title in one of them. If he had, I was out of luck. Another peek at my watch told me I had a little over four minutes left. There was no time to look carefully through hundreds of leather bound volumes.

I crossed the center hall and bounded up the circular staircase, two steps at a time. It was easy to locate the master bedroom. I followed the scent of Anne's vanilla perfume until I was standing in a large, oval room with huge windows that opened to the ocean. Decorated in stark white, I had the feeling that I had walked into a cocoon: white rugs, white curtains, white sheets and a white duvet cover. Even the couch and bureaus blended into the white walls. My footsteps made deep indentations in the thick pile rug. Trying to rake the rug with my toe, I quickly backed out into the hall.

The little room Tiffany had talked about was adjacent to the bed-room. Designed originally as a sitting room for the master bedroom, it was now clearly Andrew's. And it was clearly a mess. I edged my way past a golf bag with clubs, a tennis racket, a full size cardboard figure of Andrew in natty yachting clothes and a box full of little airline bottles of vodka and scotch. Next to the window was an old oak desk, clut-tered with papers. Magazines, brochures, books and trash littered the floor. I walked across them to get to the desk.

My heart sank. I'd never be able to find the title in all this debris, and I certainly didn't have time to tidy things up. Suddenly nervous, I glanced out the window, expecting to see Andrew appear over the dunes. From somewhere deep in the house, a grandfather clock chimed eleven times; deep mellow tones that nearly scared the socks off me. *Calm down*, I chided myself. *Just look at some of this stuff and then get out.*

I quickly determined that Andrew was incapable of throwing any-thing away. He'd saved brochures about a cruise to Alaska, the menus from a transatlantic crossing on the QE2, an outdated coupon for the Island Car Wash, several old copies of *Body Building* magazine and the latest edition of *Penthouse*.

Disgusted, I turned my attention to the desk. The drawers weren't locked, but they yielded nothing. Every single one was full of junk. As I bent down to examine the lower drawer, a sound startled me, making me bang my head against the side of the desk.

Freedom Lavender, the Roops' housekeeper, dressed in canary yel-low bicycle pants and a lilac tank top, stood in the doorway. Crossing her ebony arms, she leaned against the door and said, "Why Missus Bloom. I do believe I caught you messin' in my po' ole massa's things."

CHAPTER 7

▼

I pressed my hand to my chest, trying to make my heart stop its frantic pounding. "Good Lord, Freedom, you nearly gave me a heart attack. And don't talk that way," I said crossly. "It annoys me when you do that. I know this looks bad, but I have a really good explanation."

More amused than irritated, Freedom strode across the room and perched on the edge of the desk. "I don't doubt for one minute that you do, but you'd better make it snappy. The Madame will be back pretty soon." She eyed me skeptically. "Mr. Roop is around here somewhere. Did he let you in?"

"No. He's, ah, busy. I don't have time to explain. I was…"

"Looking for something. I figured that out all by myself. Pretty clever for an ole servant girl, don't you think?"

"Will you quit that! Honestly, I can't wait until you leave this job. Maybe then you'll stop talking like somebody's lackey. How much longer do you have?"

"Not that this is the appropriate time for this conversation," Freedom replied, "but in exactly three months and four days, I will matriculate into the graduate program at the University of South Carolina at Columbia. You may correctly assume I am counting the days."

I smiled. We had collaborated to whip up an unforgettable approach to graduate school admission. We had discarded the official

MBA application forms and produced a new, creative one in the form of a Fortune Magazine article. I'd painted a pretty good likeness of Freedom for the cover and helped her compose the text, but my artwork would have meant nothing if Freedom hadn't had excellent grades and amazing potential.

"There's so much I want to tell you," I began, "but we can't do it now."

"You can say that again. Mr. Roop and his lovely wife are the most boorish, self-centered, ignorant, elitist snobs I have ever encountered, but I need this job for three more months. If he finds you and me here in his 'office'"—she looked around the room disdainfully—"my ass will be grass."

"I certainly don't want that to happen. I'm done here anyway. It would be impossible to find anything in this pig pen."

We were almost to the stairs when we heard the front door slam and feet walk rapidly across the marble hall.

"Wait," Freedom stopped suddenly. "We can't go down there," she whispered. "Someone's on the way up."

Terrified, I banged into her back. She looked around and said, "Try not to do that again. We have to get out of here."

Deciding quickly, she pulled me back into Andrew's office. "See that door over there? It leads to a corridor that connects this room to the master bedroom. At one time all this must have been a suite. We have to go in there."

Pushing me ahead of her, she opened the door and shoved me into darkness. "Good," I heard her say. No one ever uses this, so I think we're safe."

We were in a narrow hall about twelve feet long, which was also filled with an interesting assortment of junk. There were lamps, books, silver candlesticks and many more odds and ends. At the end of it, the door to the master bedroom was open a crack.

We heard footsteps in the upstairs hall and then silence. Freedom peered through the slightly open door and motioned for me to have a look. Anne Roop strode briskly to the bedroom window and looked out. Then she did something completely out of character. She tossed her Kate Spade handbag at the elaborate mirror on her dressing table and crumpled in a torrent of tears onto the bench.

Fascinated, we watched her sob as if her heart were breaking. As quickly as she had disintegrated, she pulled herself together. She dried her eyes and began to carefully repair her makeup.

"I think we can go now," Freedom said into my ear. "We'll go back the way we came. She's too preoccupied to notice us."

This would have been a good plan if Andrew hadn't bounded up the stairs at that moment and headed for his office. We heard him moving around, obviously looking for something. His search was accompanied by several choice epitaphs of longshoreman quality. We waited, hardly daring to breathe, until he gave up the hunt. On the way out of his office, he locked the door.

"This is not good," Freedom whispered.

Not only was it not good, it was getting worse by the minute. We were, for all intents and purposes, locked in a closet, and Andrew had just entered the master bedroom.

Through the crack, we saw Anne turn to look at Andrew, a condescending smile on her face. When she spoke, we had no choice but to listen.

"You know, dear," she said, "if you're so taken with your little strumpet, perhaps you should go be with her."

"Shut up, Anne. All I did was talk to her."

"You two could live in some cozy apartment somewhere and have big nights out at Burger King. I believe she also likes to fish. That would be fun."

Anne's voice dripped with enough venom to make me glad I had never tangled with her. Andrew didn't seem to enjoy it much either. He reached for a tumbler of vodka, conveniently placed by his bed.

"I'm warning you. I'm sick and tired of you browbeating me all the time. And I'm sick of you running my life."

"Are you really? Do you have any idea what this house would look like if I left things to you? Or, for that matter, what you would look like? Your house, your belongings and you were in a perfect mess before I picked up the pieces. I've made you respectable, Andrew. Maybe you haven't noticed, but people don't snicker behind your back anymore. You can thank me for that."

I heard Freedom snicker. "She sure is wrong about that."

We watched Anne take the glass out of Andrew's hand and place it on her dressing table.

"I've even managed to temper your drinking so that people don't talk. Rarely are you allowed to make an ass of yourself. I've worked too hard on you, Andrew, and I will not allow you to embarrass me. Imagine how I felt when Stephanie called me at the beauty shop to tell me she had seen my husband and that trollop walking hand in hand on the beach past her house. I won't have it. If you try to talk to that little tramp again, you'll be a poor man. She didn't require alimony but I shall."

After this speech, Andrew was understandably upset. He sat down on the edge of the bed, and Freedom and I shifted in our cramped quarters so we could have a better view.

"I can't take this anymore," he said. "We're on the brink of bankruptcy thanks to your compulsive spending, and all you can worry about is what some nosy neighbor thinks." He laughed bitterly. "You can't get blood out of a stone, my dear wife. You precious alimony wouldn't be enough to buy you a Whopper."

Anne moved to the door. "Don't be so sure of that, Andrew. And don't test me."

Andrew pushed past her and headed for the stairs. "Get out of my sight," we heard him yell. "I don't care if I ever see you again."

We waited until there were no more sounds, and the scent of vanilla was only a faint suggestion. Telling me to stay where I was, Freedom went out to case the joint.

While I cooled my heels, I wondered where Anne had acquired such a stilted way of speaking. Her voice practically purred. Maybe she'd spent her youth talking with pebbles in her mouth to improve her diction. Heck, for all I knew, that was the way extremely wealthy people conversed. The folks I hung out with said things like "put a little mayonnaise on that squirrel sandwich, hon. It'll spice it up right nice."

"There isn't a sign of either one of them," Freedom said when she returned. She led me out of the house through the kitchen door. "Both cars are gone. Think of the lucky motorists who meet those two on the road. Talk about road rage!"

"I have to find Tiffany," I told her. "Want to come along and hear what this is all about?"

Freedom consulted her watch. "Sure. Since no one is home, I guess they won't notice I'm not here."

CHAPTER 8

▼

Tiffany was waiting for us at the Salty Dog Café in South Beach. She'd put on a pair of shorts and T-shirt and sat with her feet propped on the pier railing and her eyes closed.

I tapped her on the shoulder. "I didn't find it."

Without opening her eyes, she said, "I was afraid of that."

Freedom pulled up a chair next to her and sat down. "Would some-body like to tell me what's been going on?"

I quickly filled her in. "So you see, we thought maybe I'd be able to find the deed if I looked through Andrew's stuff. I was just trying to help Tiffy."

Freedom and Tiffany ordered sodas from a hovering waitress, and I ordered ice tea.

"How, exactly, would that have helped the situation?" Freedom asked. "It only makes the case against Joey look worse. The police will say Joey had a motive to kill Andrew because Andrew had the *Moon-dancer*."

"But he doesn't have the *Moondancer*," Tiffy almost wailed. "I would know if a lot of money was paid into our account. Believe me, there hasn't been."

"Maybe Joey was so in debt, he never put the money in the bank. Maybe he just cashed the check and gave the money to a bill collector," Freedom offered.

"That's not true, either. Don't talk like that, Freedom. I promise you, Joey would never sell the *Moondancer* to Andrew, no matter how much he needed some money."

We fell silent as the waitress served our drinks and pocketed the money. I changed the subject. "What happened with you and Andrew on the beach today? Was it awful?"

Tiffany flinched as if someone had hit her. "It was terrible. He asked me why I was sitting on his beach and I said it was a free beach, and I could sit anywhere. He touched me and said some really crude stuff. I had to pretend things were bad between me and Joey so he wouldn't suspect why I was there. He asked if he could see me again. I had to say yes." She frowned as she took a sip of orange soda. "He also said Anne never called Joey to work on the *Second Chance*. But I know she did. I heard Joey talking on the phone and when he hung up, he said it was Anne."

Unfortunately, neither Freedom nor I could offer any clarity to the situation. For a while we watched the fishing boats hurry out of the marina while the tide was still high enough. At low tide, the marina became a sandbar, with no way in or out. Finally, when we'd finished out drinks and had enough of the noonday sun, we went home.

I spent the rest of the afternoon calling dog owners about the upcoming Pooch Parade. Since I was giving them very little advance notice, I was gratified to sign up thirty-one eager participants. I explained that we would meet at the Greenwood Drive entrance to the Forest Preserve and walk a mile course with our pets. Each dog owner would pay an entry fee and elicit pledges from friends and family. All money would go to the Rescue A Dog Foundation. The lucky person who made it around the course the most times would win a lovely certificate—which I still had to create. No biting, fighting or attacking other participants would be tolerated. I'm talking about the dogs here.

Satisfied that I'd managed to successfully organize the Pooch Parade, thereby keeping the odious Winfried Burmeister off my back, I spent the next few hours wrestling with my dog painting. When the sun dipped behind Buck Island and disappeared, I gave up for the day. I fixed myself a tuna salad with asparagus spears and ate it on the front porch.

At ten o'clock, I walked outside with Wally and Willow. Foolishly, I didn't put Willow on a leash. I don't know why I do this because I know that as soon as she realizes there is nothing restraining her, she'll run for her life. But hope springs eternal in a foolish heart. I firmly believed that one day she'd sniff freedom and decide she liked it better with me. Tonight, however, wouldn't be that time.

Wally meandered around the yard, content to smell animal pee on the bushes and flowers, but Willow—and this should come as no surprise to anyone—took off. She tore around the side of the house and into the marsh. I put two fingers between my lips and blew as hard as I could, but the only sound I could produce was a disappointing pffftt. I dashed into the house, picked up a flashlight, and reluctantly made my way into the marsh.

I don't like to do this. It's bad enough in the daylight when you can see the critters, but at night it's pitch black and ominous. I parted the tall marsh grass and pointed my light at a rustling sound in front of me.

Willow stood in two inches of rising tide with her front paw lifted and her stubby tail pointed as if she were a retriever about to bag a pheasant. There are, however, no pheasants in a marsh. I didn't stop to consider what she'd found, since I knew that most things that slithered at night were either poisonous or dangerous. I ran to her, picked her up and carried her, squirming and wet, out of the water.

By the time I reached the front of the house, I was soaked and mad. I smelled like sulfur, and there was something slimy stuck to my leg. So when a car swung up my driveway and stopped in front of me, I was understandably annoyed. I think it's fair to say I wasn't in the mood to receive guests.

I shielded my eyes from the headlights as I struggled to keep Willow in my arms. Wally, always ready for any social adventure, trotted over to the car and waited for the driver to open the door. He yipped and pranced like he does when he greets an old friend, which worried me even more because I obviously knew this person and right now I looked liked something spawned in a swamp.

A figure unfolded from the front seat and long legs strode quickly towards me. I immediately recognized the smell of Brut. When he enfolded Willow and me in a sloppy hug, my heart began a little tap dance in my chest.

It was Ben Jakowski, a man I'd met in Germany.

Ben was warm, considerate, athletic, good-looking, smart and funny. In other words, he was perfect. For five months I'd been wildly happy. All the resolutions I made after the divorce, such as lifelong celibacy and a vow to consume as many double chocolate fudge brownies as I could, and who cared about the extra pounds, faded into a romantic oblivion. I lost weight, spiffed up my hair color and forgot about the celibacy thing. I even thought I was falling in love again.

And then I'd read a magazine article about *"Rebound Man—The Real Thing or Disaster? Are you grateful for all the attention he showers on you? Does he tell you you're pretty? Does he make you want to love him? Be careful you don't let your sagging self-confidence lead you into the rebound trap. Wait to find a man until your emotions are on solid ground."*

I woke up the next morning and convinced myself my emotions weren't on solid ground. My divorce from Peter was too new, and Ben was the first man I'd dated. I certainly didn't want to go through another heartbreak. What I should have done at this point was take a brisk walk, or learn to sky dive, or explore the flora of the rain forest in Costa Rica. In other words, keep myself busy until my crazy thoughts went away. Instead, I cancelled the lease on my pretty house, packed up the dogs and split for the good old United States. I hadn't seen Ben since.

I put Willow on the ground, figuring this time I'd have help hunting for her, but she didn't try to run. She sat down in front of Ben and enthusiastically offered her paw. Ben laughed and hugged me again and for a few minutes he and I bumped heads and exchanged "excuse me" as we corralled dogs and put them in the house.

Once inside, I gave him the once-over. I must admit, he looked sensational. His blue eyes crinkled when he smiled at me, and his face was tanned the color of pale copper, which contrasted nicely with his mop of sun bleached, sandy hair. He wore a blue oxford cloth shirt with the sleeves rolled up and chino pants.

"Maggie," he said. "You look wonderful."

The man was blind.

"So do you," I said as I casually tried to pull marsh scum off my leg. "I'm so surprised to see you." I thought about saying "you should have called" and decided against it.

"I'm on home leave. I wanted to find a sunny spot for a vacation, and that made me think of Hilton Head."

"You look like you've already been in the sun. Where'd you get that tan?"

"The New York Times sent me to Turkey to cover the situation there." He grinned. "They have great beaches." He looked over my head to a spot on the wall. "I was also looking for a place to relax and play a little golf."

"Of course. Hilton Head's the place for that."

So were Pebble Beach, Pinehurst and a lot of other places. We were making polite chitchat and it was killing me. I longed to ask him what he was doing here and why he was in my front hall at ten thirty at night.

For a few minutes we both made a big production of patting the dogs. Finally, I couldn't stand it any longer.

"Why are you here, Ben?" It was blunt, but I figured this was no time for subtlety.

His eyes swung to mine. "I missed you. I wanted to see you again. Why didn't you answer any of my e-mails? Or my phone calls?" He pulled me into another hug.

"What was the point?" I mumbled against his chest. "You're in Germany. I'm here. There didn't seem to be any future for us."

He held me tighter. I must say, it felt good. He was warm and solid. "You left so fast," he murmured, his breath warm against my cheek. Reluctantly, I disentangled myself from Ben and held him at arm's length.

"I'd had about enough of Germany. Being accused of murder wasn't any fun. And poor Kate. She's in a German jail. It was time to go home." This wasn't the reason I left, but he didn't need to know that just yet.

He chuckled. "Who knows what would have happened if you'd stayed. You have a talent for getting into trouble."

I dragged him to the kitchen and busied myself making coffee and hunting for something sweet and edible. My solution for awkward moments is food.

"I could fix something else, like an omelet," I said, peering into the refrigerator. "Are you hungry?"

I felt his hands on my shoulders. "Not for food."

He was moving a little fast. I hadn't seen the man for a long time, and he was ready to pick up where we left off. I managed a laugh that sounded like I had something caught in my nose. I have to admit I was hungry for the same thing, but I can't just jump into bed with the first good-looking man who appears on my doorstep in the middle of the night. Ben dropped his hands and leaned against the counter.

"Are you seeing someone, Maggie?"

"Well, it depends how you define 'seeing.' I certainly have plenty of opportunities. This place is crawling with eligible men." That wasn't exactly true. There were plenty of men, but most of them didn't want to miss their afternoon naps. "I really prefer not to tie myself down. Are you seeing anyone?"

He laughed. "No. Other women seemed a little, ah, tame after you."

In spite of my resolution to remain celibate forever more, that news made me feel good. "Where are you staying?" I asked.

"I've rented a condo in Harbour Town. I'll be here for a week. I was hoping we could spend some time together."

"That would be very nice."

I found half a marble cake that was still fresh enough to eat and put it on the counter, along with two plates, two forks and two mugs.

He stopped me on the way to the sink. "I thought we had the beginning of something good in Bonn."

"We might have," I admitted. "But how would we know? I mean, we were in the middle of a murder investigation and a plot to bomb the ambassador's residence. I wasn't feeling at my best. Maybe I was attracted to you because you were the only one who would help me."

"I see."

I could have kicked myself for behaving like an ass, but I didn't know how to tell him that the thought of romantic involvement had scared me to death. If I'd allowed myself to love him, I'd have been vulnerable to big time heartbreak when he found himself a bimbo like Peter had. Falling in love again would be like poking a sharp stick in my eye. I'd feel better if I'd stop.

But, I'd thought about him every single day. And I told him so. Relief flooded his face.

"Then why didn't you tell me? When you never answered any of my e-mails, I was afraid to call any more. I couldn't figure out what I'd done wrong."

"It's too complicated, Ben. I'm glad to see you. Let's leave it at that. What would you like to do for the next week?"

"Play some golf," he said. "Maybe a little tennis. Walk on the beach. I want to relax and be with you."

We carried the cake and coffee to the sunroom and sat next to each other on my wicker couch. After a few bites, he said, "So what have you been up to?"

"Same old, same old," I said as I pushed crumbs around on my plate. "Hilton Head is a quiet place. I paint stuff for a living." I waved my hand towards the picture of the dog and assorted pots in various stages of design.

"That's interesting. Look at me, Maggie."

I felt color spread to the freshly dyed roots of my hair. Ben slapped the couch with his hand.

"You're in trouble again, aren't you? I should have known. What is it this time? Murder? Bombs? Tell me. You can't shock me anymore."

"Nothing so interesting. And you don't have to be so dramatic. I'm simply doing a favor for a friend. Technically, I don't think you can say I'm in trouble. I may have done something slightly illegal, but there shouldn't be any repercussions." That is, as long as Andrew Roop never finds out I snuck into his house.

Ben held his head in his hands. "Want to tell me about it," he muttered.

Actually, I did. It felt good to have an impartial ear listen to the story. I chronicled the list of improbable events and waited for Ben's reaction.

"Well, I must say," he finally said with just the slightest hint of sarcasm, "I'm relieved. What we're dealing with here is a simple case of breaking and entering. That only carries a sentence of what? Two to five? I'm afraid I'm not current on American law." He took my hand and looked at me earnestly. "What is the matter with you? Why do you always feel like you can take the law into your own hands? Do you have any idea how much that worries me?"

"Ben, let me remind you that an hour ago you had no idea about any of this, so you haven't been all that worried. And, I'm not doing anything wrong. I'm simply trying to help Tiffany. Once you meet her, you'll see why. She's a nice girl who dearly loves her husband and needs someone to believe in her."

He shook his head. "Something tells me here we go again." He stood up and pulled me to my feet. "I'm going to the condo now and get a good night's sleep. I have a feeling I'm going to need it."

At the front door he kissed me goodnight: a long, warm kiss that sizzled through my body and curled my toes. It was all I could do to wave weakly as he got in the car and drove away.

That night I dreamed I was riding down Calibogue Sound on a huge oyster shell. I had long, flowing golden hair that twined strategically around my naked body. On either side of me were Ben and Peter, appropriately clothed in loincloths. They rowed in unison while chanting, "Pick me, pick me."

This celibacy thing might not work, I thought. My nocturnal fantasies were becoming bizarre.

CHAPTER 9

▼

I slept late the next morning. When I finally opened my eyes, Wally and Willow were standing on my stomach peering into my face. I got up, took them out and made a pot of coffee. While the dogs ate their breakfasts, I listened to five new messages on my answering machine: one from Peter, saying he had a big surprise for me, two from Tiffany asking me to call her immediately, a terse comment from Mrs. Jordan advising me that she absolutely needed the portrait in eleven days, and one from Ben, saying he missed me already, and he'd see me tonight for dinner.

I carried the cup of coffee to my easel and thought about mixing up some paint and getting to work, but the creative muse had deserted me. I kept thinking about Ben. He and I were operating in two different modes, I realized. He expected our relationship to resume, full speed ahead. I needed some kind of reassurance, preferably written in blood, that he would never dump me the way Peter had. I just didn't see how those two twains could ever meet.

Since I couldn't muster the slightest bit of enthusiasm for painting, I turned the picture to the wall and dialed Tiffy's number.

"I'm so glad you called," she bubbled. "You'll never guess what happened. I heard from Joey!"

I'd been prepared for a discouraged Tiffany, so this news caught me off guard. "What do you mean? Did you actually talk to him?"

"It was so exciting. I was in the cabin doing some hand washing and thinking about how I couldn't stand Andrew Roop, when that little thingy, that VHF radio, started sputtering and making all kinds of static. I tried to twiddle the knobs, but I'm not much good at getting it to work. Joey was always the one to work it. Anyway, I finally heard a voice and it was Joey. I distinctly heard him say 'May Day' three times. I tried to answer, but the static came back and then I lost him." Some of the enthusiasm went out of her voice. "May Day means trouble, doesn't it?"

"Well," I said as soon as I managed to get a word in, "it certainly means someone is having some kind of a problem. But Tiffy, I think we can assume Joey is in a," I chose my word carefully, "predicament. Otherwise he would be home. And it's good that you heard from him. At least we know he hasn't been harmed."

I crossed my fingers. A May Day call was serious and, as an experienced boater, Joey would know that. It meant grave physical danger to a person or a boat. I felt the butterflies start in my stomach. It didn't look like Joey Archer had disappeared from his own free will.

"I can't talk anymore now, Maggie. I'm going to listen to the radio all night. I'm just so happy to hear his voice and know he's trying to reach me. And guess what else? That man who had been watching the *Moondancer* is gone. You don't suppose that could mean they know where Joey is?"

"I think if they knew where he was, they'd have arrested him by now. I suspect the sheriff realizes Joey wouldn't risk coming back to Harbour Town if he had something to do with the explosion on the *Second Chance*. He'd be too visible."

"That's a relief. There was something else I wanted to ask you. Do you think you could spend the night with me on the *Moondancer*? I know I shouldn't ask, but it's spooky here without Joey. Besides, if he calls again, you'll be able to hear it too."

Oh boy, how would I get out of this? I definitely did not want to spend the night on her boat. "I don't know how I can do that, Tiffy. The dogs would be here by themselves, and I don't think they'd like that."

"You could come later—say around ten thirty—and go home real early. That way, they would hardly know you're gone. Please?" she begged. "I really do need you."

Reluctantly, I agreed. I would go out with Ben, come home and let the dogs out, stay on the *Moondancer* until dawn and be back home before the dogs realized I hadn't slept in my bed.

As I hung up, the phone rang again.

"The Madame had her shorts in a knot last night," Freedom said. "She really let Andrew have it, following him from room to room ranting and raving. I have no idea what the poor slob did, but whatever it was, no one deserves that kind of treatment. He finally took his vodka bottle and locked himself into his office."

Quickly, I filled Freedom in on the phone call with Tiffany. "She is deliriously happy to have heard Joey's voice, but I think it means he's someplace where he can't get home."

Freedom agreed. "What's the range on those VHF radios?"

"It depends. A hand held is about two to five miles. But we don't know what kind he was using. Tiffany must have stumbled onto Channel 16, the International Hailing Channel, when she was turning the dials."

"So that means anyone listening to that channel could pick up the May Day call?"

"Right. I'm sure the Coast Guard monitors it."

I steered the conversation back to the Roops. "Anne can't possibly have seen Tiffany and Andrew together, so she's going on what the nosy neighbor told her. Tiffy said they walked down the beach towards the Marina. She never went back to the Roops' house."

"Anne was gunning for trouble when she drove up the drive," Freedom said. "When I got to the house after leaving you, she was waiting for me in the hall, complaining about the way I had ironed a blouse. She also said the cleaners had lost her best silk slacks, and a cashmere sweater still had a spot on it. I think you could say she was in a prickly mood."

"I feel so stupid for breaking into the house," I admitted. "But I sure wish I had found the title to the *Moondancer*. Otherwise Andrew will have a terrible hold over Tiffany. We all thought he was over his obsession with her, but we were wrong."

"Did you ever consider that Andrew might have come by the title honestly? That perhaps Joey was in debt and Andrew lent him money, holding the *Moondancer* as collateral."

I snorted. "You don't believe that yourself. Joey wouldn't go to Andrew for money, and Andrew would have liked nothing better than to see Joey collapse in financial ruin. Besides, I saw Joey's bankbook when we searched the *Moondancer*. It didn't have a huge balance, but he didn't have outstanding debts. And he hadn't missed a payment on the boat."

For a few seconds Freedom was silent. "Then how could Andrew possibly get the title? He can't have taken it without Joey knowing, and I'll agree with you that Joey would never have given it to him. Try this theory. Andrew isn't the son of a bitch Joey was referring to. It's someone else."

"But who? Joey is a mild mannered, gentle man. There is only one person on this island who has ever made him lose his temper, and that person is Andrew. Who else would Joey call a son of a bitch?"

"Don't know, but I'll do anything I can to help. But please, Maggie," her laughter tinged voice floated over the wire, "don't lose me my job. If you do, I'll have to move in with you."

CHAPTER 10

▼

All I can say is, the devil made me do it. First, I'd given Wally and Willow a bath and brushed them until their coats gleamed, so they'd look pretty for the Pooch Parade, which was ridiculous since the Forest Preserve was full of mud and horse droppings and pine straw and ticks. Then, I decided to go to Coligny Plaza and pick up more flowerpots from the hardware store. I drove out the Ocean Gate and was whizzing down North Forest Beach Drive, minding my own business, when I spotted Anne Roop's snazzy little BMW Roadster ahead of me.

Like I said, the devil told me to ignore the turnoff to Coligny Plaza and follow the BMW down Pope Avenue, around the traffic circle and onto William Hilton Parkway, or Hwy 278, as the natives like to call it.

It began to rain; one of the sudden torrential downpours that occurs almost daily in the summer in the Lowcountry. When the first raindrops hit the windshield of Anne Roop's car, she pulled to the left lane and stepped on the gas. This was an unusual reaction for a Hilton Head resident. We all knew that a rainstorm made the William Hilton Parkway a dangerous snarl of traffic, and wise motorists proceeded with caution. Being unwise, I followed her.

Sure enough, ahead of us, at the entrance to Port Royal Plantation, there was an accident: a white Ford with New Jersey license plates had rear-ended an Ohio Chrysler minivan. A state trooper stood in the road, motioning cars around the two disabled vehicles.

Traffic moved so slowly, I was forced to pull up behind Anne. When she looked in the rearview mirror, I ducked my head, pretending to search for something on the seat beside me. I needn't have bothered. She was busy applying lipstick and fiddling with her hair. She was far too concerned about her appearance to worry about who was behind her.

Once free of the traffic jam, we moved along at a brisk speed. Anne stayed in the left lane all the way over the bridge off the island and through Bluffton.

As I drove along, I thought about Anne and her house and her relationship with Andrew. I couldn't get her lousy portrait out of my mind. The artist had painted the features but ignored the soul. Every portrait painter worth his salt knew creating a likeness was relatively easy, but capturing the essence of the person was the most gut wrenching, exhausting process imaginable. I remembered a visiting artist at college describing this experience as so debilitating, he was forced to drink straight gin for days afterward.

There was no soul in Anne's painting. And the more I thought about it, even the execution was clumsy—which made no sense. Why would the Roops, with all their money, hire an inferior artist? And why would Andrew, who so obviously had exquisite taste in art, hang it in his living room next to his true masterpieces? The answer had to be Anne. Whatever Anne wanted, Anne got.

At the intersection of highways 278 and 170, Anne turned right. She also slowed down to a legal 45 miles per hour. About two miles down the road, her speed slowed to 35. She was obviously searching for something.

She braked suddenly and turned left onto a dirt road. I drove past, turned around in a gas station and stopped at the corner where Anne had turned in. There was a small restaurant set back about fifty feet from the road. I drove up to it and parked my car. Anne's BMW was nowhere to be seen.

I climbed out, avoiding large puddles of mud caused by the rain, and approached the door. Above the door a neon sign blinked *Orville's Diner*. A smaller sign in the window said, "We catch 'em, you eat 'em. Come on in."

I went on in. A woman about sixty with white hair and sharp blue eyes stood behind a Formica counter, a handwritten menu displayed behind her head. Two people sat at a red oilcloth covered table eating heaping plates of what looked like fried fish.

The woman greeted me cheerfully. "What can I do ya for? We've got some good catfish today?" She saw me squinting at the menu. "Don't do much good to read it cuz we've only got one thing. That would be the catfish. Plus some good peach cobbler."

I hadn't intended to eat, but what the heck, it was almost lunchtime. I ordered a piece of cobbler and coffee. I sat on a stool at the counter and watched her cut a big piece of the scrumptious looking dessert from a pan and douse it with a vanilla sauce. She served the coffee and folded her arms over her chest, waiting for a reaction. I took a bite, and I can honestly say, I've never tasted any peach cobbler quite as good.

She must have read my face. "Glad you like it. Baked it myself this morning. You from the island?" She jerked her thumb in the direction of Hilton Head.

I nodded. "Actually, I'm supposed to meet a friend around here somewhere. I think it's down there." I pointed to the road Anne had taken.

The woman looked at me as if I'd taken leave of my senses. "You wouldn't be wantin' to go there. Ain't nothing there for most folks." Her lips pursed in disapproval.

I tried again. "Does that road go somewhere? I mean, are there stores down there or something?"

She guffawed and called out to Orville, who was in the kitchen. "Lady wants to know if there are stores down Nanny Goat Lane."

I waited a few minutes while they both hooted with laughter. When I heard Orville honk loudly, I figured the merriment was over and I could speak again.

"I don't understand this. I'm sure my friend said to meet her here."

This caused renewed mirth, and again I had to wait until the friendly waitress controlled a laughing fit. Finally, she dried her eyes on a napkin and said,

"Is your friend a fancy lady? The only thing down that road is Nanny's Hotel and they only have special guests, if you know get I mean."

She watched me closely as I processed this information. "You mean it's a whorehouse?" I asked incredulously. Anne Roop had driven to a whorehouse? It made no sense.

"You got it," the waitress said. "Folks around here don't call it nothing that fancy, though."

"Are you sure there isn't anything else down there? I mean, could my friend be shopping at some antique store?"

"Lady, I'm telling you, there ain't nothing for respectable folks in that place.

I thanked her, paid my bill and left. Afraid to drive all the way down Nanny Goat Lane in case Anne saw me, I went far enough to glimpse the bumper of her BMW parked in the dirt. There was no room to turn around, so I had to back out, irritating a man approaching behind me who was obviously in a hurry.

I pulled into the restaurant parking lot and called Lucy on my cell phone. "I need some info," I said as soon as she answered. "Why would Anne Roop be visiting a whore house?"

I had anticipated exclamations of delighted surprise and requests for all the details. Instead, my question was met with silence. I tried a second time. "Did you hear me?" I want to know why Anne would be visiting a disreputable place called the Nanny Hotel."

"I hear you, sweetie. I'm trying to select fabric for new curtains in the bathhouse. You caught me at a bad time."

"Excuse me? I can't believe my ears. This is juicy. You love juicy gossip. Put the fabric down and listen to me."

"Honestly, Maggie, why are you so interested in this woman? She's an insignificant player."

"How would you know that? I think she's a very significant player. She's the one who asked Joey to work on the *Second Chance*. And, she obviously wields a lot of power with Andrew Roop."

Lucy's disapproving voice floated over the wire. "She denies having called Joey. You only have Tiffany's word that she did."

"Isn't that good enough? What's wrong with you, Lucy? I don't understand this sudden affection for Anne Roop."

"It's not sudden. I mean, it's not affection. I just think we should be careful we don't judge someone without knowing the full story."

At this point, if I'd been a dog, I'd have been madly chasing my tail. This conversation was going nowhere, and I sure didn't understand my friend's sudden reluctance to dish the dirt.

"Well, thanks anyway, Lucy. I'd better be going. Maybe you should ask your new best buddy out to lunch."

"Don't be so juvenile. I do know a tidbit, if you want to hear it."

"Only if you won't be compromising your precious principles."

Lucy wisely decided to ignore my comments. "I just thought you'd like to know that Lois Tattinger told me that Anne tried to take out a loan at Rolf Tattinger's bank. She told Rolf she didn't want Andrew to know about it because Andrew was paranoid about money. Rolf said she'd need Andrew's signature on any loan application because, for the most part, the collateral was in his name. So she stalked out of the bank, vowing to take out all her money."

"Forgive me if I'm mistaken, but shouldn't this type of information be kept confidential?"

Lucy refused to sound chagrinned. "Rolf told his wife, which is perfectly permissible, and she told me. You know she shares everything."

"I'd call it blabbing."

"Call it whatever you wish. I have to go now. Julius and I are taking the boat to Charleston, and I have to tell Cook what to fix for dinner."

"I thought you were picking out curtain material."

"I'm a busy woman, Maggie. Carry on with your sleuthing. Just be careful you don't jump to any conclusions."

I opened my mouth to assure her that I intended to be fair, thorough and diligent in my search for Joey Archer, but she had already hung up the phone.

I drove slowly back to Hilton Head, pondering the implications of Anne visiting a house of ill repute. What could she possibly be doing there? Earning extra money? A mental picture of Anne's physical attributes flashed through my mind. She was lean, almost fashionably gaunt, with broad shoulders and an athletic torso. She wore expensive clothes, and her hair and makeup were always flawless. But the whole effect was cold and sterile, like a well-dressed department store mannequin.

I had trouble conjuring up an image of someone paying money to snuggle up against her washboard abs, and I'd have bet anyone who put a hand on that impeccably coiffed head would get his fingers chopped off. In other words, Anne possessed no tart-like qualities. I couldn't imagine her enjoying sex, even if she did get paid well for it. There had to be some other reason for her visit to the Nanny Hotel. Maybe she was buying diamonds on the black market, and her contact insisted on meeting in a whorehouse so he could combine business and pleasure.

I crossed the bridge onto Hilton Head, took the Cross Island Parkway to Palmetto Bay Road and was almost home before I remembered I needed dog food. I pulled into Park Plaza, intending to run into the store for a bag of Purina. As I was locking my car door, Andrew Roop tapped me on the shoulder.

"I want to talk to you for a minute."

Surprised, I whirled around, clipping him slightly on his arm. He staggered as if I'd decked him with a roundhouse punch. Andrew looked exhausted. The purple pouches under his eyes were new since I'd last seen him. His whole body sagged, as if he had a tremendous weight on his shoulders. I noticed his hands were shaking.

"I'd like you to deliver a message for me."

"Huh?"

He pawed at my arm. "I want you to tell your little friend that her scheme isn't going to work. I've had enough. You have to make her listen to reason."

I wondered if he'd been drinking. Vodka is hard to detect on someone's breath, but Andrew's behavior was so bizarre, I figured he'd probably already had a few swigs today. He was also beginning to scare me. I decided to forget the dog food and head for home. Willow and Wally could have cereal for dinner.

"I have to go now, Andrew. For the record, I have no idea what you're talking about."

"Don't give me that. You know perfectly well that little witch is trying to bankrupt me." He reached into a briefcase he was carrying, pulled out a bunch of papers and thrust them under my nose. "Look at this. My lawyers say I sold nearly all my shares of Roop Industries. But I know I didn't. I'd never do something that stupid. See this? It's a written authorization, supposedly signed by me, for my lawyer to sell all my holding in General Electric, Intel and Norfolk Southern. It's a forgery."

He suddenly grabbed his chest and uttered a groan. Terrified that he was having a heart attack, I opened the car door, eased him onto the seat and reached for my cell phone to dial 911. He batted my hand away.

"Don't call anyone. I'm okay."

"No, you're not, Andrew. You look awfully pasty."

Actually, he looked like he had already died. His face had a ghastly, distinctly unhealthy pallor. In spite of my dislike for Tiffany's ex-husband, I felt sorry for him. The man was a wreck.

"I can't figure out what's happening to me, Maggie. The bank says I have no money. That can't be true. I feel like I'm going crazy."

"Why are you telling this to me, Andrew? Isn't this something you should be discussing with Anne?"

"Anne says she doesn't know anything about this. Believe me, I've asked her. She couldn't sell stock even if she wanted to because it all belongs to me. But that little friend of your knows how to forge my name. I saw her do it when we were married. I want you to warn Tiffany that I'm on to her little scheme. I don't know how she's doing it, but I'm sure as hell going to stop it."

I was relieved to see that indignation made the color flood back into Andrew's face. I hauled him to his feet and propped him against the car. Now that his wobbly circulatory system was temporarily functioning, I wanted him to step away from the vehicle so I could be on my way.

"Are you sure you're feeling okay? I'd be happy to call for medical help if you need it, but I'm not going to stand here and listen to you accuse Tiffy of something she didn't do. She would never steal your money. I hate to tell you this, Andrew, but she doesn't want to have anything to do with you."

In one of the most repulsive gestures I've ever seen, he ran his tongue over his lips before he spoke.

"Is that what she told you? Don't believe everything you hear."

My compassion disappeared. The man made my skin crawl.

"Get lost, Andrew. And go see a doctor. You look like you could use one."

As soon as he moved away, I jumped into my car and zoomed out of the parking lot.

*   *   *   *

This time there were three new messages on my answering machine. Winfried Burmeister wondered if I'd contacted the *Island Packet*— "Wouldn't it be just delightful to see our darling babies' pictures in the paper? My little Princess will be wearing a quaint little gem stone studded collar I created myself."

Princess was an ancient Pekinese whose feet never touched the ground. Winfried carried her everywhere. The dog also had a distressing problem with gas. She could clear a room in two seconds. People would run for the door holding their noses and fanning the air, and Winfried never let on her little aromatic bundle was the cause.

The second message was from Freedom saying she would come to the Pooch Parade and help me walk the dogs.

Last, but certainly not least, Ben said he'd pick me up at 7:00. I flew into my bedroom and plowed through my closet, looking for something to wear. My intention was to look sexy. Since it had been a while since I'd thought along those lines, I had trouble finding something suitable. My closet seemed to be filled with jeans, slacks, blouses and a beige, broomstick skirt of undetermined age. I finally settle on white Capri, pants, a low cut, turquoise tank top and a pale turquoise and white chiffon shirt, which I would wear as a jacket.

By the time I washed my hair, fed the dogs and spent an inordinate amount of time applying unaccustomed makeup, it was nearly time for Ben to arrive. I added silver hoop earrings, a chunky silver bracelet and white sandals with a two-inch heel.

I viewed myself in the mirror and hoped Ben still went for the wholesome look. I was presentable, but hardly the stuff men fantasized about. I remembered I was wearing cotton Jockey underwear, but since I didn't plan to remove anything in the near future, that probably wouldn't matter.

When the doorbell rang, I checked my teeth for lipstick, tottered to the front hall and opened the door.

Ben was wearing shorts, a Pebble Beach T-shirt and a large grin on his face.

"You're looking pretty fancy for a picnic on the beach," he said.

"I thought we were going out to dinner."

"We are. At least I am. I'm not quite sure what you're dressed for." He eyed my sandals. "How do you walk in those things?"

"With great difficulty," I snapped, kicking off my shoes. "You could have told me. I don't have anything fixed for a picnic."

"Ah, but I do. Shall we go?"

Sighing, I said, "Give me a minute."

I zoomed into my bedroom, jammed my feet into a pair of canvas shoes, ditched the chiffon shirt and earrings and grabbed a sweatshirt out of my closet.

When I returned to Ben, he said, "That's better. I thought we'd take a walk after we eat." He put his arm around my shoulder as we walked to the car. "You look nice. That's the way I like you. Plain and simple."

"Peachy," I muttered. "You certainly know how to turn a girl's head with compliments."

He pretended he didn't hear me. We drove to the beach club in relative silence. I only spoke once to tell him he'd made a wrong turn on Lighthouse Road.

CHAPTER 11

▼

Ben amazed me. He had a wicker basket full of fried chicken, steamed corn on the cob, hot rolls, and a chilled bottle of chardonnay.

"Where did you get this stuff," I asked as I spread a blue and white blanket on the sand. He handed me napkins, forks and paper plates. Producing a corkscrew, he said, "At a restaurant. I said I wanted to take a special girl on a romantic picnic. They were happy to help. Look." He held up two huge pieces of chocolate fudge brownies. "They even threw these in at no charge."

As we ate, we watched dolphins frolic in the ocean. The beach was nearly deserted at this time of evening, and we had a stretch of sand all to ourselves. I had to admit, it was nice. The food was tasty and Ben was warm and eager to please. Even though I'd intended to sulk for a while about the lack of cloth napkins and chairs, I had to give it up. I was having too much fun. I stuck my bare feet into the sand and completely relaxed.

When Ben asked me how my day had been, I told him about following Anne down Hwy 278. "Why on earth do you suppose she went to a whorehouse?" I asked.

He dug in the sand with a piece of seashell. "I suppose it would be futile to suggest that you shouldn't be following anybody or breaking into houses. I don't understand you, Maggie. Do you think you're invulnerable? Or invisible? One of these days, something bad is going to happen to you if you don't stop this."

In spite of the warmth of the evening, a chill wind blew across my face. "I didn't put myself into any danger," I said defensively. "I simply drove behind the woman. She didn't see me. And you don't need to lecture me. I didn't like it in Germany and I don't like it now."

Ben got to his feet and brushed sand off his shorts. "Come on. Let's take a walk and not talk about the missing Joey or whorehouses or anything else that reminds me of how reckless you are. There must be other subjects for conversation."

There were. As the sky faded from a soft orange to a blue-gray and finally, an inky black, we walked hand in hand along the beach, allowing soft waves to break over our feet. He told me about his work in Germany, and I told him about my new artistic career. We talked about our dreams for the future, and our childhoods, and the time we spent together in Bonn. By the time we reached our blanket, I felt like we had known each other all our lives. When he kissed me, I was amazed to realize I didn't want him to stop. He must have felt the same way, because he said, "Would you like to come back to my condo? I could show you my etchings." I felt him smile in the darkness.

I slapped my forehead and said, "Damn."

"Excuse me?"

"No, no, it's not you. I have something else I have to do."

"I see," he said, pulling away."

"No, you don't. Oh dear, I can't believe I agreed to do this. I'm sorry, Ben. I have to sleep on the *Moondancer* tonight. Tiffany heard from Joey, and she wants me to be there if he calls again."

"I should have known." He gathered up the basket and blanket and stuck them under his arm. "I don't want to fight with you, Maggie. "Do whatever it is you have to do, and let me know when you'll have time for us. I know I'm an idiot to say this, but I'll be waiting."

"I'm not sleuthing tonight," I said as we walked to the car. "Tiffany is nervous being on the boat by herself, so I'm staying with her just this once." I squeezed his arm. "Don't be mad."

"I'm not mad. I'm just trying to figure out why I can't be attracted to a nice, sensible girl who spends her evenings playing with the cat."

"You know you'd hate that. Besides, you and I are dog people. We'd never be cozying up to cats."

Fortunately, I missed his reply. I think the wind swept it away.

*   *   *   *

At 10:57 I eased my car into the Harbour Town parking lot and walked past the shops to the long pier where the *Moondancer* was docked. I called out to Tiffany before I stepped onboard. At the sound of my voice, she came on deck and greeted me excitedly.

"Guess what, Maggie. I've heard from Joey two more times. I tried to talk to him, but he couldn't hear me."

She pulled me into the cabin and showed me the VHF radio. "See. I guess I don't know how to work this thing. He keeps saying 'May Day' and I keep yelling 'Joey, honey, it's me.' Maybe you can make it work." She thrust the hand held radio at me. "Anyway, make yourself comfy. Want something to drink?"

I studied my friend. She wore a cotton nightshirt with a picture of a smiling cat on the front, its ears hidden by her long, blonde hair. She looked happy.

"I don't want anything to drink."

I looked across the harbor to Ketch Court where Ben was staying. Lights twinkled in some of the condos. If I hurried, he might still be awake. We could talk some more.

"Are you sure you need me tonight?" I asked. "You seem to have everything under control."

Her smile disappeared. "I really want you to stay. It's creepy here by myself. Besides," she pointed to the radio, "what if Joey calls again? I need you for that."

Resigned to the fact I was spending the night on the *Moondancer,* I said, "Why don't we go to sleep now."

She clapped her hands. "Fine with me. I swear I haven't slept a wink since Joey left. You can have his bunk. Do you want to change into your nightie?"

I shook my head. "I'm going to sleep in my shorts and T-shirt."

To prevent further discussion about my sleeping attire, I sat down on the bunk, took my shoes off and stretched out. Tiffy turned out the light, sighed once and fell asleep. I tossed and turned, trying to get used to an unfamiliar bed. After an hour, I dozed off.

I woke up when Peanuts, Tiffy's cat, jumped onto the bed. Since I'm a dog person, I wasn't sure what the protocol was for sleeping with a cat, but Peanuts knew what to do. She curled up in the curve of my stomach and purred contentedly.

The *Moondancer* bobbed gently at the dock, and I listened to the creaks of Joey's boat. Somewhere in Harbour Town a whippoorwill called and from farther away its mate replied. For a long time the two of them sang their duet, lulling me to sleep.

An unfamiliar sound, like a thud against the stern, made my eyes snap open. For a full two or three minutes, I listened for the noise. When it didn't return, I closed my eyes and relaxed. *You're being silly,* I chided myself. *Don't be a nervous Nellie. You're not used to the sounds on this boat.* The door to the forward cabin was locked. We were safe. I glanced at Tiffany. She snored peacefully.

I was almost asleep when the noise came again, this time louder than before. Thump. And then another sound. I got out of bed, crept over to Tiffany and poked her until she sat up.

"Listen," I said softly. "There's somebody out there."

I heard Tiffy's breath catch. Together we listened in the darkness.

"You know what that reminds me of?" she whispered. "It sounds like someone is casting off. You know, you toss the line on the deck and then jump onboard. It's Joey," she yelled. "He's back!"

Without bothering to throw on a robe, Tiffany tore out of the cabin. I followed, wishing I had something I could use as a weapon, just in case it wasn't Joey. I caught up with her on the stern of the boat.

"Where can he be?" she said. "Probably planning to surprise me. Joey," she whispered, "It's okay, sugar. No one can see us."

"Well I'm glad to hear that—'sugar'—and don't go screaming or doing something stupid," said a voice. "That won't help your precious Joey."

I know my heart nearly stopped beating, so I can imagine how Tiffy must have felt. I saw her open her mouth to scream, but no sound came out.

It wasn't Joey. It was Andrew, and he was in far worse shape than I'd seen him in earlier. I could tell he was very drunk.

"You look most fetching in your T-shirt," he said as he leered at his ex-wife. She tried to pull the nightgown over her knees.

"It's not a T-shirt. It's a nightgown. What are you doing here?"

"I've come for a little chat and for that we need privacy." Andrew kicked the stern line out of the way. "Have a seat. Or do you need to put on some clothes?"

For the first time, he acknowledged me. "What are you doing here, Maggie? I thought we'd be alone."

"Get off the boat before I call the police," I threatened.

Tiffany echoed my sentiments. "What do you think you're doing, Andrew? Get off my boat right now."

"Can't do that, buttercup. See?" His finger wobbled towards the dock. "We've cast off and we're going for a little ride. Be a good girl and start the engine."

"You're crazy. What have you done? I don't know how to drive this."

"Then I'll do it."

"No. You're drunk. Get away, Andrew."

"Get away, Andrew," he mimicked. "You look so cute when you're mad." His tone changed. "Remember on the beach? You invited me to visit you."

While they chatted, I tried to concoct a plan. There were two of us, and one of him, and he was drunk. Surely Tiffy and I could put one inebriated man out of commission. I decided to sneak up and kick him in the shins. This would disable Andrew enough to allow us to wrestle him to the ground. I'd sit on his stomach and Tiffy could call the police.

He must have read my mind. As I approached, he pulled a little gun out of his pocket and pointed it at me. "I wouldn't try that if I were you. Sit there," he motioned to a bench on the deck, "and don't move."

"I didn't mean for you to visit me at night like this, Andrew," Tiffy said, ignoring the gun. "It isn't proper."

His finger grazed her arm. "You weren't worried about 'proper' on the beach. Don't tell me you've had a change of heart."

As they argued, the *Moondance*r drifted from the pier, her bow pointing straight at the retaining wall of the harbor. We had to do something or the boat would smash right into it. Ignoring Andrew's order to remain seated, I flew to the wheel, turned the ignition key and pushed the throttle forward.

"Maybe it's good you're onboard, Ms. Bloom," Andrew said. "You can drive the boat while I have a cozy talk with my bashful ex-bride."

The engine made a gratifyingly loud noise in the harbor. *Someone has to hear us leaving and notify the authorities*, I told myself. This wasn't the usual hour for departures.

The darn boat was going too fast. As I swung the wheel around, she barely cleared the wall, but I got the *Moondancer* out of the harbor and into the channel. I tried to remember where the sand bars were. I knew they were out there somewhere because the *Prime Time* had gone aground on one last week.

"I have to turn on running lights," I told Andrew.

"This isn't a romantic cruise, although we may have time for that later." He pushed me away from the wheel. "You really don't have the slightest idea how to operate a boat, do you," he said as he throttled back. "You've created a wake. That's a no no, Ms. Bloom." He took the Moondancer through the channel and headed for open water. "We won't turn on any lights. That way, no one will see us." He kept the gun pointed at us as he steered.

I, personally, thought he was crazy, because clouds scudded across a full moon that flashed like a strobe light on the water. All of Harbour Town would be able to see us.

Andrew steadied the boat on a course for Daufuskie Island. A stiff breeze whipped the flimsy nightshirt around Tiffany's body, and she hugged herself tightly. I was thankful I'd kept my clothes on. There was no way I wanted Andrew Roop leering at me, although I had a feeling it was only Tiffany he was interested in.

He didn't speak until we had passed Haig Point and were approaching the public dock. The back of Daufuskie, away from the expensive homes and fancy hotels, was in total darkness. He cut the engine and let the *Moondancer* drift in the quiet water.

"You got anything to drink on this tub?" Andrew wiped the back of his hand across his mouth and looked hopefully at Tiffany.

"No. You don't need anymore. If you want to talk, then please, let's do it now. I want to go back."

"I'll just bet you do." He settled into one of the swivel chairs. "All right. Let me tell you what I have on my mind. I know what you're trying to do, you and that no good husband of yours. And I want it to stop. It won't work, and I'm warning you, I can play rough too." His voice sounded harsh and ugly.

"What on earth are you talking about, Andrew? You know Joey is missing."

"Yeah, yeah." He leaned forward, his face close to hers. "I'm not stupid, honey, and I'm not going to buy that. You can use the innocent routine all you want, but underneath that country girl exterior I think there is a vicious alley cat ready to claw someone's eyes out. Tell me, did you think up the explosion on the *Second Chance,* or was it that son of a bitch husband of yours?"

Tiffany backed against the rail of the boat. "You're crazy, Andrew and you're scaring me."

He sat in the captain's chair and slowly moved the gun back and forth while keeping it pointed at our heads.

"Don't call me crazy," he yelled. "That's just what you'd like, isn't it? The voice on the phone, bank account withdrawals that I don't remember. All intended to make me think I'm losing my mind." His voice dropped. "You knew the family banker, Tiffany. You had access to my bank accounts. It must have been easy to forge my name."

In spite of being scared out of my wits, I was fascinated. It sounded like someone was trying to make Andrew lose his grip on sanity. Not that it would be such a difficult job. He was just about ready for a nice padded room.

"She really doesn't know what you're talking about, Andrew. Why don't you tell us?" I said.

He aimed the gun at my heart. "Not that's it any of your business, Miss Buttinski, but I'm sure your little friend knows all about phone calls telling me I'm responsible for Nathan's debts and threatening me if I don't pay up. How would all the money disappear out of my bank account? I sure as hell didn't spend it."

"As we discussed earlier today, perhaps your wife could clear this up," I murmured.

"Don't blame her. She doesn't know anything about this."

"For the last time, I don't know what you're talking about," Tiffy piped up. "Let's go back now, Andrew. I don't like this."

"What do you need all that money for?" he demanded. "Is it just revenge, or do you plan to spend it? I thought you preferred the humble way of life." He looked around the *Moondancer.* "Has this luxury yacht put you into debt?"

"Don't you dare speak to me about this boat," Tiffy retorted angrily. "You have no right to. I've told you I don't know what you're talking about, and I mean it."

Andrew grabbed her roughly by the arm. "Don't give me that, sweetheart. I can wait out here all night if I have to." His hand slid up her arm. "In fact it might be fun."

"Don't! You should be ashamed of yourself, Andrew. You already know about the boat. And taking the title wasn't fair. I still don't know how you got it. If Joey needed money, he would have told me. And talk about revenge! You just wanted to get at me by hurting Joey."

Andrew laughed scornfully. "Title? Why would I want the title to this scow? Don't try to mix me up, Tiffy. That double talk isn't charming anymore."

"I'm not talking double talk. You have the title to the *Moondancer,* and you know it. Just admit it, and tell me how you got it."

"Ah, my dear deluded ex-wife. I can assure you I neither have the title now nor do I have any wish to possess it in the future. And this isn't what we came out here to discuss."

Tiffany stood in front of Andrew with her hands on her hips. I was appalled to see that the moonlight outlined her perfect body under the cotton nightgown. Andrew smiled and put his hand around her waist. "Let's not talk anymore," he whispered. "I have a better idea." His hand caressed Tiffany's luxurious hair.

I coughed delicately. "You're a smart man, so I'm sure you realize there are two of us here. If you try anything funny with her, you'll have to put the gun down and when you do, I promise you, Andrew, I am going to hit you with the heaviest thing I can find. So whatever you're thinking, you'd better forget it."

I watched as conflicting emotions flitted across Andrew's face. Making a decision, he started the engines and pointed the bow of the boat towards Harbour Town.

"You make me sick. Both of you. I never want to see either of you again."

"That goes double for us," I told him.

Once we were back at the pier, Andrew jumped off the boat and ran toward the shadows of the parking lot. I helped Tiffy tie up the *Moondancer* and then had a serious talk with her.

"We have to call the police and tell them about Andrew. The man is a dangerous lunatic."

"No!" Tiffy said it so vehemently, I was startled.

"Why not? Come on, Tiffy. People aren't allowed to run around waving guns and commandeering boats. The police have to find him and lock him up."

"I don't want to. They'll think I've made it up because I'm protecting Joey."

"But I was there. I can verify you're telling the truth."

She shook her head. "I don't want any more trouble with the police. I just want Joey to come back. I'm not worried about Andrew. He's harmless."

Tiffany began to tremble, all the earlier bravado oozing out of her. "I need to go to sleep, Maggie. Come back and go to bed."

There was no way I was spending another minute on the *Moondancer*. I took her unresisting hand and led her around the harbor to the Ketch Court villas. Ben was asleep when I ran the bell, but he let us in and showed us to the guest bedroom without lecturing me. As I turned out the light, I heard him say, "I knew it, I knew it."

CHAPTER 12

$$\blacktriangledown$$

By 7:30 the next morning, Ben and I had taken Tiffany back to the *Moondancer*, soothed two very angry dogs and were drinking coffee in my sunroom. We'd tried to persuade Tiffy to come with us, but she insisted she felt better and wanted to be home in case Joey called again. I settled back in my chair and waited for Ben to read the riot act. Last night he'd been as upset as we were, so I figured he had a right to vent.

But, he didn't. Instead, he said, "I've come to a decision."

Well, I thought, *here it comes*. It's a damn good thing I listened to my head and didn't let myself get romantically entangled. I was already feeling just the tiniest bit fonder of Ben than I wanted to.

I prepared myself for the goodbye speech, so I was somewhat stunned when he said, "You're never going to change. I realize that wherever there is trouble, Maggie Bloom is going to be in the thick of it. So, in the future, I'm going to stop yelling at you." He looked so proud of himself, I had to smile. "My new role is to be your protector. From now on, if you intend to run off on some hare brained mission, you are taking me with you."

Relieved that I wasn't being dumped, I said, "And what do I go when you go back to Germany?"

"We'll talk about that when the time comes. But, as of this moment, it's you and me, babe."

In view of last night's events, that seemed perfectly fair to me. I was about to show him exactly how pleased I was when the phone rang. "Let it ring," I murmured into his ear. "The machine will pick up."

Unfortunately, we were both able to hear the message. It was Peter.

"Hi, Maggie. Just wanted to tell you I've sailed as far as the Chesapeake Bay. I should be hitting Hilton Head early the day after tomorrow. Can't wait to see you."

For one brief moment I considered lying to Ben and telling him I had no idea who had left that message. But I couldn't do it.

"That was my ex-husband," I tried to say nonchalantly. "It's no big deal. He's on his way to Florida and is stopping here to show me his new boat.

Ben considered this news. "This is the same ex-husband who dumped you for—and I'm quoting here—'a silicone bimbo with the IQ of a turtle'?"

"The very same. It means nothing, Ben. I can truthfully say at this moment I don't care if I ever see him again." As I spoke, I realized this was true. I'd forgotten he was coming.

"We'll see, Maggie," he said as he sipped his coffee. "We'll see."

Wisely, he changed the subject. "What are your plans for today?"

"Well, I have to do something about this dog picture, or my career as an artist is over," I said, showing him the half finished Bernese mountain dog, "Then, this afternoon is the Pooch Parade." I explained about walking the dogs in the Forest Preserve.

He gave Wally and Willow a pat and headed for the door. "Count me in for the Pooch Parade. I'll meet you there. I know where it is."

When I protested that he didn't need to come, he put a finger to his lips. "I'm coming. You and a bunch of dogs in a nature preserve? Think of the possibilities. You could be bitten by a pit bull, or fall into a lagoon, or be stung by a swarm of bees." He rubbed his hands together. "I can't wait."

"Go away," I growled. "I've got work to do.

I solved the Bernese mountain dog problem in an hour. All it needed was a perkier nose. The dog looked reasonably pleasant, so I hoped Mrs. Jordan would be able to recognize her pet's inner character, or whatever it was she wanted to see.

I took a sip of cold coffee and began to clean up the brushes and paint. As I worked, I thought about Peter. Of all the lousy times for him to be coming to Hilton Head, this was the worst. I laughed out loud. I'd had weeks of wishing I could find someone to take me out, and now there were two men at once. But, I didn't know if Peter was coming alone. So far, he hadn't mentioned that.

I shoved the paints, brushes and rags into a closet and turned the dog picture to face the hall, so I could see it every time I passed by. It wasn't too bad, I decided. But best of all, it was done.

*   *   *   *

Forty-seven people showed up to walk their pets in the Pooch Parade. By the time I gave each participant an entry number and collected a $5.00 fee, the parking lot of the Forest Preserve was jammed with barking dogs and agitated owners.

Henry, the dog in my picture, bounded over to the table where I was seated, determined to greet me with his usual gusto. To prevent being knocked into the trees behind me, I stood up, stuck out both hands and sent him sprawling into the pine straw. Disappointed that he hadn't been able to nuzzle my crotch, he attached himself to the rear end of a Sheltie. The Sheltie turned around and bit him on the nose. Mrs. Jordan shrieked, and the Sheltie owner threatened to sue.

Winfried Burmeister scuttled over to inquire about the *Island Packet* photographer. She wore red plaid jodhpurs, a white blouse with a ruffled collar and red vest. Princess wore matching plaid panties and a frilly collar. I told Winfried I'd notify her as soon as the *Island Packet* arrived. Which would be never. I'd forgotten to call them.

Wally and Willow were less than enthusiastic about the whole program. I'd tied them to the leg of the table while I worked. Wally was happy to sleep at my feet, but Willow snapped angrily at any dog that had the courage to sniff her behind.

I looked around for Freedom and Ben. Freedom stood near a parked Mercedes, explaining to a very upset woman that dog pee on a tire wouldn't necessarily ruin it forever.

Ben, looking quite wonderful in tan shorts and a blue and white polo shirt, sauntered over to me and said, "Unless you want a revolution—and I don't doubt for a minute you would find some joy in that—I think you'd better get this show on the road."

He was right. Things were getting out of hand. I blew a whistle, which set off a frenzy of barking. When things quieted down, I said, "We will start the walk at intervals of thirty seconds. Will you please line up at the entrance starting with number one? Follow the blue arrows for the one-mile course. Walk as many laps as you want. The Pooch Parade ends at 6:00."

Things went smoothly after that. Ben, Freedom and I waited until the last dog owner walked into the woods. Then we grabbed Wally and Willow's leashes and started after them.

I loved the Forest Preserve. It always amazed me that such an idyllic, peaceful place existed deep in the middle of a bustling tourist community like Sea Pines. Over 4000 years ago Indians hunted and fished in the Preserve, and you can still see traces of their lives in the mounds of shells at the Indian Shell Ring. There were also wonderful boardwalks that spanned the wetland areas of the Preserve. The dogs and I came here often to stroll along the quiet paths, and watch the egrets swoop across the marshes and the turtles sun themselves in the lagoons. Most of the time we spotted an alligator swimming lazily in the water.

We dutifully followed the blue arrows, which marked the one-mile course. Ben walked Willow and I had Wally. Freedom sauntered along between us, and we chatted pleasantly as we admired the wild life and flora. I noticed Freedom admiring Ben. Behind his back, she gave me the thumbs up sign, which I assumed meant I had her seal of approval.

At a fork in the road, we veered into thick woods on our way to Boggy Gut, my favorite place in the Forest Preserve. Boggy Gut reminded me of the setting for a Charles Addams movie: bare tree limbs dripping with Spanish moss in the middle of swamp water so filled with algae that it glowed an iridescent green. Today, to my delight, a steamy mist rose from the water, enhancing the spooky effect.

The dogs stopped to bark at Boggy Gut. Suddenly, their barking turned from the delighted yelps of two English cockers baying at invisible swamp creatures to the more urgent bark they used to announce the presence of strangers. I looked around to see what had upset them. Both dogs stood with their hind legs firmly planted, barking furiously at something.

To the left of us, about twenty feet down the path, I saw movement in the woods. I poked Ben in the ribs and said, "Do you see that? There's someone in there."

"So? What's wrong with that? Maybe it's a nature lover studying the fauna."

"That's a strange place to be walking. The woods are full of ticks."

Ben gave me a smile. "Maybe one of the dog walkers had to answer the call of nature. I don't see any bathrooms around here."

As he spoke, a man and a woman darted out of the trees and walked rapidly down the path. Too rapidly, I thought. They were almost running.

"Would you look at that," I said, stopping to watch the couple flee. "Talk about wanting to be alone. Those folks obviously don't want company."

"Maybe they don't like dogs."

"There aren't any dogs around. The others are way in front of us, and Wally and Willow are on leashes."

I shouldn't have said that. Apparently annoyed at the delay in her walk, Willow slipped her collar. Free of the leash, she tore down the path, her sturdy legs churning and her ears flapping. I yelped and ran after her, Ben hot on my heels.

Instead of heading for the parking lot as I expected, Willow rounded the corner to the boardwalk and disappeared from sight. Genuinely alarmed, I ran as fast as I could, calling her name. Alligators ate dogs, and I had no intention of allowing Willow to become some amphibian's main course. Far ahead I could see the two people now making no pretense at casual walking. They were running fast.

At the end of the boardwalk, Ben sprinted past me and caught up with Willow. He took a flying leap and tackled my dog just as she was about to head for the thick woods beyond. He and Willow lay on the ground, panting rapidly.

"You're a bad dog," I scolded as I attached the collar and leash. My own breath was coming in ragged gasps, and my hair and clothes were soaked with sweat. Ben didn't look so hot either. I helped him to his feet.

"You have got to teach that dog to obey, Maggie," he said as he brushed off his clothes. "I'm getting too old for this."

I used the edge of my shirt to wipe some dirt off Ben's chin. Out of the corner of my eye, I saw the couple stop. The woman hung heavily on the man's arm and rubbed her ankle. *Good*, I thought. *It serves you right, racing through here as if your tail were on fire.* I watched the woman wipe her face with a piece of brightly colored material and then tie it around her head before continuing down the path.

Something tugged at my memory. Somewhere I'd seen fabric like that. As Ben and I waited for Freedom and Wally to catch up with us, I remembered. Anne Roop had worn a similar scarf when I'd met her at Fashion Court. Now that I thought about it, the woman could have been Anne. She had the same compact, athletic body and same height. Excited, I shared my theory with Ben.

"It sure looked like her," I insisted. "What do you make of that? First she goes to a seedy hotel and now she's running around the Forest Preserve with a man."

"Maggie, Maggie," Ben said sadly. "Get your imagination out of high gear. Those folks were probably running from the dogs. Your animals aren't the quietest creatures, you know. Maybe they thought the dogs were loose, and they were afraid of being bitten."

I turned to Freedom, who had just joined us. "Did you see her? I think that was Anne Roop."

Freedom shook her head. "I didn't see a thing." She pointed to Wally. "Do you realize this dog absolutely refuses to run? I've never seen an animal do that. I tugged on the leash and I pleaded. Do you know what he did?"

"Yeah, yeah. He sat down. Forget about Wally. I tell you, I think that was Anne. What would the very proper Mrs. Roop be doing in the Forest Preserve with a man?"

Freedom giggled. "Having an affair? I can't say I would blame her. Living with Andrew must be a daily nightmare."

"I wouldn't pick the Forest Preserve as a likely rendezvous spot," I said. "There have to be better places."

But were there? Hilton Head wasn't big enough to hold many out of the way, discreet places. And Anne had a very high profile among the permanent residents. Everyone knew her. The more I thought about it, the more I realized the Forest Preserve was the perfect place, if you didn't mind a few pine needles in your backside.

CHAPTER 13

▼

Mrs. Dowling and her miniature Schnauzer, Fritzi, won the prize for walking the farthest in the Pooch Parade. Winfried Burmeister had to drop out at the half-mile marker because a German shepherd jumped up and tried to eat Princess. Several folks complained about soiled shoes, and one woman broke into tears when her dog ingested horse manure, but all in all, it was a huge success. So successful that Freedom, Ben and I decided to go to the Crazy Crab in Harbour Town for a celebration dinner.

I dropped the dogs off at home, fed them and took them for their usual evening walk. It was around eight o'clock before we all met again at the restaurant. Jenny, the hostess, gave us a window table so we could watch the yachts in the harbor as we drank cold Melon Coladas and nibbled on hush puppies.

Since we had a direct view of Andrew Roop's empty slip, it wasn't surprising that the conversation turned from the Pooch Parade to Joey and last night's bizarre activities.

"So, we know Joey is alive and trying to contact Tiffany, and Andrew doesn't know anything about the title to the Moondancer," I said.

"Or pretends he doesn't." Freedom reached for three hush puppies and a mound of butter. "Andrew Roop is a snake."

"Do you think Andrew was lying about the title?" I took a sip of my drink. After dealing with dog owners all afternoon, I needed something alcoholic before I thought about food.

"I think you're too trusting. You'll believe anything anyone tells you. Trust me, Andrew Roop is capable of bald-faced lies. You don't see him every day like I do. He is weak and cowardly, and I wouldn't put anything past him."

"Well, believe it or not, I just happen to agree with you. I guess I don't have to ask if, in your opinion, he has any good qualities. But, he'd been drinking last night, and you know the old saying, *'in vino veritas'*. I think in this case he was telling the truth. He doesn't know anything about the title."

Ben finished his Melon Colada in three gulps and ordered a beer. When he saw the look on my face, he said, "I'm thirsty. And I need sustenance to talk about this with you."

"Then what's going on?" Freedom asked, ignoring him. "I thought we had already established that Joey couldn't be deceitful if he wanted to be. And he told the harbormaster that Andrew had the title."

I shook my head. "He didn't say Andrew. He said 'that son of a bitch.' I think you were right when you said he might not have meant Andrew."

In deference to Ben, we talked about other things until the waiter served us plates of steamed shrimp and corn on the cob. I probed the possibility of Anne having an affair.

"I really do believe it was Anne I saw in the woods," I said as I peeled a shrimp and dipped it in cocktail sauce. "I don't know who the man was, but they both acted so guilty. I wouldn't have paid any attention to them if they hadn't loped down the path like startled deer."

Freedom chewed on her ear of corn. "Nothing would surprise me in that family. I'm about ready to quit. If I didn't need the money so badly, I would. Mrs. R is even bitchier than usual, if that's possible. She orders me around as if I'm her indentured servant. She's nervous too. Sometimes I have the feeling she's strung together so tightly, it wouldn't take much to shatter her to pieces."

"She might be worried about Andrew. It has to be horrible living with him. Ask Tiffy."

Freedom tasted my coleslaw. "I can't feel sorry for Anne. She is totally self-absorbed. And another thing; I used to be able to set my clock by her schedule, but now she disappears and I have no idea where she went or when she'll be back. Then she comes roaring in, demanding to know why her dress isn't pressed, or why I haven't prepared lunch for her bridge group, which I didn't even know about. It's driving me nuts."

"Where do you think she goes?" I grinned. "Maybe she's meeting her lover."

"Maybe. Wherever it is, it requires full makeup and designer clothes."

"But she always dresses that way. I've never seen her in anything but high fashion stuff."

Freedom eyed my cut off jeans and blue, Marco Island T-shirt. "You'd call a skirt and panty hose high fashion. Do you realize you have a glob of something yellow on your shirt?"

I inspected the offending spot. "It's paint. cadmium yellow, I believe. With just a touch of alizarin crimson. It's an honorable blob. It shows I've been working hard."

Freedom laughed. "Some people would wear an apron to paint, or at least change clothes when they were finished, but not my Maggie."

"Ladies, ladies," Ben interrupted. "If you'll pardon me saying so, you both sound a bit neurotic." He reached over to my plate and helped himself to some shrimp. "Did you ever consider there might be a very normal explanation for everything you've seen? With the possible exception of Roop's behavior," he added. "But the man just lost his brother and is apparently having a cash flow problem, so, under the circumstances, he might be a bit unhinged."

Freedom and I glared at him. "If you've got something to say, let's hear it," I snapped. "By the way, I thought you'd turned over a new leaf. No more telling me I'm crazy."

Freedom rolled her eyes.

"I said I wouldn't try to stop you," Ben said primly. "I didn't say I wouldn't tell you your theories are cockeyed." He pushed his plate away. "What I think is this: the scuttlebutt about Andrew having the deed to the *Moondancer* is hearsay. Maggie heard it from the harbormaster and…"

I opened my mouth to protest but he beat me to it.

"I know, Joey told the harbormaster so therefore, it must be true. It's still hearsay. Won't stand up in a court of law. Besides, Joey said 'the son of a bitch' had his deed. He didn't say Andrew. The son of a bitch might be his banker. So Tiffy, who is willing to ax Andrew if she gets the chance, persuades Maggie to break into Roops' house to find a deed that Andrew himself insists he doesn't have." He pointed his finger at me. "That was one stupid scheme. All you found out is that Andrew still has the hots for his ex-wife. Can't say I really blame him, either. I also have seen the lovely Tiffany."

I kicked him under the table.

He leaned back in his chair. "Now for Maggie's wild pursuit of Andrew's wife down Hwy 278. The facts are simple. Mrs. Roop had an errand which took her off the island. Maggie, her fertile imagination in high gear, decided the innocent act of traveling down the road in a vehicle demanded surveillance."

"Do you know you are beginning to sound just the tiniest bit pompous?" I asked him.

He pretended he didn't hear me. "Which brings us to her latest adventure in the Forest Preserve. Maggie, who seems incapable of participating in anything if it doesn't involve intrigue and danger, believes she sees Anne Roop fleeing down the path accompanied by a man. Maggie's logical conclusion? Mrs. Roop and an unknown companion are having an affair. The truth? A couple, out for a pleasant walk, becomes unnerved by sixty howling dogs and decides to make a run for it." He graced us with a condescending smile. "It's all very easy to sort out if you use an orderly thought process."

I crossed my arms over my chest and gave him what I hoped was a steely glare. "And how do you explain Joey's disappearance and his attempts to reach Tiffy on the radio? He's obviously being held somewhere against his will."

"I'm glad you asked. Either by accident or intention, Joey is involved in the explosion of the *Second Chance*. To escape jail, he ran away. He called Tiffy for any or all of the following reasons: to say he is okay, to ask for money, to beg her to join him, or to sell the *Moondancer*. Who knows? But he is not being held in some secret hideaway by an evil villain. Any more questions?"

I sank miserably into my chair, aware of Freedom's eyes boring into my forehead.

"When you put it like that," she began, "it does sound sensible."

"It does not," I muttered.

Ben gave his credit card to the waiter and stood up. "You girls stay here if you want to and have another drink. I still have to call some people about a story I'm writing." He patted my shoulder. "If it's okay, I'll see you later. Remember the etchings"?

"In your dreams," I sulked.

Freedom and I spent another hour in the Crazy Crab. We each had one more melon colada. I spent most of the time trying to convince her that Ben was wrong and I was right. She tried to tell me that Ben was a great guy, and I should quit doing everything in my power to screw up what could be a great relationship.

We left the restaurant together. Freedom headed to the parking lot, but I wasn't ready to go home. Still wounded by Ben's logic, I walked around the harbor, thinking about what he had said. The harbor was dark except for lights coming from the boats and the shop windows.

Ben made some sense, I reluctantly admitted. Had I possibly invented the whole scenario? Even though I wasn't prepared to say he was right, I felt slightly foolish. If I didn't watch myself, I'd scare him off, and I realized I didn't want that to happen.

When I reached Andrew's slip, I stopped. I looked down at the empty space, trying to remember what it looked like when the *Second Chance* was docked there. I listened to the music coming from the Quarterdeck restaurant and the occasional laughter floating across the water. It was hard to believe that a murder could happen in the midst of the holiday atmosphere.

I was so absorbed in my thoughts that when I hit the water, I wasn't sure what had happened. One minute I was standing on the dock, and the next thing I knew I was flailing my arms around, trying to reach the surface. In my confusion I thought I'd fallen, but when a strong hand grabbed my leg and pulled me towards the bottom, I panicked and began to fight for my life. Terrified, I punched and squirmed as the unseen hand pulled me under a boat. I felt my leg graze the propeller. With my free leg, I kicked as hard as I could and concentrated on holding my breath. Just as I felt my lungs were about to explode, the hand suddenly released me. I fought my way to the surface and heard a voice say, "Dear God, Maggie. What are you doing in the water?"

It was Ben, and I've never been so happy to see anyone in my whole life. He hauled me out of the harbor and carried me, shivering and shaking, to the side of the dock. I couldn't help it. I broke down and sobbed into his shirt, great gulpy gasps that tasted like salty tears and diesel fuel.

"I didn't fall," I said between sobs. "Someone pushed me into the water and pulled me under."

For once Ben didn't accuse me of being an overly dramatic nut. He half carried, half dragged me to his condo and didn't ask any questions until he had put me on his couch and wrapped a blanket around my shoulders.

When my shivering stopped, and I was able to breathe without gulping for air like a beached whale, he said, "It's a good thing I decided to come back and see if you were still in the restaurant. Tell me what happened."

"Somebody grabbed my leg and deliberately held me under the water." I shuddered. "I thought I was going to die."

And that wasn't being dramatic. It was the truth. As I talked, he searched my head for bumps and examined my arms and legs. Suddenly, I felt dizzy and put my head between my legs. When the room stopped spinning, I tried to stand up.

"I'll go home now. I know you probably don't believe me."

"Sit down, Maggie. You're not going anywhere. And as a matter of fact, I do believe you. Look at your leg." He pointed to a place on my right calf. "See that? It's the perfect imprint of four fingers and a thumb. Someone held you tightly enough to leave a mark."

The room started to spin again.

"But that's not what worries me the most. You've got a gash on your thigh that needs stitches, so I think we should go to the hospital. I've put a cloth around it, but the blood is seeping through."

When did he do this? I honestly couldn't remember Ben touching my thigh, and it seemed to me I wouldn't forget something like that. Or, maybe I would. It was hard to think with the room revolving in such crazy circles.

CHAPTER 14

▼

"That's a pretty nasty cut, Ms. Bloom. How'd it happen?"

Ben held my hand as the doctor gently swabbed the wound with disinfectant.

"I don't know how I scratched myself," I said. "Maybe on a nail."

I'd made Ben promise not to say anything about being pushed into the marina. Like Tiffy, I also found myself not wanting to deal with the police. At least not tonight. Tomorrow, after I'd had some sleep and some food, maybe I'd call them.

"It's certainly more than a scratch. And too jagged and wide for a nail injury. I'd have guessed something larger." The doctor smiled pleasantly.

Would you guess a boat propeller, I wanted to scream at him. I watched him poke around the gash on my thigh, swabbing and suturing. *Get a grip*, I warned myself. None of this was his fault.

Lying on my back on the examining table, I listened as the doctor and his nurse chatted while they worked. He'd had a disappointing tennis match; the nurse a disappointing meeting at a singles bar. He looked too young to be a doctor, I decided. Whoever heard of a physician with unruly blond forelocks that kept falling in his face as he worked? And I swear that was a pimple on his chin.

Thinking about the doctor kept me from dwelling on the fact that someone had tried to kill me. Every time I thought about gasping for air in the water, I felt like I was going to pass out. My chest would tighten and my heart would begin to pound. Idly, I wondered how high my blood pressure was.

The place on my calf where the hand had grasped me burned as if it had been branded with a hot poker. I closed my eyes and could feel myself being pulled once more into the dark water. Terror threatened to overwhelm me, so I concentrated on Ben's voice as he asked the doctor about a tetanus shot. I didn't even flinch as a nurse approached with a huge needle and buried it in my hip. I was numb.

Tears sprang to my eyes, which the doctor misinterpreted as pain, and promised me medication. I shook my head. I wanted to leave the sterile corridors of the hospital and go somewhere where there were no crazy men waving guns, no distraught friends with missing husbands and no unseen hands determined to kill me. Forget Tiffany, and the dysfunctional Roops, and Joey, and even my pubescent art career. What I really wanted was to get out of town.

The doctor slapped me on the leg and told me I was all patched up and could go home. Gingerly, I pulled my shorts over the wound. It didn't hurt. Maybe they had given me something for the pain in spite of my protests. Ben solicitously put his arm around my shoulder and helped me to his car. I only half listened as he talked, which was too bad because he was apologizing for not believing everything I'd said.

"Can you ever forgive me," he asked under the spotlight in the parking lot. "You've got yourself involved in something very nasty and I have to tell you, I'm very worried. Tomorrow, we call the police."

I was too numb to argue with him and he was wise enough not to press me. Without consulting me, he drove to his Ketch Court villa and escorted me to his door.

"Wally and Willow will be fine," he said as he turned down the blankets on the bed in the guest room. "Take these pills and then get some sleep." He shook two tablets out of a bottle the doctor had given him, handed me a glass of water and watched me swallow.

He kissed me on the top of the head. "Good night. I'm in the next room if you need me." In a softer voice, he said, "Go to sleep, Maggie. You're safe here."

My last thought before I drifted into a dreamless nothingness was of a highway winding through tall pine trees and rocky fields. The air was crisp and clear and the sky a cornflower blue. A road sign said, "Bangor, Maine 76 miles." The dogs and I would go there, I decided, just as soon as I got over being so sleepy.

*   *   *   *

The next morning I felt sturdy enough to pick my car up at the Harbour Town parking lot and drive it back home. Ben insisted on following me, so the two of us made our way down Plantation Drive and across Governor's Road.

A piping hot cup of coffee had cleared my head and washed away any residual effects of the pills Ben had given me. My resolve to leave, however, was as strong as ever. I figured since Ben had been so good to me last night, I probably didn't need to share this information with him right away.

A dark blue Honda Civic with a Save the Whales bumper sticker blocked my driveway. Recognizing the car as Freedom's, I looked around, but my friend was nowhere in sight. As I limped up the front steps, the door flew open and Wally ran out to greet me, a piece of kielbasa hanging from his mouth.

"They looked a little hungry so I found something in the refrigerator," Freedom called. "Don't you ever lock your door? Where have you been?"

I assumed Ben stood behind me wildly waving his arms because Freedom's eyebrows flew to the top of her hairline in bewilderment, and she stopped talking.

"We'll fill you in on the details," Ben told her. "Right now Maggie needs rest." To me he said, "I didn't have a chance to mention this before, but I have to go to Charleston today. The New York Times has asked me to write a story about the increasing migration of seniors to South Carolina. I think they figure since I'm already here, they won't have to pay my travel expenses. The good news is, I'm going to stay on Hilton Head for another week to ten days."

He brushed my lips with his. "I'm worried about you, Maggie. Promise me you'll stay in the house until I get back."

"Okey dokey," I said with my fingers crossed. I couldn't very well stay in the house if I intended to leave for Maine.

"Take care of her Freedom." He handed me a piece of paper. "You can reach me at this number any time. Make sure you call if you need me."

I bit my lip to stop the tears from coming.

As soon as he disappeared down the driveway, Freedom demanded to know what was going on. So I told her. I also told her I was running away to Maine with the dogs.

"Now, if you'll excuse me, I'm going to pack. And by the way, Freedom, if those dogs have diarrhea from all that junk you've fed them, you are going to clean it up."

I pulled a blue canvas duffel bag out of the closet and began to throw in underwear and clothes. I glanced at Freedom who sat on my bed.

"Don't try to stop me. I've made up my mind." When my friend didn't reply, I added, "Well, say something. Don't just sit there like a lump."

"I don't know what to say. I'm too shocked to say anything. This isn't funny, Maggie. You've got to go to the sheriff."

I touched my thigh. Under the thick bandage, I could feel the beginning of a throbbing pain.

"You don't have to tell me it isn't funny, but I have absolutely no intention of telling the sheriff anything." I grabbed a sequined cocktail dress and a tennis skirt from the closet and threw them into the bag.

"Look at what you're doing," Freedom pleaded. "What will you need this for?" Using two fingers, she drew out the cocktail dress. "You're not thinking clearly. Please listen to me. We've got to tell the police."

I stopped packing. "What would you like me to say to the sheriff? That I broke into Andrew Roop's house trying to find the title for the *Moondancer*? Or that Tiffany has heard from Joey on the VHF radio and we kept it to ourselves. Or that I ran like a lunatic through the Forest Preserve trying to spy on a woman who resembled Anne Roop? I think he'd charge me with breaking and entering, withholding evidence and being a busybody." I shook my head. "No thanks. I'll just leave town and come back when the sheriff solves the murder."

"But that's my point. The sheriff is so convinced the culprit is Joey Archer that he isn't doing any investigating. He'll probably manage to flush poor Joey out of wherever he's hiding, charge him with murder and close the case. Joey won't have a chance. There is someone out there trying to kill you, Maggie, and it can't be Joey. That means we know more than the sheriff."

"That makes me feel so much better," I said sarcastically.

"Well, I still maintain the sheriff needs to know what happened to you."

"And I still say no!"

Freedom flopped on her back and covered her eyes with her arm. "I almost forgot. I came here to tell you something."

I tossed a sequined evening bag and a pair of patent leather pumps into the bag and zipped it shut. "Make it snappy. The dogs and I are about to hit the trail."

"He's gone."

"Who's gone?" I asked crossly. "Honestly, Freedom, I'm beginning to think you're the one on pain killers."

She sat up and glared at me. "HE'S gone. You really are dense. Who else could I be talking about? Andrew Roop is gone."

Freedom settled herself against the headboard of the bed; fully aware of the bombshell she had just dropped.

"What do you mean 'gone'? Like on a trip? Or gone from too much vodka?"

"I mean split, out of here, vamoosed, sayonara, *auf Wiedersehen*. The Roops had another one of their world-class rows last night. The Madame came home late and offered an explanation, which would normally have satisfied him. But it didn't work because Mr. R was amazingly sober. He had called the house where his wife was supposedly attending a party and was told she had never arrived."

"He must have been terribly upset after the scene with Tiffany," I interrupted.

"But that's not what caused his exodus," Freedom continued. "At least I don't think it was, because Anne managed to calm him down, and they went to bed. Around two o'clock in the morning I heard the garage door open and felt the vibration of a car engine starting. I looked out and saw his Mercedes disappear down the drive. Well, I thought to myself, he might still be upset and is driving around until he calms down."

"Or gone to find an all night store that sells vodka," I volunteered.

"But he didn't come home. When I went to the house to fix breakfast, Anne was already up and calling everyone she knew trying to find him."

I considered this new information. "Hasn't he ever stayed out all night before? I mean, he strikes me as the sort of man who could stroll along the beach with a bottle of booze and then sleep wherever he happened to fall down."

"Apparently not. Anne kept him on a pretty short leash. He's never done this before."

"How do you know?"

Freedom squirmed slightly. I'm not proud of this," she began. "I listened to her phone conversations. She was pretty discreet with most of the calls, but one time," she shook her head, "she really let it all hang out. Said she was scared he was running around like a 'loose cannon,' whatever that means."

"Interesting," I murmured. "Maybe he finally got fed up with Anne. If she's having an affair, that would be a good enough reason."

Freedom looked smug. "You think he bolted because he suspected his wife was having an affair?" What if I told you there was a better reason?"

"I'd say you were just trying to distract me from leaving. Do you see Willow's tennis ball and rubber hamburger anywhere? I have to take them with me."

Freedom scooped the toys off the bed and tossed them to me. A malicious grin lit up her face. "I saved the best for last. This morning when I was dusting his desk in the library, I happened to look through the wastebasket."

I arched my eyebrows.

"Don't look at me like that. Anyway, there was the usual stuff; letters from bill collectors, boat advertisements, and then there was this." She reached into her pocket and pulled out a plain white envelope that had been wadded into a ball. "Take a look."

Opening the envelope, I pulled out a single sheet of white paper. Printed in block letters was the message:

At twenty three hundred hours on May 27, a boat will be waiting on Broad Creek across from Buck Island. Please be kind enough to meet us there with the painting or the money. We would hate for you to meet the same fate as your brother."

I looked at the envelope. It bore only the name 'Andrew Roop': no address and no postage. "This was hand delivered," I said. "Do you have any idea where he found it?"

"No. It could have been left under the door or on his car. I don't know. There are lots of places. I know I didn't give it to him." Excited, she bounded off the bed and grabbed my hands. "Don't you see? Andrew is in some kind of trouble, and I'd be willing to bet it has a lot to do with everything that has been going on. You can't leave now. We've got more sleuthing to do."

This was indeed interesting information. If Andrew had disappeared because of the threat in the note, this added a new dimension to the puzzle. The veiled implication was that the writer of the note was also Nathan's murderer. I could well imagine that Andrew felt like he was being pursued by demons when he received this message.

I looked my friend directly in the eye. "I genuinely regret the day I ever let Tiffy talk me into trying to find Joey." I kicked the duffel bag under the bed. "However, I will stick around a bit longer." When I saw the satisfied expression on Freedom's face, I added, "but not because of this. I have to sell the dog painting to Mrs. Jordan. And I have to tell Ben. It wouldn't be fair to leave without an explanation."

CHAPTER 15

▼

In the tiny galley on the *Moondancer*, Tiffany set the table, carefully pleating paper napkins into little paper fans. "You don't have to do that," I reminded her. "This is just a working lunch so we can figure out where we are."

"But I like to. It makes everything look nice and festive."

From her perch on the kitchen counter, Freedom yawned. "We should be doing something physical. I'm about to fall asleep and I have to be back at work in thirty five minutes."

"Even troops have to eat," I said as I chopped boiled chicken, celery and Vidalia onion into bite size pieces. I tossed these into a bowl and added fresh dill, lemon juice and ranch dressing. The activity invigorated me, and I didn't feel the least bit guilty about disobeying Ben's request to stay in the house. I would have gone crazy with only Wally and Willow to talk to.

"You could pour the iced tea, Freedom." I pointed to the refrigerator with the sharp end of the knife.

No one spoke until we had consumed nearly all the chicken salad and wedges of a perfect melon. Finally, I pushed my plate away and pulled a pad and pencil out of my purse.

"Okay," I said, "Let's get organized. We've agreed we're not going to call the sheriff because it would stir up too much trouble for Tiffany and for me."

Tiffany nodded. "I'm so grateful to y'all," she said. "I don't need any more trouble from the sheriff."

"Right," I continued, "so let's see what we know." I ticked off the facts. "The *Second Chance* explodes and Nathan is killed. Joey disappears and is accused of murder. We learn Joey does not have the title to the *Moondancer*. He tries to contact Tiffy. Anne Roop may be having an affair. Someone pushes me into the marina. Andrew Roop disappears, and persons unknown expect him to appear at a boat anchored in Broad Creek with either money or a painting. Have I forgotten anything?"

Tiffany stuck her hand in the air. "I probably should tell you this." She dabbed at a bit of chicken salad on her plate and licked her finger. "I found a little book in one of Joey's bags in the storage bin. I know it doesn't mean anything," she said nervously, "but since we're telling everything and Maggie nearly got herself killed, I thought I should too."

Annoyed, Freedom said, "For heavens sake, spit it out Tiffy, I have to go back to work soon."

"Well, it was just this little book about how to plant explosives. You know, how to make them and how to detonate them safely. Things like that. I remember a while back Joey was helping a logging company clear some land on Daufuskie, and he probably used it then. It isn't important, is it?"

Freedom pulled at her hair. "Agggh! As if we don't have enough problems. Now a little book appears that proves Joey knew how to make bombs."

Afraid of upsetting Tiffany any more than she already was, I tried to be calm. "It probably doesn't matter, Tiffy, but it's a good thing the sheriff didn't find it. Where was it? You and I searched everywhere."

Tiffany looked embarrassed. "I had it when you and I searched the *Moondancer*. It was stuck under my shirt. I just didn't want to tell you because I knew it would make Joey look bad." Her face brightened. "But I promise I've told you everything else."

Over her head, Freedom and I exchanged glances. *This was a new Tiffany*, I thought. *One who is able to lie deliberately.* I changed the subject. "What else do we have?"

"Well, I've been thinking," Freedom began, "about this title business and Andrew. We said maybe Andrew wasn't the son of a bitch Joey was referring to. But what if," she shot a glance at Tiffany, "and I don't mean to hurt you by saying this, but maybe Joey was doing something, well a little bit illegal for Andrew, and Andrew kept the title to the *Moondancer* to make sure Joey kept up his end of the bargain. Something went wrong, and Joey had to leave until things quieted down. I mean, in light of the new information we have about Andrew owing someone a painting or money, this might be a possibility. And we know from Maggie's snooping that Andrew was heavily in debt. He might have been willing to do anything to crawl out of the hole he was in. And if he needed help and Joey was willing..." She let her words trail off.

I peeked at Tiffany. The girl's back was rigid and her cheeks were flushed.

"Don't say such awful things about Joey," she whispered. "You can get off my boat right now if you think he had anything to do with all this."

Freedom patted her arm. "Don't get your shorts in a knot. I'm just trying to think of all possibilities. I didn't say he did it. I said 'what if?'"

Under the table, I thumped Freedom on the leg. She was deliberately baiting Tiffany, and I wondered why. I made a mental note to ask her as soon as I had a chance. Aloud I said, "What about Anne and the mystery man? Can we assume it was Anne I saw running in the Forest Preserve? Is it important?"

"I vote no," Freedom replied. "If it was Anne, she might have been trying out a possible replacement for Andrew. You know, a millionaire from the Country Club with a bigger yacht and a better house. Interesting, but not important. What do you think, Tiffany?"

Tiffany busied herself picking up plates and putting them in the sink. "I don't have an opinion. I'm not talking to either one of you anymore."

"Tif, sweetie, try not to be so prickly," I said, none too kindly. "We're trying to put pieces of a puzzle together. No one means to step on your toes, but if we can't speak openly, we might as well all go home and forget about the whole thing. Is that what you want?"

My stern voice made Tiffany turn around. Expecting contrite tears, I was amazed to see her steely resolve.

"All right, you two. I don't want you to stop helping, but if you say one more thing about Joey, you can get off the boat. I told you he didn't do it and I mean it."

I wasn't at all surprised to hear Freedom whistle under her breath. For the second time I chose another topic. "The note mentions a painting. Should we assume Andrew owns a painting that someone else wants?"

Freedom considered the question. "He has a fantastic art collection. Maybe it's one of those."

"But as far as I know those paintings have been there for a long time. I know they're all originals because I saw the authentication papers, and they're certainly worth a fortune. Would Andrew part with any of them?" I turned to Tiffany who was scrubbing the tiny sink with cleanser. "You know the house, Tiffy. Did Andrew ever sell any of his paintings?"

"I never paid any attention to those," she mumbled, "but as far as I can remember, the same ones were always on the walls."

I chewed the end of my pencil. "I can't help thinking it's too coincidental for the note to mention a painting and for Andrew to be in possession of such a magnificent collection. There has to be a connection."

I turned to Freedom. "I'd sure like to have a better look at those paintings. I was in a hurry the last time."

"That's the old Maggie," Freedom cheered. "We can arrange that, and this time you won't have to sneak around like a cat burglar."

"There's another thing that fascinates me about this note, and it may be the thing that caused Andrew to run," I continued. "It was hand delivered. That means the person or persons involved was here on Hilton Head, not on some boat waiting for a meeting on Broad Creek. If Andrew came to the same conclusion, he might have been panicked enough to high tail it out of here. You know, fear of imminent bodily harm. Andrew didn't strike me as having much backbone."

Freedom glanced at her watch. "I've got to go in a minute, but there's another thing we have to discuss and I know we're avoiding it. Someone tried to pull Maggie under a boat and leave her there. And that someone is on the loose and could try again. Ben didn't want her to leave the house today."

The wound on my thigh suddenly throbbed with a searing pain. "You're just a barrel of sunshine today, aren't you?" I said.

Freedom ignored me. "So, I conclude this unknown person thinks Maggie knows something that could compromise him in some way. I'd just like to ask, what if he tries again?"

I jumped up from the table, oblivious to the pain that surged through my body. "That's it, Freedom. I agreed to stay here, but not if you're going to scare me out of my wits."

Even Tiffany snapped out of her sulk and put her arm around my shoulder. "You poor thing. Here I've been worrying about my Joey so much, I forgot about what happened to you. Maybe it was Andrew who pushed you into the water and with him gone and all, you might be safe," she said hopefully.

I stared bleakly at my friends. "I wish I knew what to say. You both know everything I know about this mess. If I have some bit of information that would make some person nervous, I have no idea what it is."

Freedom gathered up her shoulder bag. "There's safety in numbers. From now on, when you go out of the house, one of us will be with you. And the dogs will protect you at home." She winked coyly. "And at night, you'll have Ben."

I smiled. The thought of two friendly English cocker spaniels, a weepy, distraught girl and a rambunctious housekeeper keeping a killer at bay actually made me laugh. As for Ben protecting me at night, well, I didn't think so.

CHAPTER 16

▼

As it turned out, my protectors were busy. Freedom had to go back to work and Tiffy mumbled something about washing clothes and tidying up the already spotless *Moondancer*. I called Lucy, thinking she might want to keep me company for a while, but her housekeeper informed me that "Mrs. Rotblumen is having her legs waxed and is not expected back soon."

Since I didn't want to be home alone, I decided to stay in Harbour Town until Ben came back. Figuring there was safety in numbers, I mingled with the throngs of harmless looking people in the marina and felt sufficiently invisible to relax. Every once in a while I looked behind me to see if I was being followed, but saw no one lurking in the geraniums, waiting for an opportunity to do me in.

For a while it was fun. I looked in the shop windows, ate an ice cream cone, and sat in a rocking chair and admired the yachts in the harbor. When I looked at my watch, I was dismayed to see I'd only wasted an hour.

I decided to stroll down the long pier and watch the boats come in. I wished I'd brought a hat. The sun was so bright that looking at the white, crushed oyster shell path almost blinded me.

I leaned against the railing and gazed out at the waters of Calibogue Sound and the islands beyond it. A sailboat tacked to the left and began its turn for the mouth of the harbor. The red and yellow para-chutes of the parasailers floated in the sky in front of Bull Island.

At the end of the pier, the *Majestic* was loading passengers. A group of Japanese tourists, cameras slung around their necks, climbed aboard. A girl with *Majestic* stenciled on her bright red T-shirt approached and asked if I'd like to take the tour to Daufuskie Island. Intending to say, "no, thank you," I was astonished to hear myself say, "that would be great."

I'd been to Daufuskie often. Every time I had a visitor from out of town, we did the obligatory tour to watch the dolphins and visit the quaint Gullah island. At least it used to be quaint. There was a time when Daufuskie consisted of dirt roads, a few homemade wooden houses, a small church, a one-room schoolhouse and poisonous snakes.

But that was before folks decided this wonderful, unspoiled island would be better with gated communities, expensive homes and paved roads. As a result, Daufuskie was divided in the middle. The front side, which faced Harbour Town, had the big homes. The back side was left largely untouched, although that, too, was changing rapidly.

I found a seat on the bow and listened as the *Majestic* captain explained the history of Daufuskie over a loud speaker. Dolphins cavorted on either side of the boat, probably hoping for something to eat. A small child tossed half a peanut butter sandwich into the water and laughed delightedly as a dolphin swallowed it.

After a short ride, we pulled into the public dock on Daufuskie. Yellow school busses were waiting to take the passengers on a tour of the island, which I knew included a trip to the schoolhouse, a drive past the original homes and ended with a stop on the beach and then back to a small restaurant for Daufuskie's famous deviled crab. I opted to stay near the dock and visit the general store.

Once inside, I admired the local folks' ingenuity. They had thought of every possible way to separate the tourists from their money. There were hand crafted ceramic bowls and pelicans, an interesting array of shells, and T-shirts with "I visited Daufuskie" emblazoned on the front.

There was also a food section with staples like bread and milk and a self-service grill with hot dogs and buns. I wandered over to a metal tub containing soft drinks on ice and selected a diet soda.

As I headed for the cash register, the captain of the *Majestic*, a large man with salt and pepper hair, entered the store and boomed, "We still have an hour and a half on Daufuskie. Don't miss the tour. Golf carts are also available, if you'd like to visit the island on you own."

A man and woman wearing matching lime green shorts and flowered shirts asked him how long we would be on Daufuskie. Patiently, he replied, "One and one half hours."

To fend off further silly questions, he turned to speak to the cashier. That's when I noticed a man dressed in filthy jeans and a torn T-shirt with a baseball cap pulled low over his head, duck behind a postcard display. He watched the *Majestic* captain. As the captain glanced around the small store, the man behind the postcards moved so he wouldn't be seen.

Finding this behavior extremely odd and thinking that perhaps the man was trying to steal something, I moved closer for a better look.

The boat captain called out, "Pay attention to the time, folks. If you miss the boat, we'll see you tomorrow," and left the store.

I saw the other man relax. He stood up, went to the grill, helped himself to a hotdog and fiddled with a little pack of relish. I watched him select a Mello Yello from the tub of soft drinks and pick up a pack of Hostess Twinkies from a shelf. As he moved to the cash register, our eyes met.

What happened next was so unexpected, I was momentarily incapable of any action. He dropped his hotdog and bolted for the door, still holding the Mello Yello and Twinkie. The cashier, unaware that some of her wares had just been pilfered, shot a look in his direction, shook her head and smiled pleasantly at me.

When the light bulb finally went off in my head, he had a good three minutes start. I had just seen Joey Archer and I was a dizzy, dumb, stupid idiot for not realizing it sooner.

Granted, he was filthy dirty. And I hadn't been able to get a good look at his face because he'd pulled the brim of the baseball cap over his eyes. But he had the same rangy build and the same reddish hair. Since I never expected to see Joey on Daufuskie, I hadn't been looking for him. But he had recognized me. And as I thought about it, that also explained his weird behavior around the *Majestic* captain. The captain knew Joey too, since both their boats were docked in Harbour Town.

I wasted another few precious minutes convincing myself I wasn't hallucinating. Ben's words of caution echoed in my ears. "You see intrigue everywhere, Maggie. Try not to be so dramatic."

I'd try another day. Right now I was going to find Joey Archer.

I tore out of the store and zoomed over to a man standing by one of the tour busses.

"Where can I rent one of those golf carts?"

He looked doubtful. "M'am, the boat leaves in an hour. I don't reckon there's hardly enough time to see the sights and get back."

What I wanted to do was grab him by the shirt and say, "Give me one right now before I shake you until your head snaps off," but that sounded a bit violent and might have caused the man to react unfavorably. Instead I said, "I don't plan to go far. I'll be back in half an hour."

The man scratched his head. "That'll still cost you the full price. Don't seem hardly reasonable."

I opened my wallet, pulled out two twenties and a ten and offered them to the man. He stuck the money in the pocket of his overalls and wordlessly led me to a golf cart. I was racing down the dirt road in pursuit of Joey Archer before he could ask me if I knew how to operate it.

I quickly realized chasing someone in a golf cart wasn't the smartest plan I've ever had. As I bounced over the bumpy dirt road, I clung to the steering wheel for dear life, afraid that if I relaxed my grip even a little bit, I'd fly head first over the front. The wheels found a deep rut in the road and for a few terrifying moments, the golf cart listed dangerously.

I also had no idea where I was going. And there was no sign of Joey. Thick, dark woods full of tangled branches and thick undergrowth lined both sides of the road. A fine covering of dust soon settled on my arms and legs and invaded my throat, making it hard to breathe. Once I had to veer sharply to avoid hitting a snake sunning itself in the road.

I was on the verge of turning back when I saw a figure ahead of me. Whoever it was ran fast. I wheeled the golf cart onto the side of the road where the footing was firmer and took off after him.

As I approached, I recognized the blue jeans and shirt. I had my quarry in sight. My golf cart was faster than he was. All I had to do was close in for the kill.

Suddenly, I saw Joey turn right and bolt into the thick woods. I skidded to a stop at the last place I'd seen him and looked around. The thicket of trees and vines looked ominous. There was no way I was going in there. I cleared my throat and called timidly, "Joey," it's me, Maggie." That sounded stupid even to my ears. He knew it was Maggie and he obviously didn't want to see me. I listened for any sound, but there was none. Either he was standing still or he could walk on air.

I got out of the golf cart, closed my eyes and stepped into the woods. Twigs and pine straw on the ground had been tramped down, indicating that someone had come this way more than once. Gingerly, I took another step.

I remembered that on previous visits the tour guide told us that every poisonous snake indigenous to South Carolina lived on Daufuskie. In the interest of safety, school children were taught how to recognize them. And here I was about to put my sandaled feet into the snake pit, so to speak.

I tried, but every time my toe tickled the pine straw, I imagined a whole horde of woodsy wildlife—from ticks to snakes—infiltrating my sandals and heading north up my legs.

I couldn't do it. Before I left, I pulled a plastic, tortoise shell clip out of my hair and clamped it onto a skinny branch. I intended to come back and search for Joey Archer, and I needed something to guide me down the right path.

CHAPTER 17

▼

Ben called at seven o'clock to say he was spending the night in Charleston.

"I hate to do this, Maggie, but I have a dinner interview and have to be here early tomorrow morning. I've worried about you all day. Are you okay?"

"I'm fine, Ben," I assured him. "No more shaky nerves. I'm back to my old self."

Boy, was that a lie.

I heard relief fill his voice as he said, "That's great. Did you call the police?"

"Well, not quite yet. But I will. All I wanted to do today was rest."

I quickly decided a phone conversation wasn't the best way to inform Ben I'd gone to Daufuskie by myself and chased Joey.

"What did you do today?"

"Read a magazine, played with the dogs, took a nap," I lied.

Ben wasn't easy to fool. I heard his voice sharpen. "That's good. You did stay in the house all day, didn't you?"

"Not strictly in the house. I had to take the dogs out. Things like that."

This was technically true. I just left out the part about visiting the *Moondancer* and my trip on the *Majestic*.

His voice floated over the wire, once again full of concern. "Stay there, Maggie. I mean it. I'll be back tomorrow and we'll go anywhere you want, but right now I don't want you traipsing around by yourself. Besides, you need rest."

It had been a while since anyone cared enough about me to tell me what to do. It was comforting to know he was concerned, but it was also a bit annoying. I was perfectly capable of taking care of myself.

"Don't worry about me, Ben. I'll stick close to home. Do your interview. I'll see you tomorrow.

As soon as we hung up, I called Lucy to see if she could meet me at the Beach Club. I had to share my news about Joey with someone. She said she would come after she had her appointment with Wanda, her "emotional interpreter". I knew what this meant. She was going to a small beauty parlor in Bluffton to tell Wanda, who did hair and nails in her kitchen, all her problems with Julius. Lucy didn't really have any problems with her husband, but sometimes, considering the difference in their ages and activity levels, she found stuff to complain about. Since I suspected it involved the kind of information that made me hold my ears, I was glad she confided in Wanda.

That evening, we sat on stools at the outside bar. The place was jumping. A bubbly, barefoot girl dressed in shorts and a tank top taught enthusiastic tourists how to shag. "Y'all are so good at this," she yelled. "I know you've done this before." The dancers laughed as they bumped into each other and stepped on sun burned toes.

The tantalizing aroma of grilled chicken and hamburgers made us realize we were hungry, so Lucy and I stood in the buffet line and filled our plates with burgers and potato salad and cole slaw.

As soon as we had polished off every bit of food, I told her about seeing Joey. "What I need to know is; do I tell Tiffy?

Lucy considered this. "I don't know. It would relieve her anxiety to hear he isn't being held captive somewhere, but it might really upset her to learn he is able to call her and hasn't done it."

"My thoughts exactly. She is so protective of him. It would kill her to think he doesn't feel the same way about her."

A gentle breeze jiggled the colored lights strung across the bar. Below us in front of the dunes, a guitar player belted out old Willie Nelson songs and encouraged the crowd to sing along.

Over the music I said to Lucy, "What I was thinking is…"

She held up her hand to cut off my words. "Don't tell me. I don't want to hear it. Every time you start a sentence with 'I was thinking', it means trouble."

"Just listen for a minute. I was thinking you and I could go to Daufuskie and see if we could find Joey. We would simply walk down the path I found, and if we don't see any sign of him, we'll leave. Nothing can possibly happen."

"Don't think so. Now, if you'll excuse me, I'm taking my drink and going for a walk on the beach."

I grabbed her hand and hauled her back. "Look at it this way. If Joey did have something to do with the explosion on the *Second Chance* and we can find him, maybe we can convince him to turn himself in. It would be helping Tiffy."

Lucy shook her head. "Your logic is faulty. I'm sure if you ask Ben, he'll agree, too." Lucy belonged to the large contingent of friends who thought I was a loony bird for not snapping Ben up.

"I'm not asking Ben and neither are you. This is very simple, Lucy. All we have to do is scout around a bit. I'm not giving up," I told her. "If you won't go with me, I'll go alone."

"I knew I should have stayed home tonight," she muttered.

"Does that mean you'll go?"

"I suppose so," she said crossly. But if a snake bites me, I'm going to make you suck out the venom."

"For heaven's sake, don't be so dramatic. There are no snakes on Daufuskie."

I was getting good at lying.

*   *   *   *

I'd just stepped out of the shower when the phone rang. Thinking it might be Ben, I wrapped a towel around me and padded to the phone.

"Maggie?"

Peter's warm, intimate voice took me by surprise and reminded me of why I had fallen for him in the first place. The man could seduce the bark off a tree. Or the panties off a willing bimbo. I'd always felt sorry for any criminal who had the misfortune to come up against him in a courtroom. He'd lean against the railing of the jury box, let that mellifluous voice work its magic, and every single female member of the jury would practically faint in ecstasy.

I, however, was beyond that. His voice had lost its magic for me.

"I've arranged for slippage in Harbour Town," he said. "Wait till you see my boat. She's a forty two foot Grand Banks Trawler, and she's a honey."

As he began a detailed description of the yacht, I wrapped the towel securely around my body and inspected the wound on my thigh. It was red and itchy. Every time I moved, the scar stretched in protest.

"I figure I'll be there tomorrow evening. This is so great, Maggie," he said enthusiastically. "This trip has made me feel like a new man. It's just what I needed. That and to see you. I'll call when I'm docked and squared away. That is, if it's okay with you."

This was an interesting dilemma. Part of me really wanted to have a look at Peter. I secretly hoped that in the months we'd been apart, he'd grown a potbelly and lost all his hair.

But Ben was coming back tomorrow and probably expected we would go out to dinner together. I wasn't quite sure how I'd go about explaining I was ditching him for my ex-husband.

Peter noticed my silence and said, "Is there a problem, Maggie. I'll only be in Hilton Head for one night, and I'd hoped to see you. But if you're not available, I can understand."

I made up my mind. Ben and I had made no commitments to each other. And I had to see Peter. One dinner was harmless. I'd check him out, eat fast and meet Ben later tomorrow evening. I pictured us toasting the ghost of my ex-husband as it finally floated away for good.

"I'll meet you at the Quarterdeck at eight o'clock," I told him. That would give me time to mollify Ben and get all the makeup on my face.

I hung up and stared at myself in the bedroom mirror. My hair hung in wet clumps, and I had dark circles under my eyes. It annoyed me that Peter sounded so young and energetic when I felt like a sleep deprived bag lady. The only thing that sounded good was sleep; long hours of undisturbed oblivion in a soft bed.

The darkness kept me awake. Even though I knew better, I imagined the raccoon running across the roof was actually the killer trying to peel off the shingles to get into the house. I put the pillow over my head to drown out the noise.

CHAPTER 18

▼

Early the next morning I rode my bike to Harris Teeter to pick up some food. I figured if I offered Ben something tasty as I told him about meeting Peter, it might soften the blow.

I wandered through the produce section, wondering how he'd feel about veggies and a dip. From across the melons, Tiffany waved to me.

"You're up bright and early," she said. "I thought you'd be sleeping late these days."

"Why?" I asked crossly. "Do I look like I need it?"

"No. It's just that with all that's been going on lately, you do look kinda tired. Not bad tired," she added hastily. "Just like maybe you could do with some extra sleep."

"Hasn't anyone ever told you it's not polite to tell people they look tired, or they don't feel well, or they need to have their hair done or their clothes don't look nice? It makes them feel bad."

Embarrassed, Tiffany stared at me. "I didn't mean anything. I just thought you maybe were a little bit sleepy."

Take it easy, I warned myself. *It won't do to have a melt down in the produce department of the grocery store. Tiffy can't help it if she looks like she's bursting with good health and vitality.* Indeed, as I inspected my friend, I realized she did look exceptionally well. Her cheeks had a rosy glow, and the drawn, tormented look was gone. This morning she wore a light pink cotton dress and white sandals and had her hair pulled back in a French braid. She looks really happy, I thought. That's the only word to describe her. Happy.

"What's new with you? Have you heard anything more from Joey on the radio?"

Tiffany picked up a honeydew melon and smelled it for ripeness. "No. Not since the last time I told you about. I'm thinking he must not be able to use it anymore." She said it matter of factly, as if it didn't bother her. It made me glance at her sharply.

"What makes you think that?"

Tiffany put three Red Delicious apples into a plastic bag. "Well, he probably would have kept calling if he could still use it. I keep it on all the time, hoping I'll hear from him again. I'm not giving up hope, though. I just know he'll come home soon."

She was acting funny. I couldn't put my finger on it, but there was something wrong. Normally, she was open and cheerful, always eager to stop and chat. This morning she was breezy and distant. It occurred to me that Tiffy might still be upset about the conversation on the *Moondancer* when Freedom had suggested Joey might have been involved in something illegal.

"Hey," I said gently. "You're not still thinking about that silly chatter yesterday, are you? You know Freedom. She always talks right off the top of her head, but she didn't mean anything by it. We were just trying to cover every possibility."

Tiffany pushed her cart towards the check out counter. Over her shoulder, she said, "I'm not worrying about that at all. I know y'all are just trying to help me and I surely do appreciate it. Be seeing you. I'm in kind of a hurry."

Puzzled, I watched her leave. I had the distinct impression she was trying to get away from me. And for someone who had recently been distraught enough to require a baby sitter so she could sleep on the *Moondancer*, she sure had changed. I wondered why she was suddenly so confident and upbeat. I was willing to bet it had something to do with Joey.

*   *   *   *

The waters of Calibogue Sound sparkled in the early morning sunlight. At precisely ten o'clock, the *Majestic* departed for Daufuskie. Lucy and I sat by ourselves on the upper deck, and we were dressed for action. Both of us wore jeans, T-shirts, socks, tennis shoes, sunglasses and hats. Lucy's jeans, however, had colored sequins running down each leg, her sunglasses had huge, red frames and covered most of her face, and she had wrapped a yellow, pink, scarlet and green silk scarf around her red hair. She was about as inconspicuous as a brightly lit Christmas tree.

"I don't suppose," I said to her, "that you could have found a less flamboyant outfit."

Lucy looked down at her clothes. "These old things? I had to rummage through old boxes to find them." She patted her jeans. "These babies were part of my wardrobe when I worked at the club. Her eyes took on a far away look. "Those were some good times."

"Don't want to know," I said, holding my ears. Lucy's good times from the old days usually involved one or two sensational looking men and tips from the Kama Sutra.

"Please tell me those aren't rip away jeans," I said peering through my fingers. "You're not going to be suddenly wearing a rhinestone encrusted g-string, are you?"

I could tell she was frowning disapprovingly behind her glasses.

"You have become such a conservative little person in your golden years."

"First of all, I am not conservative. I'll have you know I do some really radical things. And secondly, you know perfectly well I'm not in my golden years. I am exactly as old as you are."

She gave a very unladylike snort. "No one says 'radical' anymore. That's so sixties."

"How would you know what people said in the sixties? We were little kids."

Fortunately, the captain began his spiel, which made us both stop talking. When we resumed conversation, I said, "Something is up with Tiffy. She'd acting very peculiarly."

"So she's got a burr in her bustle. So what? She needs to toughen up. Sometimes I think all that innocent stuff gets a bit annoying. I mean, no one can be that sweet and naive."

"Tiffany is. It's not an act, Lucy. I've known her for nearly six months, and she's always been exactly the same. I just hope Joey isn't planning to dump her and run away with some bimbo. Hurting Tiffy would be like wounding a baby bird."

"Oh, for heaven's sake, stop with the analogies. What's the matter with you? You're all soppy and gooey."

"I am not." But I felt tears spring to my eyes. Maybe I was more exhausted than I thought I was.

"Don't worry about me. This is one cookie that doesn't crumble."

Lucy winced. "Do me a favor. Don't drink any more coffee today. You look like your eyeballs are going to come loose."

I laughed, but when Lucy wasn't looking, I pressed my fingers against my eyes to make sure they were still stuck in there.

When the *Majestic* docked at Daufuskie, Lucy and I waited until the tourists climbed into the tour busses and were on their way. Four members of the group opted for golf carts. Since we didn't want any company, we wandered through the general store until the last golf cart was ten minutes ahead of us.

I handed my money to the same man who had rented the cart to me yesterday. He looked at me strangely and scratched his head, but offered no comment when we jumped in and tore down the road.

I hoped I could drive directly to the bush holding my hair clip. This, of course, proved to be harder than I anticipated. We drove back and forth down the road, choking on dust until Lucy said, "Let me get this straight. You attached a brown hair clip to one of those brown branches and expect to locate it again?"

"Right," I answered as I wheeled the cart around. "There is a sort of path, too. We'll find it."

Actually, I wasn't terribly sure we would. The bushes all looked alike, and I was uncertain how far down the dusty road I'd driven yesterday.

Lucy crossed her arms and propped her feet against the front of the cart. "This is the mother of all wild goose chases. We are looking for a hairclip in a hay stack."

As I was about to answer her, I saw something in the bushes that flashed like a mirror. The sun had caught the metal on the hair clip. "Here it is," I shouted, relieved beyond words. Proudly, I parked the golf cart and crawled out. "Let's go. We have to get back to the *Majestic* by 2:30."

Reluctantly, my friend joined me. We took a deep breath and plunged into the bushes. Lucy walked behind me, clutching my shirt and muttering to herself, "This is a mistake. I know this is a mistake."

We followed the crushed pine straw into the dense woods. The trees blocked out any possibility of sunshine. It was as if we had stepped into a damp, earthy smelling twilight. Over my shoulder I said, "Think of this as a nature walk. Want me to describe the local flora to you?"

She gave my shirt a yank. "What I want you to do is turn around and get out of here. How do you know we'll be able to find our way back? This path twists all over the place. Maybe we're not even on a path."

I had to admit she had a point. As we walked deeper into the woods, twigs and branches covered the ground. Vines grabbed at our ankles and low tree limbs swiped our hair. I checked my watch. We had been walking for fifteen minutes and had found nothing.

Disappointed, I stopped to get my bearings. I was sure Joey had come this way, but where could he be? Had I taken the wrong turn?

"I can read your mind, you know. Are we lost?"

"Not at all," I lied once more. "I think we should go that way." I pointed to what looked like a slight gap in the dense trees. "If we don't find Joey there, we'll go back." That is, if I can find the way out of here.

Relieved, Lucy let go of my shirt and ran ahead. "I'm going to have a peek," she called. "And if there's nothing there, I'm heading to the dock."

When she raced back and grabbed my arm, I wondered what had happened.

"What's the matter," I asked. "Did you see a snake?"

Without answering, she pulled me forward and jerked her thumb in the direction of the clearing. "Go on and take a look. I'll wait here."

As I started forward, she said, "On second thought, no I won't. I'm coming with you."

A ramshackle wooden cabin stood in the small clearing. It sagged badly to the left, as if the underpinnings had given way a long time ago. The windows were broken, and most of the front steps were missing. I guessed that the original color had been a pale gray. Now it was covered with mildew and dirt. A vine from an oak tree curled around the roof like ribbon on a package.

"Oh, boy," I heard Lucy say under her breath. "You're not going in, are you?"

"We might as well have a look. It's obvious there's no one around."

"Why does your voice sound so funny?"

"Something's caught in my throat." Like fear. But I didn't say that. I stepped gingerly onto the one remaining front step and hoisted myself up to the door.

"Hello, anyone home?"

I hoped I sounded like the Welcome Wagon on a neighborly call. When no one answered me, I gathered my courage and walked in. I felt Lucy on my shirttail.

As my eyes adjusted to the dim light, I looked around. The whole cabin consisted of one room. There was no furniture except for a chair with torn upholstery and exposed springs and a dirty mattress on the floor. The dead carcasses of huge roaches, spiders and the occasional rat littered every corner.

I carefully made my way into the room, trying to avoid the rotting floorboards. I wanted to examine a pile of junk next to the dilapidated chair. There were several Whopper wrappers and a few empty plastic cups. Several million ants gnawed on the remains of a pepperoni pizza.

"There's no way to tell how old this stuff is," I said. But the wrappings looked fairly new. I picked one up and could still feel the grease.

Lucy shivered. "This place is awful. I can't imagine anybody staying here."

"You have to admit, though, if Joey is on the lam, it's the perfect hideout. No one would look for him here."

There was a newspaper partly hidden under the chair. I pulled it out for a better look. It was a copy of the *Island Packet* dated May 22, the day after the *Second Chance* exploded. On the front page was the article about the police hunting for Joey. I showed it to Lucy.

"I think we can safely assume someone has been here in the last few days, and I'd be willing to bet it was Joey."

"Well, where is he now? What if he comes back and finds us here? I don't want to wait around for that, Maggie."

"I think we should stay a while longer. I've been thinking. The only way to get off Daufuskie is on the *Majestic* or in a private boat. Even if Joey has money, he won't risk being seen on the *Majestic*. And we know his boat is still in Harbour Town. That means he has to be around somewhere."

"But he can't wander around Daufuskie either. Someone might recognize him."

"Look around, Lucy. He can hide out here until he grows a beard to his feet and his hair turns white. No one is going to find him."

"You're forgetting one thing," she said smugly, "and I'm really proud I thought of it myself. Those fast food wrappers are from Burger King, and there is no Burger King on Daufuskie. Someone brought that food over from Hilton Head. Maybe Joey isn't alone."

She had a point. I don't know why I didn't think of it. If Joey had an accomplice, who was it? Tiffany? As far as I knew, the *Moondancer* hadn't left the dock in Harbour Town. But, there was nothing to stop Tiffy from riding over on the *Majestic*. As I mulled this over in my mind, Lucy suddenly clawed my arm and whispered in my ear.

"Do you hear that? I knew we shouldn't have come here."

"Hear what?" I asked. "I don't hear anything."

"Then you're not listening. Someone is crunching the pine straw."

I crept over to the broken window and cautiously took a look. Unfortunately, Lucy was right. A man walked towards the house carrying a paper bag. He was too far away to recognize, but I was sure it wasn't Joey. This person wore tan pants and a brown windbreaker.

Terrified, Lucy and I bounced and banged into each other for a while until I said, "We've got to hide."

"Where would you want to do that," Lucy squeaked. "This is a one room cabin. With no back door."

"But there is this." I pointed to a three-foot square trap door in the floor. "Before we came in, I noticed that the cabin had been built on footers. I'll bet there's enough room under the house for us to hide. All we have to do is crawl down there and wait for the man to leave."

Lucy nearly jumped into my arms. "There's no way I'm going anywhere with copperheads and tarantulas and black widows. You go right ahead. I'll take my chances here."

"Okay," I said at I tugged at the covering. "This guy is probably the one who blew up the *Second Chance*, but I'm sure he'll be delighted to see you. By the way, who's being the 'conservative little person' now?"

A whiff of decaying animal and rot blasted me in the face as the door swung open. I sat on the edge and dangled my feet over the side.

Maybe this wasn't such a good idea. It looked dark and ominous below, and I wasn't crazy about spiders feasting on my tender skin.

"Are you going to sit there all day?" Lucy gave me a shove, and I landed on my butt in sand. She scrambled in behind me and pulled the trap door shut. We huddled together in the darkness, afraid to touch anything but each other. I swear I could feel things crawling over my body.

The sound of footsteps walking across the creaking floorboards made us hold our breath. We listened as the man stopped, uttered an interesting expletive and walked rapidly out of the cabin.

We stayed in our hiding place until our legs ached from crouching. I figured we'd given the man enough time to make a round trip to Paris. Finally, we decided confrontation seemed better than claustrophobia. If the man were still lurking about somewhere, we'd take our chances. As I reached up to push the trapdoor open and hoist myself through, I stepped on something sharp.

"Yowzza," I yipped. "Something has bitten me."

Lucy, who was clinging to my foot and therefore had a good view of the offending object, laughed scornfully. "You are standing on a plastic toy. Here. Have a look." She tossed it through the trap door, and it landed on the floor of the cabin.

First I made sure we were alone. The man had left the front door open. I stepped outside and looked around, but there was no sign of him. Then I inspected the plastic thing. It was a VHF radio with a big crack in the middle.

Well, my mother didn't raise a dummy. I held it aloft as I explained to Lucy, "This is obviously the radio Joey was using, but it's useless now."

"Why do you suppose he'd break it?"

"Maybe he didn't. It could be that our recent visitor saw Joey with the radio and destroyed it."

Lucy wasn't listening. She was busy combing her flaming hair with her fingers. "There is a rip in this Hermès scarf. I'm holding you personally responsible."

"Who in the world wears a Hermès scarf to go wandering in the woods. It serves you right."

I had to yell because she was already hightailing it out of there.

*   *   *   *

We missed the boat to Harbour Town. By the time we wiped cobwebs out of our hair and brushed unidentifiable stuff off our clothes, it was 2:45. The man at the golf cart rental was not pleased and charged us for another two hours. The *Majestic* didn't return to Daufuskie until four o'clock, which meant we wouldn't get back to Hilton Head until six thirty. Lucy and I spent the next hour and fifteen minutes sitting at a picnic table outside the general store. We kept our eyes peeled for Joey, just in case he decided he needed to do a little shopping.

CHAPTER 19

▼

By the time I finally got home, I had exactly forty-five minutes to feed, walk and water the dogs and get myself dressed to meet Peter. I checked my answering machine, but there was no message from Ben. Before I left I scribbled a hasty note and taped it to the front door, just in case he came looking for me.

Have gone to Harbour Town to meet Peter for a quick dinner. Be back soon. I underlined *quick* and *soon*, so he'd know I had no intention of dallying with my ex-husband. I added a smiley face to show him how non-serious I considered the evening.

I'm ashamed to say I almost trotted to the Quarterdeck restaurant. As I walked around the harbor, I wondered which boat was Peter's. It was too dark to read the names, but I hoped he hadn't named it something stupid like *Second Chance*. If he had, I'd figure out how to blow it up myself.

At the pier, I glanced at the *Moondancer*. The cabin lights were on, and I could see someone moving around inside. Guilty, I wondered if I should tell Tiffy about our excursion to Daufuskie. Right at the moment though, I couldn't concentrate on Joey. I had Peter on my mind.

I had agonized over what to wear. Women in the north dressed more elegantly than folks on Hilton Head. Here, we were more into the casual look. I hadn't worn a smart little afternoon outfit since my days in Germany.

I had finally settled on a long broomstick skirt in soft swirls of pink and white topped with a pink chiffon blouse. Before I went into the restaurant, I studied my reflection in the window of the Quarterdeck. I looked like a lollipop. I should have stuck with the white slacks and blue blazer.

It was show time. I took a deep breath and pushed my way through the crowded bar in search of my ex-husband. I saw him before he saw me. He leaned against the bar talking to a young blond in skin tight black pants and a Spandex top that stopped two inches above her naval.

So he'd brought someone with him. I had harbored the tiniest fantasy that he's come to Hilton Head just to see me.

I watched him laugh and cup his ear, making a big production of trying to hear over the music of the band. Grudgingly, I had to admit he looked good. He was a little heavier, but he still had all his hair. It was grayer than I remembered, but on him it looked good. He wore navy slacks, a white shirt and a navy blue sweater around his shoulders.

For a few minutes, I watched, appraising him and getting used to the idea that he was actually in Harbour Town. Months ago, I had longed for this moment. I'd dreamed about some day meeting him at my house. I'd be dressed in a flowing satin hostess gown with my hair, which had magically grown six inches, piled high on my head. I'd throw the door open and invite him in so he could see my gorgeous, muscular boy-toy lounging on the couch. Then I'd say, "Oh, it's you, Peter. I'm afraid I'm busy," as he wept and begged for forgiveness.

A waiter asked me if I wanted a drink and I said, "Margarita" without thinking. I never drank margaritas anymore. I liked wine, with the occasional Pina Colada thrown in for celebrations. The only person I ever drank margaritas with was Peter.

I saw him check his watch and glance towards the door before turning back to the blond. Good. He's looking for me. Maybe the blond is just a diversion, although I couldn't understand why the man was unable to sit in a bar for a few minutes without female company.

I finished my drink in four big gulps. I could feel the jolt of alcohol as it hit an empty stomach. *All right, old girl*, I told myself. *It's time to do it. You have the home field advantage. Now run with the ball.* As I marched toward Peter, it occurred to me that I was already slightly drunk.

It gave me a great deal of satisfaction to see the look of genuine pleasure on Peter's face when he saw me.

"Maggie." He took my hand and shyly kissed my cheek. "You look wonderful."

"You look well too, Peter." The blond disappeared in the direction of the music.

"Would you like a drink?"

"Sure."

I noticed he automatically ordered a margarita for me. One more of these was likely to lay me out on the floor, but what the heck. I took the glass from the waiter and followed Peter to a table in the corner.

"It's hard to talk," he said over the blare of the music.

"Yes," I agreed, "it is."

This was awful. We were behaving like two polite strangers. Which is what we were, I realized.

"Did you have a good trip?"

He nodded.

"No bad weather or anything?"

He shook his head and then said, "Do you mind if we get out of here? I thought we'd go to dinner somewhere. Do you know a quieter place?"

I licked the salt on the rim of my glass. "I suppose we could try the Café Europa. It's next door. I don't know if we'll be able to get in without reservations, though."

"Let's give it a try."

Taking my arm, he led me through the bar to the Café. Peter's manly charm seemed to be working because after a few words with the hostess, we were seated at a table for two against the window.

I ordered a she-crab soup as an appetizer and salmon in dill sauce. Peter settled on a shrimp cocktail and filet steak.

"Let's see," Peter said. "You need a white wine with your fish and I'd like a good Bordeaux."

"I don't need wine, Peter." I raised the margarita I'd brought with me from the Quarterdeck. "I'll just drink this." I noticed he looked a little blurry.

"Toss it down and have some wine," he urged.

I decided he was as nervous as I was. But more alcohol wasn't a good idea. After two drinks there was no telling what I would do.

Over dinner, we chatted about his boat and his job. Peter asked very few questions about my life, which wasn't surprising since he wasn't interested in it even when we were married. I'd had enough wine to make me chatty. I asked about Christine.

Peter frowned as he pushed little pieces of chocolate cake around his plate. "I don't see her any more. She's been out of my life for several months now."

I tried to think back. Would that coincide with the beginning of his phone calls?

"I'm sorry to hear that," I lied.

"How can you say that? I wouldn't blame you if you hated her."

"I don't," I said magnanimously. "That's all in the past. We've both gotten on with our lives." I peered at Peter to see whether he enthusiastically agreed with me.

"That's true. But it was a blow to me when Christine left." He looked out the window. "She really hurt me."

Good grief, holy mackerel, smack my cheeks and call me stunned! The man was actually looking for sympathy. Peter had the sensitivity of a slug. I sincerely hoped he had felt the same gut wrenching, soul searing torment I'd felt when he left me.

"That must have been hard," I said sweetly.

"Yes." He looked at his hands. "She found another man. He's a plastic surgeon in Boston, has a house on the Cape and an apartment in New York. He's not much to look at. I don't know what she sees in him."

I spit a mouthful of wine onto my plate.

"Sorry."

I patted myself on the back. Men are such idiots. Men can be such vain, self-centered idiots.

As Peter paid the bill, he asked, "Would you like to see my boat? She's right out there and she's a real beauty."

Well, why not, I thought. Might as well. We've come this far. As I rose unsteadily to my feet, I realized I felt quite dizzy. It wasn't an unpleasant sensation, but it required an enormous amount of concentration to get out the door without falling into the geranium planter.

Peter's boat was docked on the far side of the marina, a few slips away from Andrew's. As he hurried me along the dock, he told me about buying it on the Vineyard and what a steal it was. We stopped in front of a white, 40' trawler.

"I completely redecorated it myself. What do you think?" he asked proudly. Without waiting for an answer, he added, "Take your shoes off, Maggie. I don't want the deck scratched."

From the aft deck, he opened double doors leading into the salon. Someone helped him do this, I decided as my eyes took in the plush, forest green curved settee, teak entertainment center and Waverly covered chairs. He would never have put these colors together by himself.

"Beyond here is the galley. I even have a microwave. And down those four stairs is the stateroom."

He pushed the door open to reveal a queen size bed with built-in drawers on either side. In the corner to the right was a room for the head and sink. On the left was the shower room.

"All the comforts of home," he said. "Do you like it?"

"I'm stunned," I replied honestly. "It's a beautiful boat. What's her name? I forgot to look when I came aboard."

He looked shy. "It's the *Magnolia*."

I shook my head. Surely I hadn't heard correctly.

"The *Magnolia*?"

"I liked the name *Xanadu*, but that's been done so much and then I thought of this. I've been thinking about you a lot," he said quietly.

I steadied myself against the edge of the sink. The room had begun to swim, and my lips were getting numb.

"Why did you come here, Peter?" I had to hear the answer to this before I passed out.

He gathered me in his arms and crushed me against his chest. I felt a familiar twinge as I allowed him to hold me tight.

"I came to see you. That's the only reason." With his finger he tilted my chin upward so he could look into my eyes. "I've missed you, Maggie." His voice was a husky whisper. "I've missed you a lot."

I willed myself to stay motionless, to ignore the sudden desire that surged through my body, but my treacherous body acted with a will of its own. I was unable to stop myself from throwing my arms around him and responding eagerly to the kisses he planted on my neck and face and, finally, my mouth.

"Do you mean it, Peter?" I croaked when I came up for air. "Did you really miss me?"

"I'm sorry for everything, Maggie. I want you to know that. I put you through hell and I'm sorry," he said through my hair.

How long had I waited to hear these words? Right after our divorce, there had been days I believed I'd truly die if Peter didn't recognize the folly of his ways and chuck the bimbo. I'd go to sleep dreaming of the moment when he'd say, "I'm sorry, Maggie. I love you." Now, when I'd finally stopped fantasizing about it, the moment seemed to have arrived.

I buried my face in his chest. It felt good. Familiar and warm. Let me tell you, it felt really, really good. I was floating in an alcohol induced haze of happiness, and I was loving every minute of it. As far as I was concerned, it could last forever.

Sanity and sobriety returned just as Peter pulled my skirt down around my ankles and was trying to coax my feet out of the fabric.

"Oh no you don't. I'm not Rebound Woman," I yelled.

"What?" Perplexed, he tugged harder at my skirt.

"Stop it, Peter. I mean it. You didn't come here to see me. You came to get a self confidence boost." I hoisted my skirt around my waist and stepped away from him. "Don't you think I know what it's like to have someone stomp on your heart? It hurts, doesn't it? But thinking your ex-wife will come running back to you and make you feel all better is an exercise in self-delusion. And conceit. Have you really imagined I've been sitting on Hilton Head just waiting for a reconciliation?"

I was on a roll. I paced around the salon as Peter watched me in astonishment. "You haven't once asked how I'm supporting myself or how the dogs are. It's been all about you."

I headed for the door. "You're going to have to rename your pretty boat. I'm sure *Magnolia* isn't going to appeal to you anymore." Now that my sanity has returned, I realized I'd waited a long time to make that speech. I imagined I heard throngs of people cheering loudly.

Peter recovered enough to say, "You always were too dramatic. I pity the poor sap who hooks up with you."

I hustled off the boat and down the pier to my car. I hoped the poor sap wasn't back from Charleston yet, and I'd beat him to the note on my door.

Ben was sitting on my front steps. He moved out of the way so I could get the key in the lock.

"Your note said you'd be back soon. Do you realize it's nearly one o'clock in the morning?"

"No, I didn't realize that," I said crossly. "Honestly, Ben, I do kind of wish you'd quit mothering me. I'm a big girl now. I'm allowed to come home late."

"Sorry to bother you."

He was in his car and down the driveway before I could apologize for acting like a jerk.

I went to bed mad at myself. In the course of three hours, I'd managed to scare off two men, and one of them I really cared about.

CHAPTER 20

▼

I didn't have time to worry about men. Freedom called the next morning and told me to get over to the Roops' if I wanted to look at the paintings. I hastily grabbed a bagel and a cup of coffee and tore out the door, trying to avoid glancing at my dogs, who were openly hostile about the lack of attention. Willow had the TV clicker in her mouth and hid under the bed when I tried to retrieve it.

"Is the coast clear?" I asked in a soft voice, as Freedom opened the door to the Roop's sunroom.

"I don't know where she is. The BMW is still in the garage, but I've looked all over the house and I can't find her."

"She might be out for a walk or visiting a neighbor. Maybe I'd better not risk it."

"Come on in," Freedom urged. You're not going to believe this, but I think the Madam might have left the premises for good. When I was hunting for her, I noticed her jewelry box wasn't in its usual place on her dresser, and all her makeup is gone from the dressing room. Being the curious person that I am, I looked for her luggage."

"Let me guess," I interrupted. "It's gone too."

"Right. So we have the house to ourselves and, unless one of my nutty employers suddenly decides to return home, we won't be disturbed."

I shook my head. "This is getting too weird, both of them disappearing like this. I suppose you still haven't had any news from Andrew."

"Nope. Now, in his case, I can tell you he doesn't have anything with him except the clothes on his back. He must have just gotten up and walked out the door."

"Maybe Anne has gone to meet him," I suggested. When I saw how skeptical Freedom looked, I asked, "Why is that so far fetched? Just for fun, let's assume Andrew is in some kind of trouble. In a panic, he runs away. Later, he gets in touch with his wife and asks her to help him; he needs clothes, money, perhaps his passport, and he tells her where to meet him. He begs her not to let anyone know where she's going. After all, she's still his wife. She probably feels she owes him some kind of loyalty."

"Maybe. But let's hurry up and get this over with. If your theory is right, those two are crazy enough to reconcile and arrive back here expecting me to serve them champagne and crepes suzette in the Jacuzzi."

As we walked into the living room, Freedom said, "Bet you're not as nervous this time. What would you have done if the either one of them had discovered you breaking into their house? That was really a stupid thing to do. Really amateurish."

"I agree," I answered calmly. "But that was in my early sleuthing days when I hadn't thought things through."

"And now you have?"

"Really, Freedom, you're beginning to annoy me just a tinch. Now we have more clues and a little more of an idea of what we're looking for."

"But you've already been in the house, and you didn't see any mysterious painting. And I work here. Don't you think I'd notice something like that?"

"I'd doubt we'd find it propped on the grand piano. If it's here, it's cleverly hidden. I'd like to have a look at the living room and then that little sitting area of Andrew's off the master bedroom."

"Be my guest, only I'm going to stand here at the window and watch the driveway. I hate unpleasant surprises."

I turned on the individual lights above each painting. On my previous visit to the living room, the light had been too dim and I'd been too hurried to have a really good look at the art collection. Once again, I was stunned into silence by the sheer number of masterpieces. In addition to the Monet, Chagall, Renoir, Picasso and Miro I recognized from the previous visit, there was also a small Matisse, a Braque and a Cassatt.

As I viewed the paintings, I wondered how a man who had the resources and the knowledge to buy these paintings could be such a loser in every other way. I also wondered how he could disappear and leave such a priceless collection behind.

Sighing with pure pleasure, I stepped in front of the Monet and studied it closely. When I studied Art History at the University of South Carolina, Impressionism had been my favorite period. I loved the way each spontaneous brush stroke delivered a burst of color.

I moved slowly around the room, letting the colors and forms mesmerize me. I marveled at the composition of a Matisse: a portrait of a woman lounging in a chair with red and purple flowers in the foreground.

Prepared to lose myself in the sheer beauty of the paintings, I eagerly approached the Renoir, anticipating a glimpse of the artist's exquisite handling of the human body. I could feel the beginning of a smile forming on my face as my eyes swept over the *saftig* nude. The smile, however, failed to materialize. There was something wrong. The sight of a Renoir always made my heart sing, and there was definitely no singing going on in my body. Puzzled, I stepped closer to the painting, searching for the familiar Renoir handling of paint.

Then I slowly walked around the room again, pausing at each painting to give it a really thorough examination. I could hardly believe the horrifying thought that flitted through my mind.

"Why is your forehead all creased in worry lines?" Freedom asked.

"I don't understand this. I know these paintings are supposed to be originals because I saw the insurance policy on them when I looked in Andrew's desk. But, I would swear they're not."

"What are you talking about? They have to be. These paintings are the only things Andrew was genuinely proud of. He told the story over and over of how his daddy found that Picasso," she pointed to the painting of a harlequin from Picasso's blue period, "on the wall of a café in Paris. He persuaded the owner to sell it for $500. They're all real. I know they are."

I shook my head. "I can't tell you how much I wish you were right, but you're not. Listen, Freedom, not only was I a Fine Arts major in college but, just for fun, I also spent most of my summers as a docent at the Museum of Fine Arts in Boston. The techniques and styles of these artists are as familiar to me as my own handwriting, and I'm telling you, there are inconsistencies."

I dragged Freedom to the painting of a lily pad by Monet. "See this? The Impressionists used tiny brush strokes of different colors placed next to each other to create the soft effect of one color when viewed from a distance. For instance, red and yellow next to each other gave the viewer the impression of orange. Look at this area." I showed Freedom a part of the water. "It's not soft and subtle to the eye, the way it should be. It's almost garish."

Freedom shrugged her shoulder. "I don't see it. I mean, it looks okay to me."

"Well, it's not. And take a look at this leg of the nude in the Renoir. Renoir was famous for the almost mother of pearl translucency he was able to achieve in the skin tones. This isn't translucent. It's dull and flat. You don't have the impression of a sensuously rounded curve."

"Maybe he didn't always like to paint fat women. What do you want me to say? I don't see the flaws you're pointing out."

"You make me so angry," I shouted. "Any idiot can see this, and I'm telling you, something happened to the magnificent paintings that Andrew spent a fortune to collect."

"Well, I don't have any idea what could have happened," Freedom shouted back. "And don't call me an idiot. Will you calm down, for heaven's sake? I've never seen you so upset."

I realized my behavior was totally uncalled for, but I was so stunned and so angered by my discovery that I couldn't think rationally. I took a deep breath and counted to ten. When I felt like I could speak without exploding, I said, "It just makes me furious to think something has happened to all the wonderful art. Tell me this, Freedom. Did any of these paintings ever leave the house for any reason?"

Freedom's eyes widened. "Yes. To be cleaned or repaired. At least that's what I was told. Let's see. The Braque had to be repaired, the frame was damaged on the Matisse, the Madame didn't like the frame on the Renoir and wanted it changed, and the Chagall and the Picasso had to be cleaned. Those are the only ones I can remember, but I guess at one time or another most of the paintings have been out of the house." She looked dismayed. "I just never paid any attention. There was never more than one gone at a time, and I never thought anything about it."

"Why would you?" I asked. "No one would suspect something like this." My eyes scanned the room. "The forgeries are good. No one giving them a casual glance would be able to tell the difference." I nodded at the painting above the fireplace. "What about the portrait of Anne? Do you know anything about it?"

"It's fairly recent. She had it commissioned and seemed happy with the results. I think she went somewhere to sit for it because the artist didn't come here."

"When I first saw it," I said, "I thought it was grossly out of place in a room full of real masterpieces, but now that I've had a chance to study the rest of the paintings, it seems to fit in for some reason. I'd love to have a closer look at it." I stood on tiptoes and tried to make out the detail of the painting. "Do you think we could take it down?"

"That gilt frame must weigh a ton. I really don't want to be caught doing that."

"Please," I pleaded. "There's a certain similarity in the brush strokes between this and the fake paintings. Like I said, the fakes are good; the artist was able to reproduce them fairly accurately. But the portrait reminds me of someone painting out of his element. If the artist was accustomed to painting copies, I think he might have had a real problem painting from life."

"Okay. Why do I let you talk me into this stuff? Let me run to the kitchen and get the stepladder. I wouldn't feel right about putting footprints on the brocade couch."

As Freedom ran to the kitchen, I inspected each painting again. I knew I wasn't wrong, and I also knew what was missing from each painting. Although a clever forger could reproduce the style and technique of an artist, he couldn't reproduce the soul. And the soul of the artist was missing from every single painting.

*   *   *   *

Freedom stood on the ladder and lifted the painting carefully, easing it down to me. It was heavy, and we both had to hang on to keep it from falling to the floor. We propped it against the fireplace, and I stepped back to study it. As I looked at the artist's rendering of Anne's face and body, I felt my heart beat faster.

"I'm right," I said excitedly. "This painting and the others appear to be done by the same person. Look at this mouth. And look here." I pointed to the Renoir. "The artist had trouble copying the upper lip of the nude too. And this area on Anne's dress. The shading is clumsy. So is the shading on Picasso's harlequin's trousers."

I was aware that my hands were flying. I was practically running around the room and I was talking too fast, but I didn't care. "Do you begin to see what I'm talking about?"

"When you point it out like that," Freedom began, "you start to make sense."

I snorted. "I always make sense. You're just not willing to admit it. Are you willing to concede that the paintings and this portrait may have been done by the same person?"

"If you say so. But why would the Roops accept an inferior portrait when they could afford the best?"

I thought for a minute. "Maybe the commission to paint this portrait was a reward, so to speak, for painting the forgeries. The artist might be an aspiring portrait painter, and this was part of the deal; he'd do the forgeries, but he wanted a shot at his own fifteen minutes of fame. That reminds me, I didn't even look at the signature."

I bent down and searched the lower right hand corner. Tucked in a fold of Anne's chiffon skirt, I found what I was looking for.

"It says 'Haynes.' I don't recall that name around here, and I know most of the local artists."

"Something tells me this one doesn't keep a high profile," Freedom said. "I sure wish I could remember where Anne went to have this painted."

"Maybe I can ask around and see if I can find out anything about him," I offered. "You know what I think?" Without waiting for an answer, I continued. "I think Andrew Roop was so desperate for money, he was selling off his paintings and replacing them with these fakes so no one would know what he was doing."

"But why would he go to all the trouble to have these copies made," Freedom asked. "It's his collection. He could do with it as he wished."

I considered this. "Maybe he didn't want anyone to know he was so financially strapped he had to sell his paintings. What would he have told Anne? Or his brother, for that matter. Appearances mean a lot to him. He probably counted heavily on no one spotting the forgeries.

For now, let's put this back and have a look upstairs. We could also see if Anne took her appointment book with her. She might have jotted down the artist's address. And we still don't know which painting the writer of the mysterious note was referring to. I wonder if it's one of these. I can't imagine anyone being very happy about receiving a forgery."

I climbed up the ladder and positioned myself to take the painting as Freedom lifted it up to me. As I grabbed the frame, I turned it slightly.

"Holy moly, hot tamales and fry me a catfish!"

The words burst out of my mouth in one long string.

"What? Stop that," Freedom yelled. "Damn, you scared me. I nearly dropped it."

"Put it down, Freedom. Put it down on the floor and turn it around," I screeched. "And whatever you do, don't touch the back." I scrambled down the ladder and pulled Freedom next to me so we could both look.

Carefully attached with thumbtacks to the back of the wooden stretcher frames holding Anne's portrait was another painting.

The painting was a portrait of Christ seated at a table with his head bowed. On either side of him were two men, one kneeling and the other holding a bowl of food. The expression on Christ's face was serene and untroubled. A soft diffusion of light mellowed the canvas, brightening slightly behind Christ's head. The bottom fourth of the painting was unfinished, the brushstrokes running off onto the blank canvas. Even in its incomplete state, the portrait dominated Roops' living room, relegating the other works to an insignificant background.

I felt the same sensation I'd experienced in the Louvre and the Rijksmuseum in Amsterdam when I'd viewed other works by the same artist. It was an overwhelming sense of awe that a mortal man, using only paint and brushes, could capture so much of the mood and soul of a person.

Freedom's voice jerked me back to reality. "What on earth is this? You look so strange, Maggie, you're scaring me."

"I'm sorry. It's just that I'm so astonished and shocked, I can hardly speak. Do you have any idea what you're looking at?" When Freedom shook her head, I said, "Unless I'm very much mistaken, this is an oil sketch for a painting the artist did at least twice. It was called *Supper At Emmaus* and as far as I know, there are at least two finished paintings. Each one features Christ and his disciples seated at a table."

Freedom peered at the painting. "I'm not much of an art expert, but it looks Dutch. The dark colors and the play of light and dark remind me of those old Renaissance masters."

I looked at my friend approvingly. "Very good. But this isn't just any old Renaissance master. I'd be willing to bet the farm that this is a genuine Rembrandt."

"You've got to be shitting me." Freedom's hand flew to her mouth. "Pardon me. I didn't mean to say that, but really, Maggie, are you sure this isn't another fake?" She gestured to the walls. "We've got plenty of them. What makes this one so special?"

I carefully lifted an edge of the canvas. "See this material? It's so old and thin it almost crumbles in my hand. A capable forger would know how to age cloth, but it would be almost impossible to duplicate this. And look at the faint illumination around Christ's head. Rembrandt was a master at painting diffused light. As I recall, his early painting of *Supper At Emmaus* had Christ sitting in front of the light source so that his head was almost a silhouette of darkness. It produced a very dramatic effect. Later, he learned to use the light and darkness to create more of a melancholy, gentle mood. I can tell from the style of painting that this oil sketch is somewhere between the first *Supper At Emmaus* and the second one."

I sounded like a college professor but I couldn't help it. I was truly stunned, and for some reason, when I'm stunned I become extremely articulate.

Freedom chewed on her thumb. "How do you know so much about this stuff?"

"I told you. I worked in a museum. I also spent my junior year in Europe studying his work in Amsterdam and Paris. For six wonderful months I lived and breathed Rembrandt, studying his technique, his use of light and dark and, most of all, his portraits. Believe me, I know an authentic Rembrandt when I see one."

I tapped the frame of the painting. "This is a horrible thing to do to a priceless masterpiece. I can't believe Andrew, who obviously loved art, would stick a Rembrandt on the back of his wife's tacky portrait."

"You have to admit it makes a good hiding place," Freedom said. "Can we assume this is the painting referred to in the note?"

"I think we can."

I began to pull the thumbtacks out of the stretcher frame.

"Wait. What are you doing?" Freedom asked as she reached over to stop me.

"I'm certainly not going to leave this here." I glared at Freedom. "It would be irresponsible to let something happen to it. Andrew is gone, Freedom, and we don't know where Anne is. I'll put it somewhere safe, and I'll deal with Andrew Roop later."

"If he comes back looking for it and discovers it's missing, chances are he'll blame me." Freedom pointed out. "What am I supposed to tell him?"

I grabbed my friend by the shoulders. "Do you not understand that this is a priceless masterpiece? It probably shouldn't even be out of the Netherlands. How Andrew got it in the first place is beyond me, but he can't be allowed to sell it to pay off his lousy debts. Get some backbone, girl. We can take care of Andrew."

"Stop shaking me," Freedom said crossly. Rubbing her shoulders, she added, "You're crossing the line again, you know. First it was breaking into this house to help Tiffany get a boat title you felt Andrew had no right to own, and now you're stealing a painting because

Andrew shouldn't be allowed to sell it. It seems to me most of these decisions are made according to Maggie's rules."

"So call the sheriff," I replied, as I carefully removed the painting from the back of Anne's portrait. "While you're doing that, would you please bring me something soft to wrap this in? I don't want anything to happen to it."

As Freedom disappeared in the direction of the kitchen, I heard her say, "I'm not going to stay here and wait for Andrew to go berserk and stab me with a kitchen knife because he can't find his painting. If I even see him come close to this house, I'm moving in with you, Maggie."

"That would be just lovely," I called after her.

CHAPTER 21

▼

I hunted all over my house for an appropriate hiding place for the painting. I rejected the attic as too dirty and the closets as too obvious. Finally, I settled on the crawl space behind the water heater. To get there, I had to take all the junk out of the hall closet, open a trap door and wiggle on my stomach until I reached an area about two feet by two feet. It wasn't much, and it certainly wasn't a suitable resting place for a Rembrandt, but it was fairly clean and totally dry. This master-piece, I told myself as I placed the rolled painting on the floor, deserves to be framed properly and hung in some famous museum where every-one could admire it. And someday it would be, if I had anything to say about it.

The painting safely stashed away, I made a pot of coffee and checked my machine for messages. There was none from Ben. I carried the coffee and some chocolate chip cookies into the living room and sank down on the couch. From there I'd be able to see the driveway, just in case he drove up.

I crammed some cookies into my mouth and took a swig of coffee, but the food refused to move smoothly down my esophagus. In fact, I couldn't even swallow. I seemed to have a major mastication problem.

When it finally hit me that I had a Rembrandt hidden in my closet, which I had stolen—yes, let's use accurate descriptions—I felt like I was going to throw up. This wasn't a minor legal transgression. I was pretty sure Ben would call this grand theft.

I couldn't keep it in the house. And I had to have some help. Perhaps some competent psychiatric evaluation wouldn't be a bad idea either. I planned to use temporary insanity when they caught me, because I had to be out of my mind to have done this.

I glanced at the closet door. The painting had to be worth millions, and it was sharing space with my water heater. Should I have left it at the Roops'? A sane person would have admired it, clucked her tongue a few times at the horror of stealing such a masterpiece and gone on about her business. But I'd passed sanity about two days ago. I'll bet if I looked in the mirror I'd see my eyeballs spinning.

I also had no desire to get Freedom into trouble. She'd gone way out on a limb to help me and I owed her a lot.

Sighing heavily, I forced some coffee down my throat and scratched Wally's ears, ignoring the fact that both dogs, sensing my thoughts were elsewhere, had snuggled deep into the paisley down cushions on the couch.

I needed an expert evaluation of the painting. Not that I didn't trust my own ability to identify a Rembrandt, but I knew I'd feel a whole lot better about taking it from the Roops' house if someone else could verify it.

My head began to pound. As I massaged my temples, I wondered if Freedom had been right, that I had stepped over the line. If I had, it had been the sight of the Rembrandt and the knowledge that Andrew Roop would be willing to sell it for his own gain that made me do it. Not a very good excuse, but I desperately needed one, and that was as good as any.

Restless, I carried my coffee into the sunroom. I looked at the painting of Henry, the crotch sniffing Bernese, and started to laugh. Actually, I started to cackle. I had stolen a Rembrandt. There was a Rembrandt in my closet, which had probably been pilfered from a museum in Europe and smuggled into the United States, and I had it.

I looked out the window at the fishing boats on Broad Creek. Soon there would be another boat out there, waiting for Andrew to deliver the Rembrandt or return the money. What had he done to get himself into this pickle, I wondered. Where did he get the painting? And why was he willing to give it up? Had he accepted payment for the masterpiece and then decided to keep it? Double cross the mysterious note writer? That would give Andrew an excellent reason to disappear.

I had to find out about the painting. I sat down at my computer and did a Google search for stolen Rembrandts. I couldn't find any mention of a missing sketch of the *Supper At Emmaus*, but I did learn that old masterpieces could be identified by an examination of paint chips. When this mess was finally sorted out, I intended to find an expert to authenticate the painting. In the meantime, I needed to have someone else corroborate my theory. If a disinterested third party agreed with me, I'd feel a lot better about snatching the Rembrandt.

Grabbing the Hilton Head phone book, I looked up art galleries. There were several on the island. Using a local gallery might not be such a good idea, though. People talk, and the fact that I had a Rembrandt in my closet was bound to get out. I'd probably have Interpol on my doorstep before I could say, "I didn't do it."

I called Directory Assistance and jotted down the number of several galleries in Charleston. One by one, I called each number, asking if they had experience with Flemish art. On the third try, a cultured voice assured me I had found the right place. I made an appointment to meet with the owner of the gallery the following morning.

Then I called Ben. I dialed his cell phone number and waited for him to answer. I noticed my heart began an annoying thumping in my chest. Too much coffee, I decided.

When he answered I said, "Ben, it's Maggie."

"So I can hear." The phone line crackled with static.

"Where are you? Our connection is bad."

"I'm on the sixth hole of the Ocean course. Thought I'd play some golf today. That's what I came to Hilton Head for."

He sounded a little upset so I said, "I need you."

"Well, isn't that special."

"You don't have to be sarcastic, Ben. I just want to know if I can ride to Charleston with you tomorrow. That is, if you have to go back."

I heard him hesitate, then sigh. "As a matter of fact I do. You're welcome to tag along."

"Thank you. Will we see each other for dinner tonight?" I was making a peace offering I hoped he's accept.

"Afraid I can't. I have other plans."

"Oh. Okay. I'll see you tomorrow."

Maybe. This relationship, or whatever it you'd call it, was beginning to have disaster written all over.

*   *   *   *

At least Ben was still speaking to me. Now I had to worry about how I was going to describe the painting to the gallery owner in Charleston. I couldn't even contemplate taking it with me. The way my luck was running, we'd have an accident, and a priceless Rembrandt would be squashed into tiny bits under the wheels of an out of control tractor trailer. Even if we didn't have an accident, I'd still have to explain a fairly large, wrapped parcel to Ben, and I didn't want to do that.

It also occurred to me that since the painting probably came into this country illegally, Andrew Roop wouldn't raise a ruckus if he discovered it was missing. This made me feel better about Freedom. He'd be plenty mad, but I didn't think he would call the police.

I decided the best plan was to take pictures of the Rembrandt. I still had to concoct some plausible story for the gallery owner about why I had the photos, but I'd worry about that later.

I grabbed my digital camera and scrolled through the pictures. I deleted all twenty-seven exposures of Wally and made sure the camera was set to take "high quality" photos. I could always photograph my puppy, but how often did a person get to take pictures of a Rembrandt?.

Once again I tossed the tennis rackets and golf clubs out of the closet and retrieved the Rembrandt from its hiding place. I carried it into the sunroom and gingerly placed it on my easel, using as few thumbtacks as possible and sticking them into the old holes.

Heaven help me, I couldn't stop a huge smile from creeping over my face. Here I was, Maggie Bloom, standing in my house, looking at a picture of Henry, the dog, and a Rembrandt, side by side. It was so bizarre, it seemed surreal.

Knowing there was some reason you never used a flash with old paintings but not being able to remember why, I used it anyway, taking ten pictures of different areas of the masterpiece and five shots of the whole painting. I saved them to my computer, sized the best ones to 8"x10" and printed them on glossy paper. Since my hand had been shaking, the photos weren't examples of my best work, but they showed enough to give the gallery owner a decent representation of the painting.

After I tucked the Rembrandt safely away for a second time, I tried to take a nap. Life was becoming very stressful and I needed to recharge my batteries. I also needed to lay off the coffee. My eyes wouldn't stay closed. They kept flying open and looking towards the hall closet.

CHAPTER 22

▼

"So what are you up to in Charleston today?"

Ben and I were being very civil to each other. He'd asked about the wound on my leg, which I'd nearly forgotten, and I said I hoped his article about Senior migration was going well. He didn't say a word about calling the police or the obvious fact that I wasn't sticking close to my house. Neither one of us mentioned Peter.

I'd been waiting for him to inquire about my trip to Charleston. Since he was basically nosy, I knew sooner or later he would.

I'd prepared a little speech, which I hoped would satisfy him, so when he finally asked the question, I said, "When I was in Germany, I took a trip to Brussels and went to a little art gallery. I saw the most amazing sketch hanging on a wall. I told the gallery owner I was interested in buying it but wanted to think about it for a while, so he let me take some photos. The other day when I was straightening up my bedroom, I found them in the closet. I thought maybe a gallery in Charleston could give me more information about the sketch."

I smiled at him to show I was being honest and open. I noticed my hands were as cold as Popsicles. Lying is not without its drawbacks.

Ben drummed the steering wheel with his finger, and for a few minutes we raced down I-95 in silence.

"Let's see them."

"Excuse me?"

"The photos. Let's see them. I'm interested in art, too. I'd like to see what has you so excited."

"Ben, I don't think now is a good time to look at pictures. You're driving a car. I'll be happy to tell you what the gallery owner says." By then I'll have had enough time to invent another story.

He crooked his index finger at me. "Hand 'em over, Maggie. This has me intrigued."

Reluctantly, I pulled the photos out of a manila envelope and gave them to him. "It's really just a simple little sketch, Ben," I said, praying he knew nothing about art.

He held them in his left hand and steered the car with his right. Out of the corner of my eye, I watched him glance at the photos and then at the road. He seemed to be taking an awfully long time to study them. When he pulled into a rest stop and killed the engine, I thought he suddenly had to go to the bathroom.

"Okay, Maggie, what's up?" His voice was low and intense.

"I don't know what you mean."

I wondered if he could tell I was lying. I knew I was using that falsely cheery voice that indicated the truth was nowhere in sight, but I hoped he didn't know me well enough to recognize it.

"You know damn well what I mean. Where'd you take these photos?"

"I told you. In a little gallery.

"I see. Didn't you tell me you were a Fine Arts major? What do you suppose this painting is? You must have an idea, since you're racing to Charleston with it."

I searched Ben's face trying to read his thoughts. I sure didn't want to tell him my suspicions about the oil sketch. "I think it might have been done by a Dutch painter and before I buy it, I want to make sure."

His knuckles turned white as he gripped the steering wheel. "Let me get this straight. You're suddenly interested in buying a painting you saw over a year ago in a gallery in Brussels and are racing to Charleston to authenticate it even though you have no idea if the painting is still for sale."

"That's about it," I mumbled miserably. "Can we go now?"

"I think not. Let me point out a glaring flaw in your statement." He shoved one of the pictures under my nose. "First of all, this is from the Flemish school. Even I know that. And, it's extremely well done. You did not, however, photograph it in a little gallery in Brussels. If I had to guess, I'd say this picture was taken in your sunroom."

"What?" Genuinely surprised, I snatched the photo out of Ben's hand so I could have a closer look.

"Right here." He pointed to an area at the left of the picture. Is that not the ear and red collar of your Bernese mountain dog? If you're going to lie, Maggie, make sure you don't have photographic evidence to the contrary."

That's the trouble with bending the truth. Once you take the big plunge and fabricate a story, you have to pay attention to every tiny detail. Obviously, I'd overlooked one. I couldn't think of another adequate fib so I said, "I guess I can't show the folks in Charleston this photo."

He put his arm around my shoulder and pulled me close. "Look, I know we got off on the wrong foot. If I apologize for coming on too strong and promise not to pontificate, no matter what you tell me, will you let me in on what's going on? I really do care about you, and I want to help if I can."

I rubbed a throbbing spot on my temple while I thought about this. Since I was sitting in his car in the middle of a busy highway, it didn't seem I had much choice. I could refuse, of course, but I had a feeling that would signal the end of any possible relationship with Ben. And I didn't want that to happen.

"If I tell you, will you promise you won't call the police?"

"You mean this is bad enough to require the attention of the authorities?" Ben always sounded a bit pompous when he was upset.

"Well, maybe not, but I have the feeling you're going to throw around words like "grand theft" and "prison term," and I just want to make sure you don't."

He promised but I could see it was killing him.

I told him about the forgeries in Andrew Roop's collection and about finding the oil sketch on the back of Anne's portrait and how I thought it might possibly be a Rembrandt. Then, I told him about stashing the painting in my closet. "For safe keeping," I assured him. 'I don't intend to keep it."

His face turned a bright purple and he smacked the steering wheel so hard with his hand, I jumped about ten feet. "Damn," he said over and over, "Damn, damn, damn."

"For a New York Times reporter, you have become extremely monosyllabic. Do you have any other comments that require two or more syllables to express?"

"I don't know what kind of hot water you're going to find yourself in when this is all over, Maggie. If you go to jail, I'll come on visiting days. But this is a story. A really big one."

"Come again?" I was confused. In spite of his promises, I'd expected a stern lecture. "What do you mean, 'a really big story?'"

He rubbed his hands together in glee, and I could swear I saw his nose quivering. "You know, the New York Times. I write stuff for a living, remember? I'd love to blow the lid off an art smuggling ring and help return a Rembrandt to its rightful owner." He turned the key in the ignition, put the car in gear and careened out of the rest stop towards Charleston.

"Hey, wait a minute," I protested. "I have no intention of providing you with fodder so you can see your by-line on the front page. And I could be wrong about the paintings in Andrew's collection being forgeries and wrong about the Rembrandt, you know. If I am mistaken, you'll look very foolish. So you can drop me off here." I indicated a gas station. "I'll find my own way."

"Nope. Either I stop and call the cops, or I go with you and become your willing accomplice. What will it be?"

A willing accomplice sounded better than a stint in jail. But I didn't speak to him for another five minutes, just to show him he didn't have the upper hand.

CHAPTER 23

▼

"So, what's your plan? I'm sure you've got one."

We were on the outskirts of Charleston and I was very nervous.

"Basically the same thing I told you, with some embellishment." I fished the address for the gallery out of my purse and showed it to Ben. "Can I catch a ride back to Hilton Head with you later this afternoon? I'll talk to the gallery owner and do a little shopping until you've finished working."

He laughed. "Forget my work. I wouldn't miss this for the world. I'll tag along, if you don't mind."

This didn't suit me because I can't lie when Ben is listening. If I went into the gallery without him, though, I was sure he'd barge in after me and create some sort of scene. Resigned to the fact I wasn't going to be able to ditch him, we tried to concoct a reasonable story. It was he who suggested we should pretend to be married.

"I've made an appointment using the name Natalie Pickins," I told him.

"Quite an original moniker. How'd you come up with it?"

"While I was on the phone with the gallery, I saw an ad in the paper that said, 'Pickins' are slim at Baxter's Book Bag for customers looking for *Natalie's World,* the best seller that's charming the nation.' I had to think fast, so I just picked out some words and used them."

Ben shot me what I hoped was an admiring glance. "You really do have a devious mind. We will be Natalie and Bradford Pickins from Mobile."

"How'd you come up with that so fast?"

"God help me, I'm beginning to think like you." He squeezed my hand. "I'm with you all the way, Maggie. Whether you believe it or not."

Ben found a parking space in front of the gallery. The sign out front said, "Dogwood Gallery. Specialists in Conservation and Restorations. Hours by appointment."

I smoothed the wrinkles out of my navy linen skirt and straightened the collar of my white blazer. This was it. Soon I'd know whether I had a competent fake or a genuine masterpiece stashed in my crawl space. I glanced at Ben. He raked his fingers through his hair and made sure his shirt was tucked in his pants. My heart was beating so fast, I was afraid it was going to jump out of my chest.

The inside of the gallery was cool and sparsely furnished. A massive pine desk stood against the far wall. An enormous marble statue of a nude woman, her arms twisted in what looked to me like excruciating pain, occupied a large space by the door. On the polished, heart of pine floor was a breathtaking Tabriz rug.

Ben poked me in the ribs, pointed to the marble statue and said, "Can you do that?"

I poked him back. "This is not the time for frivolity."

At the sound of the tinkling bell above the door, a woman appeared from the back. Around sixty, she was dressed in a severe, steel gray skirt and high collared white cotton blouse. She wore no make up and as she approached us, she adjusted the hairpins in a tight bun.

I extended my hand and introduced Ben and myself. Ben bowed from the waist and said," I'm pleased to meet such a lovely lady." His accent was thick and southern.

"I'm Pamela Chalmer, I must admit, I've been thinking about you ever since you called. I'm very curious about what you have to show me." She looked at my empty hands. "You didn't bring it with you?"

Unprepared for such directness, I hesitated. Apparently this woman was not even going to ask us to sit down. She must think she's on to something big.

"I don't own the oil sketch, Miss Chalmer. I thought I made that clear. I said I've seen it, but I don't actually have it."

Miss Chalmer seemed disappointed. "How am I to determine its authenticity if I can't see it?" Her lips curved into a frown, implying we were wasting her time.

Ben held up his hand and said. "Might my bride sit down for a moment, Miss Chalmer? She is expecting our first child in six months and tires easily." He put his arm around me protectively. "She is extremely delicate."

I tried to dig my elbow into his ribs without Miss Chalmer noticing.

Once we were both seated, I opened my shoulder bag and pulled out the photos. "As I explained on the phone, when I was in Europe a few months ago, I saw a partially finished oil sketch in a small antique shop in Brussels. I felt it had certain characteristics of a genuine Rembrandt. The owner of the shop seemed to think it was a fake, done possibly by an art student. In any event, he wasn't very interested in it and was willing to let me photograph it."

I offered the photos to Miss Chalmer whose enthusiasm had cooled considerably. The woman probably had other plans for a Sunday afternoon, like bird watching or poetry reading and had canceled them for me.

"I thought the painting might be the real thing, possibly a sketch Rembrandt made for another painting of the *Supper at Emmaus*."

When Miss Chalmer raised her eyebrows indicating skepticism that I would be able to distinguish a Rembrandt from a Grandma Moses, I said, "By way of explanation, I should add that I was a professor of Art History at Boston University. I did my Master's thesis on Rembrandt's interpretation of the human soul. So I am familiar with his work." I prayed Ben wouldn't laugh out loud and was pleased to see he was able to control himself.

Miss Chalmer's eyebrows floated to a position somewhere between her hairline and her eyes.

"If you could just have a look, I'd be most grateful. I know you're a busy woman, and I don't want to waste your time."

I hated myself for sounding so wishy-washy. I was willing to bet I had a more thorough knowledge of Rembrandt than the formidable art gallery owner.

Miss Chalmer sat down behind the desk and placed the photos side by side on the highly polished desktop. Pulling a magnifying glass from the top drawer, she examined the photos. For a full ten minutes the only sound we heard was our own uneven breathing.

To break the silence, Ben said, "We most surely do appreciate you taking the time to see us. We're over from Mobile on our little boat. Which reminds me, sweetest, the captain said the crew would like to have tonight off. Something about a concert they want to attend." He caressed my hair fondly. "Cook will leave us something for dinner. I know how you hate being on your feet after 7:00."

It occurred to me I'd forgotten to use a southern accent. I wondered if Miss Chalmer noticed. If she did, I could always tell the truth and say I'd lost my drawl years ago.

I knew it was difficult to assess a painting from photographs, but at least two of the pictures adequately showed good examples of Rembrandt's treatment of dark and light. An expert should be able to recognize that right away. I was beginning to doubt Miss Chalmer's qualifications.

I tried not to fidget. And I was annoyed at being made to feel like an incompetent schoolgirl. I considered grabbing the photos and leaving. I was convinced the painting was genuine. Why did I need this woman's opinion?

Finally, Miss Chalmer put down her magnifying glass and cleared her throat. "You say you saw this in a shop in Brussels?"

I nodded.

"Why didn't you buy it?"

I felt Ben put a warning hand on my leg.

"I didn't want it if it were a fake. Look, Miss Chalmer," I said as I leaned on the desk, "you and I both know the likelihood of finding an authentic Rembrandt is extremely remote. Ridiculously remote. I was in the shop looking around. There were lots of dark, old paintings and interesting curios, but most of them were junk. There was something about this oil sketch, however, that made me look at it twice. I thought it bore amazing similarities to a genuine Rembrandt but surrounded by all that worthless stuff, I didn't really believe it. Am I making any sense?"

I hoped I was. In fact, it sounded so good, I almost believed the story myself. Ben beamed in approval.

Miss Chalmer smoothed the hair on her upper lip. "What would your intentions be if this were a genuine Rembrandt?"

"What do you mean, my intentions? I don't own this, Miss Chalmer. My curiosity is now merely a scholarly one."

"You wouldn't, then, be planning to return to, ah, Brussels to purchase the sketch?"

"No, I hadn't considered it."

I knew this part of my story was weak. If the painting were a Rembrandt, any normal person would have been on the next flight to Brussels, checkbook in hand.

"I really am only interested in knowing whether or not it is a Rembrandt. I think my curiosity is understandable given my background."

Miss Chalmer stood up. "Would you excuse me for a moment?" She disappeared into the back and in a few minutes we heard her voice, low and insistent.

Ben took this opportunity to say, "You're doing a great job. Since she hasn't dismissed us outright, there must be a possibility that it's a

Rembrandt." He winked at me. "How do you like my southern accent, sugar?"

"How could you tell her I'm pregnant? And delicate? Couldn't you have thought of something else?"

He patted my stomach. "Don't get the little one upset, buttercup. You know what the doctor said. You mustn't have any stress."

I was peeling his hand from my mid-section when Miss Chalmer returned carrying a bottle of Perrier Jouet and three long stemmed glasses. For the first time she smiled, exposing large yellow teeth.

"Mrs. Pickins, I won't beat around the bush," she said as she poured the champagne and set the glasses in front of us. "I'm prepared to offer you one million dollars for the oil sketch, but only after I have seen the original."

I almost laughed out loud. If this were an original Rembrandt, it was worth several millions, not the piddling amount this woman was offering.

"I believe I told you I don't have it," I said.

Ben felt compelled to add, "You sure don't, my sweet magnolia." He was getting frisky so I shot him a sharp glance to calm him down.

"Yes, yes." Miss Chalmer waved my protest away. "I know you say you don't. But it's hard to believe you would leave a painting you thought had even the remotest possibility of being an authentic Rembrandt. You have a solid background in Flemish art. Surely you would have purchased this, or at least secured it with a down payment until you could substantiate your beliefs."

She lowered her voice. "I can imagine there would be a bit of a problem getting it out of the country. There might be all kinds of difficulties with the Dutch government if it knew a priceless treasure was being removed."

"Are you saying you also believe it is a Rembrandt?" I asked.

"I'm saying there are characteristics reminiscent of Rembrandt," the woman said cautiously. "Enough for me to offer payment as if it were an original. Let's be honest with each other, Mrs. Pickins. You have it and we would like to buy it. It's as simple as that."

I was so excited, I wanted to get up and dance a jig around the room. Uncannily, Ben was able to read my mind. He pressed hard on my leg to make sure I stayed seated.

I had to admit, I admired Andrew's cunning. This woman was trying to cheat me by offering only a million dollars. I'd be willing to bet Andrew's buyer had offered much, much more. I folded my hands and looked at Miss Chalmer with what I hoped was a sincere expression.

"I'm afraid I am telling the truth. I don't own it. Walking out of that shop in Brussels without the painting is probably the dumbest thing I've ever done in my life, but I really don't have it."

Miss Chalmer tried another tack. "Would you be able to provide me with the name of the antique shop in Brussels? Perhaps if you really aren't interested, we would be able to contact them directly."

I was ready for this question. "I'm fairly certain I'd be able to find it again. But the address?" I shook my head. "It's in a little village on the outskirts of Waterloo. Let me see if I remember. You drive through Waterloo to the battlefield. After the lion statue—you know, that famous Waterloo landmark—turn left at either the second or third road and drive out into the country."

Ben interrupted. "Sugarplum, I think you're wrong. I'm pretty certain the driver turned at the fourth road. I remember there was a quaint restaurant on the corner, and you said you wanted to stop for something to drink. That was the day you were having those pesky fainting spells." He smiled benignly.

"I had forgotten about that, dumpling," I said through clenched teeth. "Anyway, on the right about ten miles down the road, there is a new housing development. Turn right; drive about three miles until you come to a crossroad. Turn left, go about one and a half miles and at the sugar beet field, turn left."

Miss Chalmer, who had been writing rapidly, put down her pen. "Mrs. Pickins, this isn't very helpful." She looked at her notes. "Left at a sugar beet field is hardly a valid direction."

"It's the best I can do, Miss Chalmer. I believe the shop is called *Le Petit Couchon.*"

The older woman considered this information. "I believe that means little pig."

"Exactly. The shop is in the country. Perhaps the owner felt that name fit in with the rural atmosphere." I stood up. "In any event, you should be able to find it. I'd suggest calling Brussels information. I'm sorry I can't give you the name of the village. There are so many of them in the countryside around Brussels, and I just didn't pay attention."

"Come, my little muffin, we must go," I said to Ben. "Isn't it almost time for your mother's daily call from the institution?"

Miss Chalmer scooped up the photos and opened a drawer. "I'd like to keep these for further study," she said.

I plucked them out of her hand. "I'd like to keep them too. You know, as a souvenir of my European trip."

"But Mrs. Pickins…"

"They're mine, Miss Chalmer. I thank you for your time. You've helped me immensely. I wish you luck in locating the antique store."

"At least I sent her on a plausible wild goose chase," I told Ben as we walked out of the gallery. "There really was an antique store named *Le Petit Couchon* in a village on the outskirts of Waterloo. I saw it when I went to visit friends in Rhodes St. Genese. I can imagine the owner will be stunned to hear he had a possible Rembrandt in his inventory. As far as I can remember, he sold hand-painted wooden figurines of Napoleon and metal replicas of battle weapons."

We were almost to Ben's car when we heard footsteps pounding on the pavement. Miss Chalmer skidded to a stop beside us, breathing hard.

"I just wondered," she said, "if I might have an address and phone number from you. Just in case you should be able to secure the painting and would be interested in selling it."

She held a pad of paper in front of me and offered me a pen.

"Apple fritter," I said to Ben, "won't we be spending the next few months at our house on the Cape?"

"That's up to you, plum cake." He patted my stomach again. "Do you think little Bradford would like that?"

"You're having a boy? How nice," Miss Chalmer said, staring at Ben's hand. She obviously thought we were candidates for a mental ward but was too interested in the Rembrandt to offend us.

I scribbled Christine, the bimbo's, address in Sudbury, MA. It wasn't on the Cape, but the gallery owner wouldn't know that.

If Miss Chalmer decided to pursue the matter, she'd have to deal with her. By the time she explained to Christine that Rembrandt was an artist and not a toothpaste, she'd be so frustrated she would more than likely give up. This was one time I was happy Peter had taken up with a dim witted Barbie doll.

CHAPTER 24

▼

Neither dog met us at the door. I found them in the dining room, hard at work on things they had found in my bedroom. Willow chewed on a terry cloth slipper, while Wally tore up a roll of toilet paper. Wet globs of the stuff littered the floor.

"If you can't behave in the future, I'm going to lock you up," I yelled, but I was too excited about the Rembrandt to get really upset. Ben stepped over my panties and a partially chewed hairbrush.

"I think the dogs are trying to tell you something, Maggie. You've been leaving them alone too much. Let me see the Rembrandt."

"What? No foreplay? No sweet talk or cuddling? You want to plunge right into the main event. A girl likes a little bit of coaxing before she puts out."

"Very funny." He snapped his fingers impatiently. "Let's see it. Knowing your talent for attracting trouble, it's probably been eaten by palmetto bugs."

That thought scared me just a bit. I flew into the closet, delighted to see his eyes widen in disbelief as I pulled the priceless painting from its hiding place next to the water heater. He started to say something and thought better of it. This time I didn't tack it onto the easel. I carefully held it in front of me so he could have a look.

"It's magnificent," he whispered, as awestruck as I'd been. "It would be a crime to allow someone to sell this."

Since he seemed to agree with me, I spent the next hour telling him about the rest of my adventures. I told him about the cabin on Daufuskie and about how I believed I'd seen Joey and about how Anne and Andrew Roop both seemed to have disappeared.

"This all has to be connected somehow," I said, "and I think I'm close to having it figured out. All I need is a bit more time. Do you still promise me you won't call the police?"

To my utter astonishment, Ben completely capitulated.

"I promise," he said. "In fact, I'm going to go to Savannah and do a little research. I'll talk to a friend of mine who lives there and used to work for the Times as the art editor. He'll be able to give me more information. I seem to remember a Rembrandt was stolen from a museum in Cologne, Germany a few years ago. I'll check it out. By the way, tonight I have to go out to dinner with someone from the Del Webb Corporation. He's going to give me some details about the Sun City development. Want to come along?"

I shook my head. "I'd better take the dogs for a walk. Otherwise, I'm not going to have any underwear left."

There was also something else I had to do. As soon as Ben left, I called Freedom.

"Any sign of the Roops?" I asked when she answered the phone.

"Nope. I've had the house to myself. What have you been up to?"

"Funny you should ask." I told her about going to Charleston. "The painting is probably a real Rembrandt," I explained. "The woman wouldn't have offered me money for a good fake. So, I've been thinking," I began, waiting for her to say, "I don't want to hear it."

Instead, she said nothing.

"Are you still there?"

"Does this thinking involve me?"

"Absolutely," I replied cheerfully. "I wouldn't think of leaving you behind."

I heard Freedom sigh. "All right. Tell me what it is. I can always say no."

"I'm thinking, since we know we have a real Rembrandt on our hands..."

"Your hands," Freedom interrupted. "You can leave me out of that."

"Okay, my hands. And we know that a boat is going to be waiting on Broad Creek tonight to take delivery of the painting." I paused. "Do you realize I can see Broad Creek from my window, Freedom? I can also see Buck Island. They're really not that far away."

"So?"

"Did you also know that there is a functional row boat under my house?"

"Oh, no you don't, Maggie Bloom. I see where you're going with this. There's no way I'm rowing with you out to Broad Creek to meet a boat. Find somebody else."

"Don't be silly, Freedom," I said briskly. "There is nobody else. Ben went to Savannah to research the painting, and I don't know when he'll be back. Lucy doesn't have any clothes suitable for night skulking. I need you. Here's what I'm suggesting. We simply row out and have a look. That way, we can tell the sheriff what kind of a boat it is and possibly even give him the name. If we tell the sheriff everything and can back it up with a good description of the boat, he might be more inclined to believe us."

When Freedom didn't say anything, I took that as a sign she was willing to listen. "I think you'll agree with me that we can't keep the Rembrandt stashed in my closet forever."

"You're the one who can't keep it stashed," Freedom reminded me. "I don't have anything to do with that painting."

"Whatever," I said impatiently. "Work with me here, Freedom. I need to have a look at that boat."

"I know I'm going to hate myself for this."

"Great. I'll consider that a yes. Be at my house no later than 10:15. And wear something sensible. There are mosquitoes at night in the marsh."

I hung up, feeling the tiniest bit guilty. I hadn't given my friend a chance to decline. But, if we did manage to identify the boat and report our findings to the sheriff, Freedom might be off the hook for allowing the painting to leave the Roop residence, and I might be able to escape a long prison term for grand theft.

Satisfied, I began to clean up Wally and Willow's mess. Full of nervous energy, I took them for a long walk and fed them a good dinner. Still too restless to sit still, I cleaned large gobs of green stuff out of the vegetable bin in the refrigerator, did a load of laundry and swept the front porch. Realizing I hadn't talked to Tiffany for a while, I dialed her number. She answered on the first ring.

"Am I catching you at a bad time, Tif?"

"Not at all," she said, when she recognized my voice. "I can't talk long though. I've got some stuff to do."

"Have you heard again from Joey," I asked, knowing full well he couldn't call her on a broken VHF radio. I suppose he could walk to a pay phone by the dock, but I was willing to bet he wouldn't.

"No. I guess he doesn't have the radio anymore."

I thought her voice sounded funny, as if she were trying too hard to be nonchalant. I also noticed she didn't sound very concerned about Joey's well being. Something was up, but I had no idea what.

"Well, I'm busy too. I'll talk to you later."

She had hung up the phone before I finished my sentence.

CHAPTER 25

▼

Dark clouds had formed to the south, sending sudden gusts of wind across the porch, rippling the newspapers and magazines on the table. The wind whistled through the pine trees and made the marsh grass wave like spectators at a baseball game.

Not a good night for a moon dance, I told myself as I looked out at the marsh. The blob of sun sitting on the horizon suddenly dipped from sight, leaving the sky a faint orange afterglow. For several minutes I watched a hawk glide and then flap its wings as the strengthening air currents interrupted its flight.

As I stood there, the wind increased, screaming through the pines and the screening on my porch. Clouds raced across the sky until there was nothing left but ominous black. The islands on the other side of the Intracoastal turned from green to a gray shadow against the darkening sky. Then the rain came, heavy drops at first, spattering sand below my house and sending a rabbit scurrying for cover. The wind blew sheets of rain across the marsh until even Buck Island was a hazy, faint outline against the sky.

When the lights came on in the house next door, I realized I was wet and chilly and went inside.

*　　*　　*　　*

At 10:30 the marsh throbbed with the night symphony of frogs and crickets. The rain had washed away the humidity of the day, and the air smelled clean and fresh. Occasionally in the darkness an unseen critter splashed into the water, sending ripples around our ankles.

We both wore jeans, long sleeved shirts and rubber boots. In spite of the warm air, Freedom shivered. "It's spooky down here," she said. I hate to think of the things slithering around my feet."

I had to agree with her. "I'd rather be on the deck myself."

I looked at my home. Built on brick footers, it rose fourteen feet above sea level. From the deck, the marsh was a serene vista of green marsh grass and water. At ground level, where we were now, the wax myrtle bushes, pine trees and marsh grasses towered above our heads.

Freedom swatted at them in frustration. "How are we ever going to get the boat through this stuff? It's so thick, I can't even see the water."

"We'll manage," I assured her. "Help me lift the boat off the saw-horse. The tide is in, so once we've pushed out a little way, we should be able to find a channel."

Freedom let the beam of the flashlight play on the old boat. "Have you ever used this thing? It looks pretty dilapidated."

"No, it came with the house, but it looks okay to me."

I was relieved Freedom hadn't thought to ask if the boat was seaworthy. I mentally kicked myself for not checking it before now. I'd been too busy thinking about the Rembrandt. And I had to admit, I'd been thinking about Ben. He really was a genuinely good person, and he cared about me in a way Peter never had. When all this was over, I'd let him know how I felt—just as soon as I figured it out myself.

As we turned the boat upright at the edge of the marsh, I tried to stop worrying about possible holes in the bottom. We would know soon enough. If it took on water, we would still be able to slog back to the house.

I stowed a heavy-duty flashlight, mosquito repellent, a Swiss Army knife, binoculars and the cell phone under the bench in the bow of the boat. I also included the only weapon I could find; a BB gun I'd found in the attic when I bought the house. I suspected the previous owner had used it to shoot at pesky raccoons.

"Now we have to push," I said. "And keep your voice down. Remember, voices carry on the water. When I sit on my deck at night, I can hear every word people are saying out here. We don't want anyone to know what we're doing."

In the darkness, Freedom gestured towards my house. "You don't think that racket might alert the neighbors that something is up?"

I listened to Wally and Willow. Both dogs howled as if they were being pierced with a barbecue fork.

"They always do that when I go away. They'll settle down in a few minutes. The neighbors are used to it."

But I wasn't so sure about that. They'd been left alone too much lately and were protesting the only way they knew how. I could see Wally at the window, his head thrown back as he wailed in indignation. He knew I was out there, and he might keep it up until I came back.

Wading into the water, I said, "I'll pull, you push."

"No thanks," Freedom replied. "I'm not stepping into anything I can't see."

"Oh, for heaven's sake, just push. All the marsh inhabitants are asleep now."

I hoped Freedom didn't know that South Carolina's coastal region was heavily populated with nearly every kind of poisonous snake known to man.

"Really? Then what's that noise? It sounds like an alligator."

"There are no alligators in the marsh. Let's go."

I was glad I'd worn jeans and long sleeves. The Spartina grass swiped my arms and legs and scratched my face. When this was over, I was going to look like I've been in a prizefight. My hand automatically went to the wound on my thigh. But it didn't hurt. And, in all the excitement of finding the Rembrandt, I'd also forgotten that someone tried to kill me. Now wasn't a good time to think about it.

Freedom and I pushed and pulled the boat through the heavy grasses. It was going mighty slowly. At times the boat stuck on the sand, and I had to wade to the stern and help Freedom push. When we reached a dead tree in the marsh that looked like driftwood, I stopped. Wiping my brow with the palm of my hand, I looked back at my house. We'd gone about forty feet and the backs of my legs had already begun to hurt.

My foot nudged something soft that moved out of my way when I touched it. *Probably a crab*, I reassured myself, knowing full well it was too big to be a crab.

After twenty yards of wading and pushing through ankle deep water, we abruptly broke through the marsh grass into deeper water. Freedom and I both sank in to our knees. Frightened, she grabbed the side of the boat and hoisted herself up, falling face first into the stern. The boat rocked wildly, drenching me.

"That's not how to get into a boat," I informed her.

"Don't start lecturing me. My boots are filled with water and my jeans are soaked. This was a lousy idea."

"I'm sorry you're so uncomfortable. I, on the other hand, am toasty warm and having a wonderful time."

Reaching forward, Freedom extended her hand to me. "Get in. Maybe once you're out of the water, you'll stop with the sarcasm."

I motioned to Freedom to change places with me. With the flashlight I inspected the bottom of the boat. Good. No water. If it were going to leak, it would have started by now.

"I'll row for a while," I said. "You keep a look out."

The old oars protested loudly as they turned in the oarlocks, and I felt splinters dig into my hands. As I rowed, Freedom sat rigidly in the bow, her hands clenching the sides. Slowly, a mist fell over the marsh making the moon look fuzzy.

"Unpredictable weather," I told her, hoping thunder and lightning weren't next on the agenda.

In the darkness Freedom said, "I don't feel comfortable, Maggie. It's too eerie. I'd like to go back."

"We're almost there. Turn around and look. The lights from Buck Island are much closer."

"Then row faster. I want to get out of this swamp."

"This isn't a swamp. It's a saltwater marsh. There's a big difference."

"I don't feel like splitting hairs right now, Maggie," she said through her teeth. "I just want to get out of here."

To get Freedom's mind off her misery, I said, "This is hard going. The oars keep getting caught on the undergrowth. If the tide were out, we'd be sitting in bushes. Does that make you feel better?"

As I spoke, the boat lurched suddenly forward. "Thank God," I announced. "We're in one of the channels near Calibogue Cay. I've seen fairly large boats come through here, so that means we're in deeper water."

It also means we can't get out and walk, but I didn't tell Freedom. At the edge of the marsh, I stopped rowing. Broad Creek was straight ahead.

"I don't want to go out there," I whispered to Freedom. "We'd better stay in the marsh where there is at least a little protection. The note said the rendezvous point was on Broad Creek across from Buck Island. That's right there." I pointed to a spot fifty yards away. "We'll swing a little to the left and find a place where we can stop."

I maneuvered the boat into a clump of grass and hauled in the oars. "We'll sit here and wait."

Looking around, I felt fairly secure. We could see Broad Creek, but the marsh grass hid us well.

I rubbed my arms. "My muscles are going to hurt tomorrow," I said to Freedom. "Try the binoculars and tell me what you see."

Freedom slipped the strap over her neck and lifted the binoculars to her eyes. "Should I stand up?"

"I think not."

She tried to peer through an opening in the marsh grass. "This won't work. I'll only be a second," she said as she stood up and scanned the water. The boat rocked dangerously. "Nothing coming from Harbour Town and nothing from the direction of the bridge. Wait a minute." I held my breath. "Nope, false alarm. There is a boat, but it's on the other side of Buck Island on the Intracoastal. It's very small, probably a fishing boat."

I stretched my legs and checked my watch. "It's after eleven. Maybe the boat isn't coming."

"I've been thinking that, too, Maggie," Freedom said as she scrambled to her seat. "This whole thing might have been a big hoax designed to torment Andrew. Wouldn't we feel like fools if we'd rowed out here for nothing?"

"True. I won't tell anyone if you don't."

I yawned. The combination of exercise and fresh air was making me sleepy. "Let's wait for a few more minutes and then go home. Speaking of Andrew, where do you suppose he is?"

"Probably in a foreign country living high on the hog. I think Andrew snapped. Guilt about the death of his brother, too much booze, I don't know. It was more than he could cope with so he took the money and ran."

"See, that's what bothers me. Why would he leave the Rembrandt behind? If he blew up the *Second Chance* and sold off his collection, why wouldn't he take the biggest prize of all? It would have only taken a few minutes to remove the sketch from the back of Anne's portrait."

"He left in a hurry," Freedom suggested. He was probably terrified the tough guys were going to rough him up or even worse. Speaking of tough guys, we should finally let the sheriff in on our detective work."

"We've been over that, Freedom. I don't know how to explain everything without landing Tiffy and me in deep trouble. We should have called him as soon as Tiffy heard from Joey. But now?" In the darkness, I shrugged my shoulders. "Too much has happened. I don't want to tell him I have the Rembrandt in my crawl space."

Both of us froze at the sound of a diesel engine. Coming from the direction of the bridge leading to Hilton Head, it throttled back as it approached Point Comfort and coasted toward Buck Island. The rowboat nearly capsized as I grabbed the binoculars and stood up.

"It's running without lights," I whispered. "I can't believe it. There is actually a boat out there and it's a big one." I felt my heart race as I watched a large, black shape, bigger than some of the boats I'd seen in the harbor silently stop within one hundred feet of our rowboat.

Freedom's hands flew to her throat. "I'm scared," she said softly.

Me too, I thought. *Scared enough to wet my pants.* This was no longer a sleuthing game. There was a very real boat very close to us. The note to Andrew had been real, not a hoax as I had half hoped, and whoever had threatened Andrew was in that boat. He probably wasn't a nice person.

In the still of the night, Freedom and I waited. We could hear low male voices, too indistinct to understand, coming from the boat. I put my mouth next to Freedom's ear.

"If we can hear them," I whispered, "they'll be able to hear us too. We have to be absolutely silent."

Freedom nodded in agreement. We sat like granite statues, afraid to move a muscle as we listened to the water lap around the rowboat. I felt my foot fall asleep, and I resisted the urge to shake it. I realized my hand was clenching the binoculars tightly, and I slowly relaxed my grip, allowing blood to flow through paralyzed fingers.

The boat was so much bigger than I'd had expected. It was a yacht. You couldn't call something that significant a boat. It looked menacing, like a sinister intruder on the quiet water.

Do something, I urged myself. *Either take a good look at the thing so you can tell the sheriff about it or get the hell out of here.* But I couldn't make myself move. My body was frozen in terror as I listened for even the slightest sound.

When the phone rang, I jumped as if I'd been stung by a swarm of bees. Accustomed to the silence, the ring of my cell phone sounded like Big Ben peeling across the water. At first I didn't know what had caused the noise, but as Freedom grabbed my hand in fright, I remembered the phone. It rang five times before I found it beneath the seat. To stop the ringing, I had to answer.

"Hello?" It wasn't even a whisper, more of a breathless gasp.

"Maggie, I'm glad I found you."

Ben's voice was so vibrant, I pressed the phone to my ear to muffle the sound. I could hear the tinkle of glasses and the hum of voices in the background.

"I just called to say I've got great news about the Rembrandt. I was right about the theft from the museum in Cologne. My friend described the painting, and it matches the one you have in your, ah, hiding place. I think the German government would be very happy to learn it's safe and sound." He laughed. "Relatively speaking, that is."

I felt tears spring to my eyes. Right then I'd have given anything I owned to be with Ben. I'd even let him lecture me about my foolhardy ways. I was pretty sure sitting in a rowboat at night with the bad guys a few yards away would qualify as foolhardy in his book.

"I can't talk right now," I murmured into the phone.

"What? I can't hear you. I think we have a bad connection."

"We don't have a bad connection. I just can't talk."

Please understand, Ben, I prayed. But how could he? He didn't know where I was.

"Are you okay?" I heard the happiness fade from his voice and concern replace it.

"No, I'm not okay. I'm out in the marsh. Help me, Ben."

I glanced at Freedom who was holding her ears and mumbling, "Hang up. Hang up."

"Can you hear me?" I asked. I heard voices in the background. Ben must be having fun. Nice, non-dangerous fun. The line crackled.

"Did you say you need help?" His voice faded and then came back. "Tell me where you are. I don't understand."

"I'm in the marsh. The boat is here about the Rembrandt. I can't talk anymore." I pushed the power button, and the phone died. Turning to Freedom, I said, "I'm sorry. I didn't know the darn thing was turned on."

Freedom swayed back and forth, hugging herself. "I should have stayed home. I knew I should have stayed home. Something bad is going to happen."

"Will you stop that? I'll just have one more quick look and we'll be on our way."

Freedom grabbed the phone out of my hand and flung it into the water. "I'm finished. Let's go now. This isn't funny. I have to tell you, I'm scared to death."

Suddenly the rowboat, Freedom and I were bathed in a glaring light. It was so bright, I could clearly see the fear on my friend's face. Trying to shield my own eyes with one hand, I frantically swung an oar into the water. For the first time in my life, I could taste real fear. It filled my throat, threatening to stop my breathing.

"We've got to get out of here. Grab the other oar, Freedom."

Incapable of action, Freedom screamed, "What is this? What's happening, Maggie?"

Hearing the panic in Freedom's voice, I struggled to stay calm. "They turned a search light on us. We've got to try to get back into the marsh."

As I swung the boat around, I saw a distant light on the shore. I knew it came from my house; from the floor lamp in my living room, and that Wally and Willow were curled up on the couch next to it, waiting for me to come home. It made me want to cry.

With a strength I didn't know I possessed, I dug the oar into the water and rowed toward the safety of my home. When I felt Freedom at my side, I gratefully gave up an oar and, like dancers on a black stage, she and I rowed, the spotlight following our every move.

My arms hurt beyond endurance. When a male voice said, "Good evening, ladies," I was almost glad to drop the oar.

CHAPTER 26

▼

A black rubber dinghy, the kind used to tow customers to a parasailing float and almost invisible in the darkness, bumped against our boat. Two men dressed in black turtleneck shirts, dark pants and ski caps greeted Freedom and me politely. Using a grappling hook attached to a rope, one man secured the hook onto the edge of the rowboat while the other kept a flashlight trained on us as we cowered in the bow.

An outboard motor on the dinghy roared to life and the rope attached to the rowboat straightened into a taut line. Both the rowboat and my stomach lurched, the rowboat in the direction of the waiting yacht and my stomach in the direction of my throat.

It had all happened so fast I had no time to feel anything but disbelief. My mind was not willing to comprehend what had just occurred. It wasn't until the rowboat began to move steadily into the open water of Broad Creek that absolute terror threatened to stop my heart.

I felt Freedom's cold and clammy hand grab mine in the darkness, and I held it tightly, unable to speak. When I did find my voice, it came out as a bleating cry that I didn't recognize.

"Hey. What are you doing?"

The men didn't reply. I heard them talking. One laughed, a deep, throaty sound that made the hair stand up on the back of my neck.

Next to me, Freedom began to shake, her whole body trembling like someone with a terrible chill. When she said, "I think I'm going to faint," I knew I had to pull myself together.

I noticed they had slowed down a bit, as if the dinghy were having trouble pulling the heavier rowboat. It makes most sense, I decided, to try to pull out the grappling hook. I grabbed it with both hands and, bracing my feet against the bow of the boat, tugged as hard as I could. I soon realized that the pull of the line had imbedded the hook into the wood. I couldn't budge it.

In a panic, I tried to find another option. "We could jump," I whispered to Freedom. "We could jump and swim back to the marsh."

Freedom's hand tightened around mine. "I can't do that. I can't swim."

"That's okay," I reassured my friend. "I wasn't really eager to do that myself. It was a dumb idea."

Think, I urged myself. *You have to think of something.* That's when I remembered the Swiss Army knife. Leaning forward, I rummaged under the seat until my fingers felt the solid, smooth surface of the knife.

Freedom's eyes widened. "What are you going to do with that?"

"I've got to try this. I think they intend to haul us out to the yacht and maybe even take us on board." I flicked the knife open, displaying the gleaming blade. "Maybe I can cut through the rope. It's too bad you threw the phone in the water. We could call for help."

Freedom began to cry.

"I'm sorry, Freedom. I really didn't mean to say that. I'm too scared to think straight," I said as I sawed at the thick, twisted hemp. "This won't cut. It has some kind of plastic on it, and the knife won't even put a nick in it."

"It doesn't matter. Look!" Freedom said in a resigned voice.

I looked up to see the solid side of the yacht not more than twenty feet away. I estimated the ship to be about one hundred feet long, as high as a two-story house and sleek as a torpedo. Silhouetted by an interior light, a massive dark shape leaned over the railing.

"Pull it in tight, boys and urge the little ladies to come aboard," a voice said.

A ladder clattered over the side. And a sudden jerk on the line told me we were being reeled in like hapless fish.

In spite of my fear, a stubborn sense of survival made me decide to fight. My mother hadn't raised a wimp. They could take us on board, but not until I was too exhausted to resist.

Keeping my voice low, I said, "It's now or never, Freedom. As soon as we're close enough, I'm going to stick the knife into the dinghy. You get ready to grab the oars and row as fast as you can."

A muffled gasp told me that Freedom had heard me.

I tensed, the handle of the Swiss Army knife gripped firmly in my right hand, as I inched my way forward, ready to strike.

The rowboat banged into the dinghy. One of the men threw a cigarette into the water, its lighted end dropping in a graceful glowing arc. He stood up and began to haul in the rope.

"Now," I yelled.

I thrust the blade as hard as I could into the rubber dinghy and was rewarded with a satisfying hiss. When I felt the line slacken, I struggled frantically with the grappling hook, trying to pull it loose. With clenched teeth and eyes closed, I pulled until I thought my arms would pop out of their sockets. The hook came free, sending me sprawling.

"Shit," I heard one man say. "She busted the dinghy. Get them, Lenny. Use your gun."

"Don't shoot them," the man on the deck warned. "At least don't shoot to kill. I need to talk to them."

"We're sinking here, boss," the man called Lenny yelled. "I'm getting all wet."

Both men grabbed the ladder, abandoning the sinking dinghy. Freedom turned the rowboat around and headed for the marsh, the oars cutting through the water with a speed born of panic.

"Row," I yelled at her. "We can get away."

"I don't think so," came the voice from the deck. The searchlight came alive again, pinpointing us like butterflies in a lepidopterist's collection. "It seems I have to do everything myself," the voice continued. "I'd advise you to row to the ladder and come aboard. I'd hate to have to shoot you."

Uncertain what to do, Freedom faltered, lifting the oars momentarily out of the water.

"Keep rowing," I screamed. "He won't shoot."

A shot rang out, echoing across the marsh and landing with a plop in the water beside us. So much for that theory.

"Oh, but I will. Let's stop this nonsense, ladies, before someone gets hurt."

"I can't do it, Maggie," Freedom cried. "I'm too scared. He really will shoot."

I looked at the light from my living room beckoning in the distance. This was absolutely ridiculous. I felt indignation sweep through me. I certainly was not going to let some boorish thug intimidate me. We were on Broad Creek within sight of my house. This kind of thing simply did not happen on Hilton Head. If this were a nightmare or some surrealistic dream, I needed to wake up right now. After I pinched myself a few times and still found myself sitting in a rowboat in the middle of the night, I took the oars from Freedom and began to row towards the marsh. I was going home. I was going home and find Ben and call the sheriff and end this nonsense once and for all.

When the next shot landed so close to the boat, it sprayed me with water, I stopped rowing. I really had no desire to have bullets make nasty holes in my tender body. I had to reluctantly admit they probably would shoot us if they had to. Hating myself for giving up, I turned around and headed for the yacht.

"Hold the ladder with both hands and step up. It's quite simple," the voice said pleasantly as if he were greeting guests at a cocktail party. The men from the dinghy stood silently on either side of him.

I reached under the seat, found the BB gun and stuck it down my jeans. It wouldn't be any match for a real weapon, but it was better than nothing.

"You go first, Maggie," Freedom said. "I'll be right behind you."

Thinking furiously, I grabbed a rung of the swaying ladder and prepared to step off. Could I still do something? Jump into the water and swim around to the other side of the yacht? That would leave Freedom alone to fend for herself. A bad plan. Think of something else.

"Come on, little lady. You seem to be stalling." A hand reached down to steady the ladder. The voice turned cold. "I'll not tolerate this much longer. Lenny, give her a hand."

"With pleasure, boss."

The man named Lenny started down the ladder, a grin on his face. My skin crawled. If he touched me, I'd kick him where it would do the most harm.

"Get away, I'm coming," I called and was surprised to hear my voice sound so resolute and in control. Slowly I eased one foot and then the other onto a rung and began to climb.

Four rungs from the top, a beefy hand reached for my wrist. I jerked away. "Don't touch me. If you do, I'll jump off."

The voice laughed. "A feisty one. I find feisty women a challenge. I'm looking forward to our conversation."

My head cleared the railing, and I had my first look at the man behind the voice. He was enormous, probably close to four hundred pounds, I estimated. Dressed completely in white, he wore a thick, gold chain around a neck that looked like the trunk of a redwood tree. He also had an amazing number of gold and diamond rings on his fingers. His thin, dark hair was swept back from his forehead and plastered down with something greasy. He smelled of sweat and whiskey.

"Welcome aboard the *Old Master*." He grabbed me by the arm and hauled me onto the deck as easily as if he were lifting a rag doll. "Now tell your friend to come up."

Realizing that, at the moment, he was calling the shots, I motioned for Freedom to follow me.

At the door to the salon, the man turned to us and said, "Please don't interpret this remark as intended to be offensive, but I can't help noting the condition of your clothes. His eyes traveled up and down our bodies. "You are both wet and," his lips curled in disapproval, "dirty." "Might I ask you to follow my man here," he indicated Lenny, "to one of our guest staterooms where you will find fresh towels, soap and comfortable robes."

This wasn't such a good turn of events. I stepped forward and said, "Now listen here, whoever you are. We have no intention of taking our clothes off. And I'd like to inform you that we are expected back on the island by now. When we don't appear, people will come looking for us."

"I see. You have called the authorities? Then we must hurry." He dismissed me. "Please follow Lenny."

"I said…"

I stopped when Lenny pointed a gun at my stomach. We were obviously dealing with a nut case. Nevertheless, the pointed pistol had its desired effect. I had no intention of being shot full of holes.

"All right. Just tell him not to touch me."

The man's full lips curved into what I assumed was a smile. It was hard to tell. Freedom and I followed Lenny down a corridor. He opened a door and motioned us inside.

"The boss said for you to strip down and throw out your clothes."

"In your dreams, Jocko," I said as I tried to shut the door.

"Or else we can help you if that's what you want."

"Try that and you'll be missing some crucial appendage," I yelled as I slammed the door. I could hear Lenny laughing.

The stateroom was obviously decorated for a woman's taste. There was a dressing table with a variety of perfumes and make-up, a pink and mint green upholstered couch and a pink, white and green striped quilt on the circular bed. The sliding closet door stood open, revealing white, Christian Dior terry cloth robes.

"What should we do, Maggie?" Freedom asked. "I don't want to take off my clothes."

"I don't either, but I don't think we have much of a choice. I don't want these thugs doing it for us."

"This is crazy, and that man is repulsive. He gives me the creeps."

I peeled off my T-shirt and stepped out of my jeans. "That's as far as I go," I said as I slipped on a robe. "If he wants the rest, he's going to have to fight me for it."

I put the BB gun under the robe and tied the belt tightly around it.

"What good is that going to do?" Freedom asked. "That won't make a hole in anyone."

"I know it won't, but I feel a lot better having it with me."

I realized that by robbing us of our clothes, the man gained a huge psychological advantage. As soon as we put on the robes, Freedom and I immediately became more vulnerable.

We fooled around in the room as long as we could, trying to figure out if there was anything we could do. I sensed that Freedom was very close to collapsing, and I felt terrible about dragging her into this situation. Suddenly, the whole hunt for Joey, Andrew Roop's forgeries and the Rembrandt had ceased to be fun. Ben was right. I was a reckless idiot.

When someone banged on the door, I had no choice but to open it. Lenny stood in the corridor grinning. I suspected his intelligence level didn't permit him to do much more.

He motioned us into the salon and, by waving the gun in our direction, indicated we should sit. Freedom and I took seats next to each other on a white plush couch so deep our feet didn't touch the ground. On a gold-rimmed glass coffee table big enough to accommodate a large picnic comfortably was a crystal decanter and several fluted glasses. Our host, if you can call him that, was waiting for us.

"May I offer you something to drink? I am not an uncivilized man, and you certainly must be thirsty after your adventure," he added with a chuckle. He stood in front of us, a giant of a man, his girth so amazing it completely blocked the light from the Waterford table lamp behind him. His face was baby smooth and his jowls wobbled as he spoke.

"I didn't realize I'd be receiving ladies this evening." He looked down at his white Mandarin shirt and baggy pants. "If I had, I would have dressed more appropriately."

I shuddered. In a bathrobe with my feet sticking off the couch, I felt like a small child listening to a parent's lecture. And I was sure the man realized this. He was good, but I wasn't going to let him wreck what little self-composure I had left.

"I should introduce myself," he continued. My name is Leonard Baron. I deal in imports and exports."

He poured two glasses of whiskey from the decanter and offered them to Freedom and me. When I shook my head, he said, "I must insist. It would be rude to refuse me and it will relax you for our conversation."

"I don't drink."

Particularly not when the stuff might have knockout drops in it.

"Really? How unfortunate. Again, I must insist."

I saw Lenny steady his gun at a spot on my chest. I raised the glass to my lips and took a tiny sip. I planned to hold it in my mouth until it evaporated.

"Good."

Satisfied, he stood with his hands clasped behind his back. The two goons receded to the back of the room. I noticed their feet left wet shoe imprints on the white carpet. Leonard Baron frowned. "Would you excuse me for a minute? I need to speak to my men."

My eyes roamed around the room. It was done completely in white; plush, white semi-circular sofa and matching armchairs with white drapes at the windows. A lighted curio cabinet in one corner held a collection of Boehme birds. On the two end tables were white porcelain figurines of nudes, one sitting cross-legged playing a flute and the other resting her chin in her hand. I recognized them as German Rosenthal. The only splash of color came from a vibrant Matisse painting on one wall.

I nudged Freedom. "This guy has a white fetish."

"I'm not interested in him," Freedom said softly. "How are we going to get out of here?"

Good question. At the moment, I had no idea.

The two goons left the room as Leonard Baron returned to have a cozy chat with us.

"We don't need them, do we? I'm sure we'll be just fine together. Now," he said briskly, "how am I to interpret this? I was to meet someone else here tonight to consummate a business deal and instead of him, I find you two waiting in a rowboat. Explain, please."

I put my glass on the table, pulled the robe firmly across my legs and folded my arms. Leonard looked grieved.

"Please don't tell me you don't want to talk. That could make things quite unpleasant. Perhaps your friend here would be more willing to cooperate." He glanced at Freedom. "Tell me, my dear, were you perhaps fishing?"

I pressed my leg against Freedom's thigh, warning her to remain silent.

Leonard looked from one of us to the other. "Will one of you be kind enough to speak?"

I cleared my throat. "We were in the marsh for reasons of our own. It had nothing to do with you. As I told you, very soon people will be looking for us. We'd appreciate having our clothes returned and we'll be on our way."

Leonard looked unhappy. "You disappoint me. I anticipated a livelier discussion." He looked toward the door. "Shall I call my men?"

I didn't just fall off the turnip truck, so I knew what he was talking about. If I didn't chat with him, he'd let his men play with us. At least that's what I thought he meant. Maybe I'd read too many mysteries. I made a decision.

"All right. If I tell you what we know, will you let us go?"

Leonard stroked his chin. "Possibly. It depends on how accommodating you are."

"A friend of ours has disappeared and we've been hunting for him."

"The friend's name is?"

"Joey Archer," I filled in. "We think Joey was somehow involved with a man named Andrew Roop. We also searched Andrew's house," I said, feeling foolish as I did so, "and found a message saying a boat would be at Broad Creek tonight expecting money or a painting. We hoped by coming here, we might find our friend. I tried a smile. "You see," I added with false sincerity, "our only concern is Joey. He's the husband of a good friend. She used to be married to Andrew. It's a long story and probably not relevant to," I hesitated, "your, ah, business."

"And what exactly is my business?"

"You mentioned import and export." Throwing caution to the wind, I said, "For instance, the excellent Matisse on the wall. Would that be an import?"

Leonard eyed me shrewdly. "If I answered yes, what would you say?"

"I'd say you have superb taste and a lot of money," I answered blandly.

"Maybe your friend would say something else. She hasn't opened her mouth yet."

I put a hand out as if to protect Freedom. "She doesn't know anything. The rowboat thing was all my idea. I needed help."

"It's okay, Maggie. He's not going to bully me."

"Bravo. The other one has some spunk too." He clapped his pudgy hands together like a child.

Emboldened by Freedom's courage and curious about the painting, I continued, "Andrew Roop had a very valuable collection of master-

pieces that has been replaced by fakes. We think Andrew sold the originals to pay off his debts." I raised my eyebrows in a question. "Are we
right?"

Leonard Baron didn't answer. He began to pace back and forth with
his head down. He seemed to be having a conversation with himself.
Finally, he eased his huge girth into an oversized chair across from us.

"Let me tell you what I'm so angry about. I have been promised a
Rembrandt."

As I opened my mouth to speak, he waved dismissively. "I anticipate
your question, but it doesn't matter where it came from. When I was
informed the painting had been obtained and I saw the authentication,
I forwarded three million dollars as a down payment. The painting was
to be delivered upon receipt of the money. That was on May 21."

I stole a look at Freedom. May 21 was the day the *Second Chance*
exploded.

"I can't tell you how distressed I was when the courier never
arrived."

In spite of my fear, I felt a little bit of exaltation. I knew Miss
Chalmer was trying to cheat us. I couldn't wait to tell Ben. But first
things first.

"This courier. You wouldn't happen to know his name, would
you?"

Leonard folded his hands across his broad middle. "It was that
Archer chap. The one you're looking for."

I tried to keep my face impassive. I needed more information. "Did
Joey Archer often act as a courier? I mean, was this some sort of a regular routine for him?"

The huge man looked bored. "He may have. The courier was unimportant, dear lady. I was only interested in the package he was to have
delivered."

Poor Tiffy, I thought. *This would kill her.* "Would you be able to tell
us what happened to Joey," I asked.

He made a tent with his fingers. "Unfortunately I can't. I'd like to have a word with him myself."

I continued to press ahead. "And the man Joey worked for? Would that be Andrew Roop?"

"I have business dealings with many people. Names are unimportant. Let me ask a question for a change. Would either of you ladies happen to know where I could find my Rembrandt?"

He locked eyes with mine and when I didn't flinch, he turned to Freedom who suddenly began to shake. Leonard settled back in his chair.

"I see. I'm afraid this is going to be more complicated than I thought."

He was interrupted by one of his men returning to the salon.

"Boss," the man yelled breathlessly. "I've got to talk to you."

Leonard waved him off. "Not now, Lenny. I'm busy at the moment."

"But boss. There's a boat coming fast from the north. The guy has to be a nut; either that or a cop. He's waving a search light and yelling something in a megaphone."

Annoyed, Leonard lifted himself out of the chair. He did it slowly, as if his back hurt. "Pardon me, ladies. I won't be a minute."

As soon as he left the salon, I jumped to my feet and pulled Freedom up. "Come on. While he's busy, we'll go out onto the deck and jump over. Anything is better than sitting here with this nut."

"But, Maggie. I can't swim," Freedom reminded me with fear in her voice.

"I'll pull you. I think we can make it to Buck Island and once on shore we can hide in the trees. There's a house, too. Maybe we'll be lucky and find somebody at home who can help us."

I opened the sliding doors, and we stepped out onto the deck. We could hear a commotion coming from the bow and a voice scream, "The guy is crazy, boss. Look at him come. He's gonna ram us."

From the stern, I watched the speeding boat clip the bow of the *Old Master*. As the yacht lurched, I grabbed the railing and yelled for Freedom to do the same. We watched as the mystery boat slowly circled and approached from the rear, a searchlight bouncing on the deck as if it were held by an unsteady hand.

"Quick," I urged, "find some place to hide. And lose the bathrobe," I said as I peeled off my robe. I didn't feel all that great about running around in my undies, but I didn't want the weight of the robe to pull me under the water. I held the BB gun in my hand like some female commando and yelled, "When I give the signal, we'll jump."

Footsteps thundered along the deck as Freedom and I crouched behind a chair, but the men were too preoccupied to notice us. From my hiding place, I peeked through the railing. The boat had stopped twenty feet behind the stern, its engine idling. It reminded me of a bull pawing the ground ready to charge.

Lenny must have thought so too. "He's gonna ram us again, boss. Let me pop him one.

The other man clambered up to the flying bridge and yanked the search light around to shine on the waiting boat. As the beacon reached the bow of the smaller boat, a shot rang out. The bullet zinged over my head and buried itself into the teak bulkhead. I ducked, covering my eyes with my hands.

A man appeared in front of me and shouted, "Hey, them broads are out here."

I whipped the BB gun around and fired at his fat stomach. He yelped in pain and tried to catch me, so I aimed the gun lower and fired again. He grabbed his crotch and screamed like a banshee.

A hail of bullets came from the circling boat. One hit the searchlight, which exploded in a burst of sizzling electricity and crashing glass. Somewhere, a man groaned in pain.

A megaphoned voice called across the water, "There's more where that came from. Now get your damn boat out of here."

I jumped to my feet. "Holy Batman, Freedom. That's Andrew's voice." I grabbed her arm. "Andrew is in that boat. We've got to do something."

Looking toward the bridge of the *Old Master*, I saw the outline of two men. Neither was bulky enough to be Leonard. I wished I knew where he was. If he was on his way to find us, that could be bad.

I made up my mind in a hurry. I cupped my hands and yelled. "Andrew, it's me. Maggie. Freedom's here too. Get us off."

In reply, a bullet ricocheted off the salon door and landed with a thud in a chaise lounge cushion. Another bullet missed the stern completely as it sailed past the deck and landed in the water.

"I'm going to fix you bastards," Andrew shouted, as his boat moved to the bow of the *Old Master*. A hail of rapid-fire bullets tore into the wheelhouse, blasting delicate instruments and ripping through the electric wiring in a series of ear shattering explosions.

From the other boat I heard a scuffle and a thump, then a female voice screaming, "No!"

"My God," I yelled at Freedom. "That's the *Moondancer*. He's got Tiffy with him."

I watched in horror as Andrew gunned the engine and prepared to ram the *Old Master* again. He had to be insane. Tiffany's boat was no match for the huge yacht. But an armed Andrew was.

"Andrew don't," I screamed as loudly as I could. "Freedom, take my hand and jump."

We hit the water between the stern of the *Old Master* and the bow of the *Moondancer*. "Just relax and let me pull you," I told Freedom. "Try to keep your head out of the water."

From the bow of the *Moondancer* a frantic Tiffany yelled, "Come to the side, Maggie. I'll throw the ladder over. Please hurry up."

I certainly didn't need to be told to hurry. The men on *the Old Master* had found flashlights, and they stood on the stern, training the beams on the water.

At the top of the railing, a hand reached out to grab mine. "Andrew's in the bow with some kind of machine gun. He's been drinking, and I'm so scared he's going to do something dumb."

With surprising strength, Tiffy pulled Freedom and me to safety. She then ran to the controls, threw the engine into gear and applying full throttle headed for open waters, creating a wake that hardly rocked the disabled *Old Master*.

CHAPTER 27

▼

Tiffany giggled. "I forgot to tell Andrew to sit down. I hope he didn't fall overboard."

"I didn't." Andrew appeared from the bow, soaking wet, but somewhat sobered. "You little bitch. There's nothing you'd like better than to throw me into the drink. Too bad for you it didn't work." He stared at my wet Jockey panties and cotton bra and at Freedom's black bikini briefs and lacy top. "Are we going to have some kind of kinky party?"

"Andrew, will you please be quiet," Tiffany begged. "Leave them alone. I wasn't trying to drown you. I had to get them out of the water," she said, looking at Freedom and me, "and get us out of there. Are they coming after us? Somebody go take a look."

Looking back toward Buck Island, the only thing I saw was the wake from the *Moondancer* as it plowed full speed through the water. After Andrew's crazy Rambo style rampage, I didn't think the *Old Master* was in any shape to come after us. Relaxing, I tried to smile.

"Are you okay, Freedom?"

"I think so. My right ankle hurts like hell, but otherwise I'm fine."

Wiggling my arms and legs, I checked my own body. Everything seemed to work, although my shoulders ached badly. I felt a bump on my lower back that made me wince when I touched it. I was also shivering.

"Tiffy, could we borrow some clothes? It's too cold to stand around in our underwear."

"Help yourselves to anything you can find," the girl called. "I don't think my shorts will fit you, Maggie, but I have a skirt you can wear. It's real full and has cute little hearts on it." She looked at our bare feet. "And some bedroom slippers, I guess. They're kind of stretched out, so they might be okay."

I was too miserable and exhausted to worry about what I wore or what I looked like in Tiffy's clothes. *Probably like a stuffed sausage*, I thought as I tugged the skirt over my hips. But the bulges didn't seem to bother Ben. Although, he had told that gallery owner I was pregnant. I ran my hand over my fairly flat stomach and remembered that Ben's hand had done the same thing a few hours ago. I wondered if he'd heard me ask for help. It didn't matter now. We were safe on the *Moondancer*. All we had to cope with was a drunk Andrew, but after the experience with Leonard Baron, Tiffy's ex-husband would be a piece of cake.

I added a plain white T-shirt to the skirt and ran Tiffany's comb through my hair. Freedom found a pair of navy shorts and a Salty Dog tank top.

The pockets of the borrowed skirt sagged. As my fingers explored the contents, an amused smile spread over my face. Tiffy seemed to use her pocket as a carryall. My hands touched a lipstick, two picture hooks, a pack of gum and some other stuff. I didn't stop to remove the items. Freedom and I hurried back to the stern, anxious to learn what had been going on.

On deck Tiffany was still at the wheel while Andrew sulked in a chair. Speaking to Tiffany, I asked, "How did you know we were out there on that boat? I shudder to think what might have happened if you hadn't come along."

"I didn't know. Andrew, here, hijacked my boat. He was ranting about some voice on the phone and a note, and then he got some crazy idea about settling the score with someone. I have to tell you, Maggie, he really scared me, waving a gun around and all."

"Don't start that again, buttercup. I'm fed up with you. At least I got the bastard." Andrew blew on his forefinger. "Bang, bang."

"I'll say you did," I retorted. "What in the world were you thinking of, Andrew? Some of that firepower sounded like a semi-automatic. Where did you get something like that? And by the way, where is it?"

It made me nervous to think Andrew might still have his weapon stashed somewhere.

Andrew smiled. "You'd be surprised what you can buy at a pawn shop these days. You have to admit, it did the trick. But I threw my weapons overboard," he said with a theatrical gesture. "I won't need them anymore.

"We should call the sheriff. There may be someone hurt back there on that boat," Freedom said.

I agreed. "Could we use the VHF radio, Tiffy? Freedom's right. If someone is hurt, we have to report it."

Tiffany didn't answer.

"Is it okay if I get it?" I repeated.

"Not right now, Maggie. I'm having trouble making the boat steer properly. Something's broken on the starboard side. I can't leave the wheel to hunt for the radio. Besides, I have to go somewhere."

"I knew it." Andrew slapped the arm of the chair. "She was all set to cast off when I got to the pier. She was all prettied up, too. Lipstick, and some stuff on her eyes. Where were you going, sweetheart?"

"None of your business, Andrew, but I've got to get there now."

He put his arm around her shoulder. "You can tell me, Tiffy. Were you going to meet a man? Maybe get a little? Who's the lucky guy?"

"Get your hand off me, Andrew, right this minute." Tiffany aimed a kick at Andrew's shin.

I decided to put an end to the bickering. There was a shot up, disabled yacht sitting on Broad Creek, possibly with injured people aboard, and these two were squabbling like school children.

"Stop it, Andrew. You too, Tiffy." I said as firmly as I could. "Maybe I didn't make the situation clear. This isn't something we can keep to ourselves. Soon someone will find the people on that boat, or they'll be able to call for help themselves. In any event, don't you understand? The sheriff will be looking for the *Moondancer*. I think it would be much better if we find the sheriff before he finds us. I'm sorry, folks, but the jig's up."

"You're damned right it is," Andrew yelled. "I don't know what's going on here, but whatever it is, it's not going to work." He grabbed my arm, twisting it cruelly. "What in the hell were you doing on that boat? Are you in on it too?"

"In on what? You're not making any sense. If you'll behave yourself, I'll tell you everything," I said, as I pried my arm loose.

Andrew alarmed me. His eyes had the crazed look of a man on the brink of disintegration. I began to speak as softly and reasonably as I could, hoping I could calm him down.

"First of all, where have you been, Andrew? We've been worried about you."

"After she," he pointed a finger at Tiffany, "tried to make me think I was going crazy and the note came saying I had to give back some money or a painting, I decided to get out of town for a while. Think things over. Things were too confusing."

I nodded. "I can understand that you were also very concerned about money. We know you sold your fabulous art collection and replaced each painting with a forgery. That man on the yacht was just another customer."

I touched him lightly. "It's not illegal to sell your own paintings. It's just sad that you decided to do it. I don't know what to say about the Rembrandt."

I expected anger, denial or vicious threats of retaliation for breaking into his house, so I wasn't prepared for bewilderment and confusion. He looked absolutely stunned.

"My paintings are not forgeries. What in the hell are you talking about? Those paintings are the result of years of careful buying. I know they're authentic. You're a damn liar trying to drive me crazy." He clenched the railing. "Christ. This is rich. On top of everything else, now she thinks my paintings are fakes." With his back to us, he began to laugh. It was a shaky, high-pitched sound that reminded me of a child close to hysterics. Suddenly he whirled around. "Are you sure you're right?"

I nodded my head. "I'm sorry, Andrew."

He seemed so genuinely upset, I almost believed him. He was either doing a darned good job of acting, or my theory about the sale of the originals was way off base.

"Tell me about the Rembrandt on the back of Anne's portrait."

At the mention of his wife's name, Andrew's face darkened. "That damn lousy portrait. I didn't want it in the house, but she insisted. And what Rembrandt? You're a loony bird, Bloom. Where would I find a Rembrandt?"

"It was tacked to the back of the picture of Anne. You have to know what I'm talking about."

"Like I said, you're loony," he snarled. "You need medication."

"This probably isn't a good time, Andrew," Freedom interjected, "but I should mention I think your wife is gone. Some of her clothes are missing. Her jewelry and luggage, too.

He rubbed his eyes. "That's great. I go away for a few days to think things over, and she runs out on me. Where did she go?"

Freedom spread her hands helplessly. "I don't know. She just disappeared."

"Andrew," I began, "are you telling us you really don't know about the fake paintings or the Rembrandt?"

"That's exactly what I'm telling you. Do you think I'd be crass enough to thumbtack a masterpiece to the back of a hideous portrait? I'd never do that."

Puzzled, I looked at Freedom. "Then who did?" I asked.

"I'll tell you who. If money is involved, then so is my lovely wife," Andrew said. "They go together, you see, like love and marriage." He glanced at Tiffany. "Although, I guess I wouldn't know about the love and marriage part."

"Then why did you swipe the *Moondancer* and go out to meet the yacht?" I demanded. "Weren't you trying to save the Rembrandt?"

"Because I wanted to end the voices on the phone and the threatening notes. I thought she was responsible," he said, scowling at Tiffany. "And that bastard of a husband. I thought I'd find Archer on some boat on Broad Creek."

I suddenly remembered I'd forgotten about Joey. I'd better tell Tiffany now about how I'd seen him on Daufuskie. Get it out and get it over with. Sighing, I said, "Tiffy, I have to tell you something and you're not going to like it, but please try to stay calm."

Tiffy shoved the throttle into neutral and let the boat idle as she turned to listen to me.

"Joey was the courier for the sale of some of the paintings." When she looked at me blankly, I said, "He delivered the paintings to the buyer."

She considered this information. "That's not against the law, is it? All he did was deliver paintings." She looked relieved. Then, like a cat with its claws out, she pounced on Andrew. "Where did you take him? And why? You're a horrible, horrible man, Andrew Roop. I hate you."

Andrew pushed her away. "Hold on, sweetheart. I didn't take him anywhere because I don't know what in the hell is going on. I didn't sell my paintings either. So if that bastard Archer delivered them anywhere, he broke the law for somebody else. And trust me, as soon as we find him, I'll have his ass thrown in jail."

"You're a liar," Tiffany screamed as she flailed at him with her fists. "You'd do anything to get back at me for leaving you. You want to see Joey in trouble. That would make you happy, wouldn't it, Andrew?" Tears flowed down her cheeks.

"Don't flatter yourself." To me he said, "Get her out of my way before she gets hurt."

Andrew wisely retreated to the stern of the boat. I watched Tiffy play with the zipper on her windbreaker, running it up and down. Her face was pale and drawn. *Tonight has been a shock for her,* I thought. *First, the shoot out on Broad Creek and now the news about Joey.*

We had reached an impasse. Andrew professed ignorance about the paintings and the Rembrandt. There was such tension between Andrew and Tiffany, I was afraid one might hurt the other. We had to call the sheriff, I reminded myself. The call was very overdue.

"Let me have the VHF radio, Tiffy." I looked around trying to figure out our location. While we had been busy talking, Tiffany had taken the *Moondancer* out into deep water. Far to the right, I saw the lights from Tybee Island. "Where should I tell the sheriff to meet us?"

"Don't tell him anything. We're not calling the sheriff just yet."

"We're not? What's the matter with you, Tiffy? We don't have any choice."

Tiffany threw the *Moondancer* into gear, brought the boat about and said. "I'd hoped to be able to drop you all off at Harbour Town before I did this, but now you've got to go with me. Don't worry," she called over her shoulder. "I'll let you off somewhere close to Hilton Head."

"What are you talking about?"

Alarmed, I tried to put my hand on the wheel, but Tiffany shook me off.

"I'm so mad at all of you. You've made me late, what with your shooting and arguing. If he's not there, I'm gonna be very mad."

"If who's not there?" She was making me crazy enough to tear my hair out. I had had more than enough for one day, and now Tiffany was acting like a nut.

"Joey," the girl said. "I'm going to get him and don't try to stop me."

CHAPTER 28

▼

"He's on Daufuskie," Tiffany shouted over the roar of the engine. The wind carried her voice to my unbelieving ears. "Just think; he's been there the whole time."

I gripped a railing for support and confronted Tiffany. "How do you know?" Or better yet, when did you find out?"

"He sent me a message, but it was all in a kind of a code. Only me and him knew about our special picnic place." Tiffany straightened her back in the pilot's chair, her blond hair blowing behind her. "We're gonna meet him at Bloody Point."

"I'm glad you know about Joey hiding out on Daufuskie, Tif. Freedom and I were afraid to tell you."

"You mean you knew? Were you going to mention this to me? I mean, weren't we all supposed to share information with each other?"

"I was afraid you'd be upset if you knew he wasn't being held captive. I can't imagine why he called May Day. He didn't look like he was in any distress to us."

Tiffy turned her back to me. "He was being held captive. He told me so. I don't like you anymore, Maggie Bloom."

"I'm sorry, Tif."

This was crazy. I was apologizing to someone who was about to load a wanted fugitive on board and make a run for the border.

"Where are you going to go after you get Joey? Listen to me. You can't run away. They'll find you, and it will be much worse for him."

"No, It won't. We'll go out into the ocean where no one can see us. I've got a full tank of fuel, or at least I had before Andrew decided to play commando with my boat."

"But Tiffany. There's the Coast Guard and other ships at sea. Someone will spot you."

I could tell by the determined set of Tiffy's chin that my words were falling on deaf ears. Defeated, I gave up.

*   *   *   *

There were no houses on Bloody Point, only the beach, washed tonight in silver moonlight, and the thick border of pine trees beyond the dunes. Tiffany brought the *Moondancer* as close to the shore as she could. Cutting the engine, she let the boat drift as she wrestled with the anchor.

"Y'all can stay here," she said as she removed the key from the ignition and put the VHF radio in her pocket, "or come with me." Without waiting for a reply, she jumped off the stern into the water. "I don't see him anywhere," she said. "He'd better still be here."

I watched as Tiffany ran in zigzags, softly calling Joey's name. When she started toward the dark trees beyond the beach, I poked Andrew in the ribs. "Go after her. We can't let her wander around all by herself."

"There is no way in hell I'll do anything to help that witch. I'm going to walk to Haig Point and get myself out of this loony bin."

"Might I remind you," I said, "that you are the one who shot up the yacht back there. I'm sure the sheriff will be delighted to see you."

"I said no," he repeated sharply.

"Then I'll go," I told him, knowing it was another stupid decision. For some reason, I felt a responsibility for Tiffany. The girl seemed too naïve to be able to take care of herself.

"Count me in, too." Freedom gave Andrew a withering look. "I just love strong, brave men," she said sarcastically.

"By the way, you're fired, Miss Lavender," Andrew said with no emotion.

"I've already quit, Mr. Roop."

Freedom and I were halfway across the beach before Andrew caught up with us. Bursting between us, he took each of us by the arm. "Changed my mind," he said as we walked three abreast. "I decided you needed help."

"Don't give us that," I said. "You're afraid to stay by yourself."

I had a question I needed to ask. "Andrew, is it possible Anne sold the paintings without you knowing it?" I was thinking about her rendezvous at the Nanny Hotel. She could have been meeting a buyer.

"I owned the paintings. She couldn't have sold them without my signature."

Unwilling to give up, I said, "What about the portrait of Anne? Did you commission it?"

He snorted. "Don't make me laugh. That thing was a pile of shit. She arranged for it and she sat for it. All I did was pay good money for crap. I don't know anything about the artist."

"Then Anne had to have something to do with the sale of your paintings, because I would swear the forgeries and the portrait were painted by the same person."

"What would you know about art? You paint crap too."

He was an absolutely charming man.

*   *   *   *

The three of us caught up with Tiffany at a dirt road.

"Please stop and tell me where you're going," I whispered even though there was no reason to be quiet. "Do you plan to roam around Daufuskie until you find him?"

"Yes, I do." I heard the determination in her voice. "I'm not leaving without him."

From behind, Andrew mumbled, "I don't know what you see in that loser. He's got himself into trouble and now we're wandering around trying to get him out. He doesn't deserve it."

"Shut up, Andrew," Tiffany shot back. "It's your fault we weren't here on time. If anything has happened to him, I'm going to blame you."

"Go ahead. Do you think I give a damn what you do?"

Tiffany turned and walked backwards so she could shout at Andrew. "Are you telling me you don't still want me? How about that day on the beach when you practically drooled all over me?" she taunted.

"You're a slut. A cheap, greedy little slut. I hope you and your husband get what you deserve."

I pressed my fingers to my temples. That's it. No more! They were driving me crazy. To Tiffany I said, "I'm willing to walk another hundred feet with you. After that, I'm going to figure out how to reach Haig Point or the Melrose Club and ask for help. I'm not going to plod around Daufuskie in the middle of the night with no idea whatsoever where Joey might be. I know you want to find him, but you have to realize he may not be here."

"Suit yourself," Tiffany replied as she moved away from our group. "I'm staying."

As we walked in silence, the wind picked up. Against the moonlit sky, branches of the oak trees lining the road swayed like goblins in a ghostly dance.

"You know," Andrew said, "this looks familiar to me. I used to come to Daufuskie with my dad when I was a kid. We stayed around here somewhere. This part of the island hasn't changed much." Talking more to himself than to any one else, he said, "Maybe, the cabin is still here."

"We're not on a sightseeing trip," I reminded him. "A few more feet and I'm turning back."

Suddenly a scream pierced the night.

"Joey!"

As we ran to catch up with her, I saw Tiffany throw her arms around a man's neck and hug him. Freedom, Andrew and I stood a few feet from the couple, allowing them a chance to greet each other.

"Let's get out of here now, Joey. I've got the *Moondancer* waiting, just like you said."

Instead of leading his wife in the direction of the boat, Joey buried his head in her neck and said, "I'm so sorry, Tif. He made me do it."

"Do what, honey? You mean this courier thing? We can talk about that later when we're safely out of here."

"No, I don't mean that," he said in an agonized voice. "I mean him."

From behind them, a man stepped out of the shadows into the moonlight. I had to blink several times to make sure I wasn't hallucinating.

Nathan Roop stood in front of us with a gun in his hands.

Tiffany shrieked, both hands flying to her mouth. Andrew raised his hand as if he were warding off a demon. Freedom and I simply stared.

"Sorry, brother dear. I guess you thought I was dead." When Andrew didn't reply, Nathan continued. "Too stunned to talk? Did the news of my death really affect you that much? Funny. I never thought we were very close." He took a step forward and pointed the gun at the group. "Could I ask you all to step into the cabin? We have some things to discuss."

Tiffany clutched Joey's arm, "What does he mean, honey? I don't understand."

Out of pity, I reached for Andrew's hand. The man looked like he's had all the air knocked out of him. He stood motionlessly with his shoulders slumped and his head bowed. I could only imagine the shock that he felt. I also couldn't believe we were tramping up the same path Lucy and I had explored yesterday. I carefully avoided the broken front steps.

"Get moving," Nathan ordered. In the cabin he motioned for us to be seated on the filthy mattress. "I hadn't expected so many of you," he said, a pleasant smile on his face, "but luckily, I've come prepared. Archer," he commanded, "light this kerosene lamp and tie them up." He tossed Joey a rope. "Tie my brother's wrist to your wife's and so on. Make it a nice tight chain."

When we were all bound to his satisfaction, Nathan tied Joey's wrist to Freedom's. "Do you remember this place, Andrew? We used to come here with our dear daddy. I'll bet you never thought about it."

As he talked, I watched Nathan. He looked exactly like Andrew: same thick curly hair, same facial features, but Nathan was more muscular. Where Andrew's jaw was weak, Nathan's was firm. He stood erect with his shoulders squared, exuding confidence and a touch of arrogance.

"So," he continued, "the question is, what am I going to do with all of you. Needless to say, you are in my way."

"I had to tell him," Joey blurted out. "He was at Bloody Point waiting for me," he said to Tiffany. "And then he said he was going to shoot me. I had to tell him you were coming to pick me up."

"You are such a fool, Archer. Did you think I didn't realize you were planning something? You are transparent, my friend. I simply followed you through the woods and waited for you to make a move."

Nathan dismissed Joey and turned his attention to Andrew. "I never thought we'd see each other again so I don't have an explanation prepared, but you're a smart man. You can figure it out."

Andrew found his voice. "No, I can't. Who died on the *Second Chance?*"

Nathan smiled. "A beach bum looking for a place to sleep. He was extremely grateful when I gave him my gold chain and Rado watch."

Tiffany gasped. "I should have known when I saw the foot."

"What are you talking about?" Nathan snarled.

"The dead man's foot. It was all dirty and tan and had dark hair on it. I knew it wasn't Joey or you, Andrew. Your legs are real white and they don't have hair. I'll bet, since you are twins, his don't either. I was really dumb not to think of that."

Nathan appraised Tiffany. "I'm glad you didn't. That would have been very inconvenient."

For the first time since we had entered the cabin, I spoke up. "You switched the paintings, didn't you? You had fakes painted of the originals and then sold the real ones."

"Very clever," Nathan sighed. Did you notice, Andrew, that your collection had diminished in quality?"

Andrew tried to lunge at his brother, but the rope held him back. "You had copies made of my paintings? But how? They were always there."

"It was easy. One needed to be cleaned, another repaired. For one reason or another, and at one time or another, every single painting left your living room." He chuckled. "My artist worked quickly. I think you will have to admit, the reproductions are very good."

"The bank account and the company stock? That was you too?"

"It was a simple matter to forge your signature. After all, we are twins. We look alike, we sound alike, and we can write alike."

"But, why, Nathan? I would have given you money if you'd asked. Why take everything I own?"

Nathan sneered. "Your charitable gift wouldn't have helped me at all. I needed big money, Andrew. Besides, I didn't want your charity. Where's the sport in that? It was a game and I won. You were too busy lusting after her," he waved the gun at Tiffany, "or drinking yourself into oblivion. You didn't realize what was going on. You didn't deserve those paintings."

"But why did you have to take everything I own? And make me feel like I was going crazy."

"I'm planning a new life. An expensive new life. Let's just say I found it great fun bilking you out of your money and watching you try to figure out what was happening." His lips curved into a smile. "You never did know how to live, brother, but I do. Sad, really. Now you'll never have the chance."

Nathan turned out the kerosene lamp and in the sudden darkness said, "At first I was upset to see you all here, but this may work out quite nicely. There will be another boating accident, I think. The Coast Guard will find Joey Archer and all of you on the *Moondancer* and decide Archer, a wanted fugitive, was making a run for it and forced you all to go with him. What an unfortunate explosion."

"You're a mad man," I said in a low voice. He really was. And not in a wild, uninhibited way, like my friend Lucy. Nathan was mad in the certifiable, padded cell, heavy medication sense.

"Do you think so?" he asked. "Perhaps you're right. But I'm a clever mad man. You'll grant me that, won't you?"

"Listen, Roop." Joey spoke up. "Take me, but leave Tiffy out of this. She didn't do anything."

"Ah, yes. The innocent Mrs. Roop. Forgive me, I mean Mrs. Archer. How noble of you. But no, I think you all must die. You've helped me out a lot, Archer. Much obliged. Now, please stand up and let's be on our way."

We filed out of the cabin like prisoners on a chain gang, with Nathan following, his gun against our backs.

CHAPTER 29

▼

I began to panic when Nathan slowed the boat to a crawl. Surely he doesn't mean to kill us here. We were in sight of land. The lights of South Beach marina flickered in the distance. He wouldn't risk blowing up the *Moondancer* where someone might see the explosion.

I had never felt so helpless. We were five against one and we couldn't overcome him. Nathan had us strung up in the bow like wet wash on a clothesline. Andrew's and Joey's wrists were attached to the railing on either side of the boat so that the most any of us could move was a few feet.

"I'll have to ask you all to come with me," Nathan said as he headed the boat to shore. He untied Andrew and Joey and indicated we should all move to the stern. "We're going to stop here for a few minutes," he said as dropped the *Moondancer's* anchor in the ocean across from Andrew's South Beach home.

As we trooped through the surf and across the dunes, I whispered to Freedom, "I'm dead if he looks for the Rembrandt. What are we going to do?"

"I'm going to hold my breath and hope I pass out," she replied. "That way, I won't see him shoot me."

In the living room, Nathan flicked on the lights and said, "You know the routine. Everyone on the floor."

Like a professor lecturing his class, he moved around the room pointing out certain details in the paintings. "You never noticed this, Andrew?" His hand stroked a portion of the nude's hair in the fake Renoir. "The colors don't blend well and the brush strokes are too heavy." He frowned. "The artist disappointed me on this one, but it fooled you, didn't it?"

I glanced at Andrew, who looked absolutely miserable. He sat on the floor in a dejected heap, shaking his head over and over as if he couldn't believe what was happening. I felt sorry that he was forced to listen to Nathan gloat over what a fool Andrew had been.

"Why did you bring us here, Nathan?' I asked. "To show us how clever you are? I noticed they were fakes the first time I saw them." That wasn't quite true, but I didn't feel guilty about lying to Nathan.

Nathan tickled my chin with the barrel of his gun. The cold metal made me jump. "I always worried someone would blow the whistle before I was ready to leave. It's a good thing you weren't a frequent guest." He glanced at the portrait of Anne. "Now it really doesn't matter."

I had to stall him. If he looked at that portrait and discovered the Rembrandt was missing, I was afraid what would happen.

"So you planned to fake your own death by blowing up the *Second Chance* and having the police identify the body as yours. That much I understand," I said. "But where have you been all this time? It can't have been easy to hide."

"It wasn't as hard as you might imagine. I used motels off the island, and once I even slept in my own bed in the guest house." He saw the astonished look on Freedom's face. "You walked right past me on the way to your room. I'd forgotten to close the door, and I thought you had noticed. But you didn't." He rubbed his hands together. "Everything worked perfectly."

Nathan touched the frame on Anne's portrait. "Now you are about to witness my greatest triumph, my greatest acquisition if you will. The sale of this alone would make me a very rich man, even without," he nodded to Andrew, "your little contribution. However, I don't plan to sell it. It will be my insurance for the future."

He continued his lecture. "Behind this inadequate portrait is a masterpiece, the likes of which most people have never seen except in world renowned museums." His eyes glazed. "Even I was astonished when I first saw it."

He's demented, I thought. *Demented and dangerous*. Beside me, I felt Freedom begin to shake. I willed my friend to control herself. *Please don't say anything, Freedom*, I prayed. *Please don't*.

"Where did you find this masterpiece, Nathan?" I asked. "I'm curious."

He stroked his chin. "I suppose it wouldn't hurt to tell. I was on a trip to Germany and visited a small private gallery in Cologne. The featured exhibition was of *Die Wilden* but, in a smaller side room, they had hung a group of lesser Dutch painters. The one I have here," he tapped Anne's portrait, "wasn't signed, but I knew who had painted it."

I didn't believe him. He was implying he had bought the priceless masterpiece in a gallery. That would mean he was the rightful owner of the Rembrandt and could legally sell it. I hoped Ben could prove otherwise. I had to keep him talking, so he didn't discover the Rembrandt was gone.

"How do you know so much about art?"

"Your questions are beginning to bore me, Maggie. We both know, my brother and I, a great deal about art. Our daddy saw to that. Remember the summers in Europe, Andrew? All those tedious summers of sitting in musty museums while our friends were blowing their minds with drugs. It paid off," he concluded proudly. "It was a simple matter to buy this from the gallery. The owner was a fool. He didn't deserve to keep it."

"How did you find buyers for all the forgeries?" I asked.

"That's no problem. You would be surprised at the number of people with almost unlimited resources who are anxious to add a masterpiece to their private collections with no questions asked."

Andrew tried to get to his feet, dragging Tiffany with him. "You set me up, you bastard. You were going to disappear and let me take the fall. Your buddies out there in the boat tried to kill me."

"Andrew," I said sharply as I shot him a warning look, "let Nathan finish. I want to know when he stole the painting."

I was afraid Andrew was going to blow it. Up until now, no one had mentioned the note or the yacht, and Nathan didn't know we knew about the Rembrandt.

"I'm sick of listening to him talk," Andrew bellowed. "He set me up." Andrew looked as if he were going to cry. "When I got that note, I had no idea what it meant. It scared the shit out of me."

Nathan stroked the barrel of the gun with his hand and smiled. "I assume our friend, Mr. Baron, made contact with you. I can imagine he was a bit upset, but tell me this, brother, would you have parted with such a priceless masterpiece?" Nathan shook his head. "That would have been unthinkable. I received a sizeable payment from Mr. Baron, which was meant to reserve the painting for him. I never had any intention of actually delivering it to him. I was very clever. I pretended to be you, knowing full well that when the deal went sour, and Mr. Baron didn't receive his masterpiece, he would come after you. I'd be in the clear, with the Rembrandt and a sizeable amount of money."

"I want to see this painting you say you have," Andrew mumbled.

"No, you don't," I yelled.

"With pleasure," Nathan said. "We can consider it your last wish." He reached for the portrait.

I closed my eyes. I had run out of questions and I couldn't think of any way to stop him from looking at the Rembrandt.

"You people are only a temporary glitch in my plans," Nathan said as he lifted the portrait from its hook. "The accident on the *Moon-*

dancer will tidy everything up and then I'll be free. Free, rich and unencumbered." He closed his eyes as if he were previewing the future.

"Ladies and gentlemen, I present to you a genuine Rembrandt." Smiling, he turned to Anne's portrait.

I held my breath and lowered my head. If he's going to kill me, I'd prefer not to see it coming. Poor Wally and Willow. I hoped Ben would take care of them.

I waited with my head bowed for the bullets to slam into my body. Instead, I felt Nathan rush past me. When I heard Andrew scream in pain, I opened my eyes. Nathan, his face an ugly red, stood over his brother with the butt of the gun raised above Andrew's head. Blood gushed from Andrew's temple onto the elaborate needlepoint rug.

"Where is it, you bastard? What have you done with the Rembrandt? Do you want me to hit you again?" Nathan shouted.

Groaning, Andrew fell back on the floor and tried to shield his head from more blows. The pull on the rope forced Tiffany to fall against him, her hand scraping his wound and her hair mixing with the blood.

When Joey saw what was happening, he tried to get to his feet. "Get her away from him," he yelled. "I'm coming, Tif."

Nathan pointed the gun at Joey. "Sit down! All of you!" A blue vein throbbed in his neck. "It would be quite foolish for anyone to move even a finger."

Maddened with rage, Joey ignored Nathan. "Come on, stand up. We can take him. He can't shoot all of us at once."

As Joey dragged me to my feet, Nathan fired. The bullet grazed Joey's shoulder. I watched in horror as a crimson stain spread over his shirt.

Tiffany began to cry hysterically. "You've killed him. You're a monster."

"He's not dead, at least not yet, and he's not going to die from this wound." Nathan aimed the gun at Joey's head. "Are you going to sit down and behave yourself, or should I let you have it again? The next time, I won't graze you. I'll shoot you dead!"

Nathan next turned his attention to Andrew. "I need the Rembrandt, brother. I need it right now. I'm not going to waste any more time with you. If you won't willingly tell me where it is, I'll beat it out of you." He raised the gun to strike Andrew.

"Stop it, Nathan. I'll tell you what you want to know," I shouted. "Leave him alone."

Nathan didn't hear me. "Hurry up. One last chance. You're holding me up, Andrew. I have a plane to catch to South America."

"Oh, really, Nathan? That's not what my itinerary says. Silly me. I packed for the south of France."

Anne Roop stood in the doorway of the living room, a small pearl handled revolver in her hand.

The blood drained from Nathan's face.

"You seem surprised to see me," Anne smiled. Did you think I was safely tucked away on the Air France flight to Paris? That would have been convenient, wouldn't it?" She surveyed the room, taking in Joey's wound and her husband on the floor. "Things seem to be a bit out of control, don't they Nathan? And you had it all planned so well."

"I never intended to leave without you, Anne," Nathan began.

"Oh? I think we would have ended up at quite different destinations. I waited for you at the Plaza and then at Kennedy. I have to tell you, I almost boarded the plane to Paris. At the last minute, however, I thought maybe something had happened to you. Luckily there was a Delta flight leaving for Savannah. I was able to get on it, and here I am. I was worried out of my mind, Nathan."

"The conversation in this room over the last twenty minutes has brought me to my senses," Anne rambled on. "I've been in the hall, listening."

"What are you talking about, babe?" Nathan attempted an appealing smile. "I have a temporary problem here. I always intended to meet you in Paris."

"You're a liar. I distinctly heard you say you were going to be free, rich and unencumbered." She inspected her fingernails. "Somehow I don't feel your new life would have included me." Anne waved her gun at the portrait. "And the Rembrandt you seem to be missing. You forgot to tell me about that, Nathan."

He took a step toward her. "I didn't forget. It was to be the last big sale. I wanted to surprise you."

"Get back! I don't believe you." Anne glanced at Andrew. "What did you do to him, Nathan?"

At the sound of his wife's voice, Andrew tried to sit up. "Help me, Anne. Get a cloth or something to stop the bleeding."

Anne stared with distaste at the blood on the carpet. "You really have made a mess, Nathan. You disappoint me. You were always such a meticulous man. So different from your brother.

I couldn't stand it any longer. From my place on the floor, I yelled at Anne, "For God's sake, do something about your husband. What kind of a woman are you? Can't you see he's really hurt?"

Anne's eyes narrowed. "Why do I have the feeling you are largely to blame for this situation, Maggie? You have an annoying habit of turning up at the most inopportune times. You and those damned dogs."

I nudged Freedom. "So I was right. And it was Nathan I saw with Anne in the Forest Preserve," I said under my breath. I felt Freedom press against my arm indicating she also understood.

"Just out of curiosity, Anne, did you meet Nathan at the Nanny Hotel? Is that where he was staying?"

One tweezed eyebrow lifted in surprise. "You saw me there? That disturbs me, since we'd been so careful. But it really doesn't matter now, does it?"

Anne smiled at Tiffany. "I see you have your little trollop with you, Andrew. Perhaps she can do something about your pain."

"Don't you care about me at all?" Andrew asked in a low voice.

"I'm afraid not, dear. You were much too difficult to manage. You know how I detest sloppiness. My life with you was just one continuous sloppy mess." She smiled at her clever use of words.

"Well, Nathan. I can see we have a problem here," Anne continued. "A Rembrandt seems to be missing and we need to find it. Notice I said 'we.' I have gone to far too much trouble for you, so I'm not going to let you abandon me. Don't forget it was I who arranged for all of Andrew's paintings to be spirited out of the house to your artist friend, and it was I who made sure Andrew never noticed. You owe me quite a bit." Her steely demeanor faltered somewhat. "I did everything you asked."

Eager to appease Anne, Nathan nodded. "You certainly did. I couldn't have done it without you." He reached for her gun. "Just give me that, and we can decide what we're going to do."

As Anne and Nathan chatted, I looked beyond them to the sunroom. Had I seen a shadowy figure moving out there? Since the principal players were in the room, I couldn't imagine who else would be skulking about. When a face appeared at the door and put a finger to his lips, I knew. Ben looked terrified, but he had brought a weapon. He waved the poker from my fireplace in the air and gave me a thumbs-up sign.

Feeling vastly relieved, I turned my attention back to Anne, who was now pointing the revolver at Nathan's stomach. "I'm not giving you my gun. I don't trust you, Nathan."

Frustrated, Nathan ran his fingers through his hair. "We're really not getting anywhere." With his foot, he tapped Andrew's leg. "He knows where the Rembrandt is. If we use a little more persuasion, Anne, he'll tell us."

"Give me your gun, Nathan. You can untie Andrew and take him somewhere to talk. I dislike violence." Anne paced in front of us. Her elegant, brown, patent leather Ferragamo pumps were a foot from my knee.

I jerked up my shackled arm and waved madly at Ben. Anne turned to deal with me as Ben burst into the room brandishing the poker and yelling, "Everyone get your hands up."

Behind him stood Lucy, wearing a long, strapless red evening gown, shocking pink boa and an orange, red and white turban on her head. She tapped Anne on the shoulder.

Anne whirled around to see what was happening and Lucy socked her with a very impressive right hook. Arms outstretched to brace herself, Anne uttered a very unladylike oath and pitched into Nathan, knocking him against the sharp edge of the mantle. He went down with a thud, crumpling into an unconscious heap on the hearth.

Anne's revolver flew into a corner of the room. Ben picked it up and said, "I've got you all covered." I noticed his hand was shaking. Lucy relieved him of the gun and, with impressive steadiness, pointed it at Anne.

"Don't move, sweetie." She squinted down the barrel. "Unless you want me to drill you. I haven't done that for a while."

She reached under her skirt, extracted a penknife from heaven only knows where and tossed it to my honey. "Here. Make yourself useful and cut these nice folks loose."

I was gratified to see Ben's first concern for me. As soon as I was free, I hurled myself into his arms and hung on for dear life. Under his shirt, I could feel his heart beating far too rapidly. He stroked my hair and murmured, "It's okay, it's okay," as if he were comforting a small child. At that moment, I didn't much mind having someone take care of me.

Andrew whacked the rope binding him and Tiffy together and then, in spite of his injuries, hurled himself on top of his wife, pinning her to the ground. His free hand flailed at her head.

"You're a bitch. A deceitful, lying, conniving bitch."

"Stop, Andrew." Tiffany pulled at his arm. "You'll kill her."

"She deserves it." Andrew grabbed Anne's hair and yanked her head back. "You are worse than dirt. You're lower than the lowest scum on the earth."

Anne tried to jerk away. I was horrified to see that one eye was swollen shut, and a trickle of blood oozed from a cut on her lip.

"Help me, Andrew," she moaned.

In disgust, he let her head drop to the floor. "You're beyond help, Anne. I wish I'd never laid eyes on you.

"That's probably enough, honey."

Lucy stepped over the prone bodies and moved Andrew aside. Drawing a silk hankie out of her décolleté, she gently swabbed Anne's face.

"So, how's it going, Ruby? Long time no see."

Through swollen lips, Anne tried to tell Lucy where she could stuff her hankie. Fascinated, I let go of Ben and moved over to the two women.

"Why are you calling her Ruby?"

"Because that was her name. Isn't that true, toots?"

Anne's reply was unintelligible.

"Remember the Purple Pelican, that nifty club near Savannah? As you know, I was a dancer. Those were good times. Really uninhibited and fulfilling. But I digress. Anne worked there too. Her professional name was Ruby."

"Was she also a dancer?"

"Not exactly, although there was probably a good bit of rhythmic movement involved in her line of work. She was a hooker. She picked up customers at the bar and took them to a motel down the road."

"Get out of town!"

"We had sort of a code among all the girls who worked there. We tried to keep our professional and private lives separated. If we saw one of the working girls," she inclined her head towards Anne, "outside the work setting, we would pretend we didn't know each other. All these years I've kept her secret, but pointing a gun at my friends negates all former agreements."

"Ruby, or Anne, as she now calls herself, left the island just about the time Andrew flew the coop. It doesn't take much imagination to figure out what happened. She "accidentally" ran into him at some club or party, he was lonely and unhappy, she was sympathetic and willing. And voila! We have the next Mrs. Roop."

Anne looked like she was going to be sick. She uttered a string of obscenities so anatomically explicit, I wondered if she'd had medical training. I have to say, I was stunned. I couldn't imagine the proper, articulate and extremely fastidious Mrs. Roop turning tricks for a living. But this wasn't the time to ponder the vagaries of life. We needed to get this mess straightened out.

I helped Ben bind Anne and Nathan together.

Andrew checked for a pulse on his brother's neck. "He's alive. Good. I want them to stand trial. Maybe I can recover some of my money."

I felt Ben's arms around my waist. Wordlessly, we hugged each other. I never wanted to let him go. But I had to. On wobbly legs, I tottered across the hall to the library. I had to call the sheriff. *There would be a lot of explaining to do*, I thought, as I picked up the phone.

CHAPTER 30

▼

Sheriff Griffey was not amused. As he settled himself on the brocade couch in the living room, I watched a scowl form on his face. I noticed the bottom of his pants were wet. Water trickled onto the sofa fabric, turning it a dark yellow. He pulled a ballpoint pen from his shirt pocket and used it to scratch a spot behind his ear.

"I've just come from Broad Creek," he began. "Would any of you happen to know anything about a very large, disabled yacht out there?" He gazed at our group.

Tiffany sat in a wing chair with her hands folded. Freedom and I were each perched on an arm of the same chair. Ben stood behind me, a protective hand on my shoulder. Lucy was in the kitchen, making coffee. Nathan, who was now conscious, sat on the floor, handcuffed to Anne. Technicians from the Emergency Rescue Squad worked on Joey and Andrew. Two deputies stood at the door, their hands on their guns. When no one spoke, I figured I'd better get the ball rolling.

"A man brought the yacht to Broad Creek to settle a business dispute with him." I pointed at Andrew and then moved my finger to Nathan.

"By him, you mean the recently deceased Nathan Roop, who is not dead after all?" the sheriff asked, looking for confirmation.

I nodded in the affirmative. "It's a fairly long story and a bit compli-cated, officer."

The sheriff tapped his knee with a clipboard. "Someone had better start talking soon, or I'm taking the whole bunch of you to the Beau-fort jail. Maybe a stay in the pokey will make you all more coopera-tive." After letting his last threat sink in, the sheriff began again. "Let's try this one more time. Which one of you shot up the boat in Broad Creek?"

Tiffany's eyes slid to Andrew.

"I did," he managed weakly. "I thought the person on the boat was trying to drive me crazy, and I wanted to stop the voices."

The sheriff looked disgusted. "Let me get this straight. You com-pletely destroyed a four million dollar yacht because you were afraid of voices? Mr. Roop, you'll need some serious psychological help after the State gets through with you. Anyone else want to help me out, or should I bring around the van for the ride to Beaufort?"

I held up my hand. "If you'll give me a chance to explain, I'll be happy to. I would like to begin, however, by saying I know we should have called you a long time ago." I gave him what I hoped was a win-ning smile. "I guess we all did some things that might be construed as being outside the law, but we didn't want to get each other into trou-ble." I glanced hopefully at the sheriff, trying to see if he was succumb-ing to my charm. "They weren't very significant," I assured him. When he didn't reply, I continued.

"It began the day Joey Archer disappeared. Tiffany asked me to help her find him. You were so convinced, Sheriff Griffey, that he had blown up the *Second Chance*, we were afraid you weren't looking for any other suspects."

After that, I told him everything, inwardly wincing when I came to the part about breaking into the Roop's house and taking the Rem-brandt.

"When someone pushed me into the marina and tried to pin me under a boat, I knew Joey wasn't the bad guy because he had disappeared. It had to be someone else."

"It was Anne," Nathan said in a whining voice. "She followed you from the Crazy Crab and when you walked around the dock, you made it easy for her. She was going to kill you."

"You mean to tell me you actually jumped into the water and pulled me under?" I asked her. In disbelief, I eyed her immaculate clothes and hair.

Apparently proud of what she had done, she said, "Of course not. As your big mouth friend pointed out, I don't have any trouble finding men who are willing to do small favors for me. Guess how I pay them." A frown of annoyance clouded her face. "Unfortunately, he bungled the job. You kicked him and managed to get loose. He hid behind a boat in the harbor until your boyfriend hauled you out."

"And shut up," she spat at Nathan. "You told me to take care of her because she saw us in the Forest Preserve and recognized you. You're just like your brother. Weak and spineless. I should have known."

The sheriff scribbled furiously on his pad, either raising his eyebrows or shaking his head as I continued my story. Nervous and worried about how he was digesting it, I stuck my hand in the pocket of my borrowed skirt and fiddled with the junk Tiffy had put there. I rolled my fingers around a piece of smooth metal. I pulled it out and held it in the palm of my hand, rubbing it back and forth. Finally, I finished my story and Sheriff Griffey stopped writing.

"Where is the Rembrandt, Ms. Bloom? You said it's in a safe place. Where would that be?"

"In the crawl space of my closet," I answered in a small voice, not daring to look at Nathan. "It's safe, don't worry. And it's dry," I added unnecessarily.

The sheriff tossed the clipboard onto the couch next to him and folded his arms across his chest. "As far as I can tell, you are all in trouble with the law to one degree or another. Nathan Roop for grand larceny and international theft, Andrew Roop for malicious destruction of private property, and Anne Roop for attempted murder and perhaps more. As for you, Ms. Bloom, I don't know where to begin. It will be up to the court to sort it out. You and Ms. Lavender did some pretty unorthodox things."

He looked at Joey. "You will be charged with malicious destruction of private property for blowing up the *Second Chance* and murder. Only Mrs. Archer seems to be fairly in the clear," the sheriff said. "I don't think a judge will punish her for trying to help her husband."

I gulped. "I didn't actually steal anything. I took the Rembrandt so that it couldn't be sold. Wouldn't that be considered protecting it? I certainly had no intention of keeping it."

"That's for the court to decide," he said brusquely. "You did remove it from this house."

"But it didn't belong to Nathan. He stole it," I protested.

Ben cleared his throat. "I think I can shed some light on the history of the Rembrandt."

"And who are you, sir?" the sheriff asked.

After he had identified himself, Ben said, "When Maggie told me about the Rembrandt, I went to Savannah to talk to an ex-colleague of mine, and he verified what I suspected. The masterpiece, which is resting at the moment in Maggie's closet, was one of three works, stolen from the Amadeus Museum in Cologne, Germany in 1997."

"German authorities felt it was an inside job because no alarm was tripped. Last year, an employee of the museum, who had been arrested on another matter, confessed he'd been paid $10,000 to turn the alarm off and allow two men to enter the museum at night."

Here, he paused to make sure everyone was listening. "One of the men fits Nathan Roop's description."

I nudged Freedom. "Can you believe that? He stole the painting himself."

Lucy appeared with a silver tray full of cups and a pot of steaming coffee. As she distributed the beverage, she said, "So, Bertie, I don't mean to hurry you, but are you about finished here? I'd like to get Maggie home. She's looking a bit frazzled. I know you'll have this tidied up soon. You've always been right competent."

Sheriff Griffey turned the color of a ripe tomato. "Sure enough, Flame, ah, I mean Mrs. Rotblumen. We're done. We'd appreciate it if you'd make yourself available for any further questions, Mr. Jakowski." The waiting deputies moved to take Anne, Nathan, Joey and Andrew into custody.

"Wait a minute," I said. "It's about the *Second Chance*. Something just occurred to me. Joey was on Daufuskie. How could he have blown up Andrew's yacht?"

The sheriff looked unconcerned. "He planted the explosive before he went. He and Roop, Nathan that is, cooked it up together and then Roop spirited Archer off the island. Roop needed a fall guy. Someone he could blame for the murder. Archer had no idea Roop was going to turn against him."

I shook my head. "Let me talk to Joey for a minute," I begged. I was all for tidying this mess up, but something didn't jibe.

"Joey," I said to the miserable looking young man, "You told Tiffany you had a call from Anne asking you to fix an engine on the *Second Choice*. Was that true?"

He shook his head. "It was Nathan on the phone. He told me to meet him at the *Second Chance* at nine o'clock. But I never got there."

"Why did you lie to Tiffany?

He hung his head. "I should have made up another story, but I couldn't think of one fast enough. I just thought Nathan wanted me to make another run." He looked up at me, his eyes as sad a Basset hound's. "He paid me good money for those delivery jobs and I needed the cash badly. I was gonna lose the *Moondancer.*"

"Joey, listen to me. This is important." I knelt in front of him and took his hands. "Did you plant an explosive on the *Second Chance?*" When he didn't answer, I said, "Tell me the truth, Joey. Did you?"

"No," he whispered. "But what chance do I have? He thinks I'm guilty." Joey nodded at the sheriff. "You won't believe this, but that morning I decided not to do any more jobs for Nathan. I was getting too worried about what Tiffy would say if she ever found out. After I started out to the *Second Chance*, I turned around to go back to the *Moondancer* and tell her everything, but Nathan made me get in a boat with him and go to Daufuskie."

"I don't know where you're going with this, Ms. Bloom," the sheriff interjected, "but you're chasing your tail. Who else had a motive? Archer was jealous of Andrew Roop. Maybe he found out Roop was trying to ruin his charter business. It's a clear cut case of anger and revenge. Stop trying to muddy it up."

As the sheriff talked, I looked at the metal object I'd been holding in my hand. I felt a cold chill settle over my body as the most unthinkable idea formed in my mind. Once again I looked at the object, rolling it between my fingers and hoping I was wrong.

With genuine sadness, I said, "He didn't do it, Sheriff Griffey, but I think I know who did." I turned to my friend. "You did, didn't you, Tiffy? You blew up the *Second Chance*. I'm right aren't I?"

Tiffy sat very still, looking around the room at the others. Every pair of eyes stared back at her. "What in the world are you talking about, Maggie. You think I did that to the *Second Chance*?" Tears filled her eyes. "How could you suspect such a thing? You're supposed to be my friend."

I rubbed a knot in my shoulder, which had begun to ache unbearably. "I am your friend. But all of a sudden, things begin to fall into place. You were even clever enough to try to throw all of us off the track."

Tiffany put her hand on Freedom's arm. "What's the matter with her? She's acting so funny."

Freedom pulled slightly away and gave me a quizzical look.

"It's a whole bunch of stuff, Tiffy," I continued. "First of all, and this is what surprised me, you're physically much stronger than you want anyone to know. I saw it on the *Moondancer* when you argued with Freedom, and certainly last night again when you took charge of Joey's rescue mission. That was no timid girl stomping through the woods. After spending the last day with you, I know you have a deep hatred of Andrew. Whether you realized it or not, you were constantly at his throat."

I tried to determine what effect my words were having on Tiffany, but the girl sat quietly, a wary look on her face. "Maybe you found out Andrew was trying to ruin Joey's business, maybe it was just because you hated Andrew, but I think you did it, Tiffy. And it breaks my heart."

"You're ranting and raving, Maggie, but you can't prove any of this nonsense."

"That's where you're wrong. I think I can." I held up the metal object and showed it to Tiffany. "Do you recognize it?" It's part of one of those flowered hammers with four screwdrivers inside. You know, like they sell at Fashion Court. If you look carefully, you'll see that the two inch screw driver is missing."

"So what?" asked Tiffany. "What does this have to do with me?"

"This was in the pocket of your skirt. I've been playing with it; you know, screwing and unscrewing the metal end, without paying much attention to what I was doing. Look," I said handing the handle of the hammer to Tiffany, "here's the big screwdriver, here's a Philips and the tiny one for jewelry. There's one missing. And another thing: each screwdriver here is daubed with a bit of red nail polish. I don't know why you did that: maybe to remind yourself that they all belonged to the same set. Whatever the reason, the screwdriver I found in the Andrew's empty slip also had a daub of red enamel."

I turned to the sheriff. "I'd be willing to bet I have the two inch screw driver that fits into this. I found it imbedded in the side of the pier where the *Second Chance* had been docked. I think you used it when you planted the explosive device, Tiffy, and somehow lost it while you were still on the boat."

Tiffany jumped up and threw the metal piece at me. It hit me in the face, stinging my cheek.

"You're a horrid person, Maggie Bloom," she yelled. Then Tiffany buried her face in her hands and began to cry. "He said he'd pay me five thousand dollars if I'd put the bomb on board. Hide it in the washing machine or somewhere, he told me."

"Who told you, Tiffy?" I asked gently.

"Him." She pointed at Nathan. "He told me Andrew was going to run Joey out of Harbour Town, and this would be my chance to get even with him." She ran her hand through Joey's hair. "I didn't have any idea my Joey was working for Nathan too."

"You promised me the boat would be empty," she screamed at Nathan. "I've felt so awful all this time thinking you had been killed. I just couldn't figure out why you were on the *Second Chance,* because you knew all about the bomb set to go off."

"Where did you get the bomb?" I remembered the book about explosives Tiffy said she found on the *Moondancer.*

"He gave it to me. Nathan. It was timed to go off hours later. I was so worried about Joey that day because I didn't know where he was."

I felt totally exhausted. My arms and legs were so heavy I could hardly move them. "Do you really hate Andrew so much that you'd want to destroy his yacht?"

"He wanted to destroy us, Maggie. Me and Joey." She gazed fondly at her husband who had begun to weep. "And I couldn't let that happen."

I felt tears on my own cheeks as a deputy led Tiffany away.

CHAPTER 31

▼

Brightly colored umbrellas dotted the beach, and sailboats dipped and rose on the sparkling ocean under a deep blue sky. Near the shore, sea gulls circled a shrimp boat, swooping occasionally to pick up tasty morsels.

I inhaled deeply, smelling the mingled odors of suntan lotion, French fries and sea air. I pulled my wide brimmed sun hat firmly over my head and stepped out of my blue beach cover up. My body had an interesting collection of bruises in various stages of purple and yellow, but I didn't care. It felt so good to be normal again. No unseen killer lurking in the shadows, no worries about a missing husband or an unfaithful wife and, above all, no bullets flying over my head scaring me to death. I took Ben's hand and we walked from the beach club towards Shipyard, Wally and Willow running ahead.

"You shouldn't have let them off their leashes," I said. "First of all, it's not allowed and secondly, Willow will run to Savannah if you give her a chance."

Ben squeezed my hand. "Will you stop worrying. You have to learn to relax. Nothing is going to happen. Look at them. They're not going anywhere."

It was true. Willow was almost underfoot, while Wally stayed close by, looking back at us every once in a while to make sure we were still there. They must have known something was wrong last night, and they're making sure I didn't disappear again.

"By the way, I saw an interesting boat leave Harbour Town the other day," Ben said. He watched a pelican swoop into the water and retrieve a fish. "It was named the *Magnolia*. Pretty serious stuff when a guy names a boat after a woman. Was it Peter's?"

I laughed. "It was. And I have a feeling he's going to be changing the name very soon. Peter didn't really want to see me. He just wanted some ego stroking. He's out of my life forever."

"Really?" With a sudden burst of energy he picked up a shell and tossed it into the tide. "Well," he said. "What do you know about that?"

I glanced at Ben. His tan face was happy and contented. A little smile played around his lips. I realized I owed him a lot. If it hadn't been for him, I'd probably be in jail.

As soon as Andrew had been released on bail, Ben had gone to him and persuaded Andrew not to press charges against me for breaking and entering. He's promised Andrew he's write a full story in the New York Times, describing the missing paintings and mentioning Andrew's generous reward for getting them back.

Andrew was so thankful he'd been able to get back most of his money from Nathan, he'd slapped Ben on the back and said of course he wasn't interested in prosecuting me. Or Freedom either.

He and Lucy had convinced the sheriff that I only had the Rembrandt's best interests at heart when I took the oil sketch. Then Ben had gone with me to my house, retrieved the Rembrandt from the crawl space and delivered it to the sheriff for safekeeping. Furthermore, he had called the museum in Cologne and advised them the stolen masterpiece had been found. The astonished museum director was already on his way to Hilton Head to pick it up.

Yes indeed. He was quite a guy. Ben began to smile.

"What are you laughing at?" I asked.

"I was just thinking about the mess you managed to mix yourself up in." He laughed out loud. "Rowing a boat out to Broad Creek to intercept a yacht? Do you know how insane that sounds? And how dangerous?"

"It really isn't anything to laugh at, Ben. I was scared to death."

"I'll bet you were. Why didn't you tell me what you were planning to do? I'd have helped you."

It was my turn to laugh. "You know that's not true. You also know what you would have said if I'd told you. I'll never forget the sound of my cell phone blaring across the water. I'm just happy you heard me say we were in trouble."

Ben tucked his arm around my waist. "And when you weren't at home and you weren't at Lucy's, she and I figured the next logical place to look for you was at the Roops'. You need me around, Maggie, to keep you out of trouble." He kept his voice light, but I knew he meant what he said.

That night we had dinner at Stripes restaurant, my favorite eating establishment on the island. Over chilled gazpacho and a wonderful grilled salmon, I relaxed completely.

"I'm so happy Freedom can keep her job. She really needs the money," I said. "Andrew needs someone to look after the house. He's out on bail, but I'm sure he doesn't want to bother with housekeeping details."

Ben took a bite of his steak. "It will be interesting to see what this Baron character decides to do. From what I've been able to learn, his hands certainly aren't lily white either. He knowingly bought stolen art, and some of his import business involved smuggling ivory elephant tusks out of Africa. I'd be willing to bet he won't prosecute. Baron may want to cut his losses and run, although I'm sure Andrew won't get off scot-free. There is probably an ordinance prohibiting semi-automatic fire on Broad Creek."

"You can bet on that," I said, my mouth full of fresh asparagus.

"And Tiffany? What do you think will happen to her?"

"Well, it won't be murder one, because it wasn't premeditated. Tiffany didn't know there was a man on the yacht when she placed the bomb. She might be able to get off with a manslaughter charge if she's lucky."

"Where is she now?"

He took a healthy bite of his grilled to perfection filet mignon. "As far as I know she's still at the detention center in Beaufort. I don't think she will be denied bail, but I don't know if she and Joey will be able to come up with enough money to get her out."

"I just can't believe it," I said. "I mean, Tiffy of all people. If you knew her Ben, you would understand how unlikely it is that she could do something so violent. We drank iced tea together right after the explosion and she acted perfectly normal. Of course, by then she knew Joey wasn't on the *Second Chance*. How could she behave that way, knowing she had planted a bomb and had killed someone? By the way, Lucy told me it was Nathan who had the title to the Joey's boat. He took it to guarantee Joey wouldn't get any ideas about turning Nathan in to the police."

I scraped up the last bit of scrumptious fish. "Tiffany told the sheriff that after she hid the bomb in the washing machine, she jumped overboard and swam to the mouth of the harbor. Do you know how far that is, Ben? You have to be really strong to do that."

He motioned for the waiter. "Who knows what motivates people, Maggie. Tiffany obviously had a very deep hatred for Andrew. And hate is a powerful motivator."

"I wonder why she didn't just step off the *Second Chance* and walk away," I mused.

"Probably because she didn't want anyone to see her near the yacht. From what I understand, she swam out to the boat, too." Ben ordered Stripes' famous bread pudding for two.

"But then she paddled all the way back to South Beach in a kayak. She must have been exhausted," I said, "but she looked so fresh and pretty when I met her."

Ben laughed. "She's young. What can I tell you?"

Over coffee, I had another thought. "Tiffy showed Freedom and me a book she found on the *Moondancer*. It was about explosives. "Why would she do that? It implicated Joey."

"Maybe she isn't as innocent and naïve as you think. It sounds to me like she was setting her husband up."

I shook my head. "That can't be true." But I realized it could be.

Ben drew little pictures on the tablecloth with the edge of his spoon. He obviously had something on his mind. Finally he said, "I've been thinking, Maggie. Hilton Head isn't such a bad place to visit. What would you say if I came back, say in October? I could rent the condo again and this time, maybe we could have an uninterrupted vacation. That is, if you can stay out of trouble." He shook his head. "I don't mean that. I mean, if you'd like me to come. I know I should have called and told you I was coming, and I shouldn't have criticized you so much, or taken so much for granted. I made a lot of mistakes, but I couldn't help it." He spread his hands helplessly. "I really care about you."

It was quite a speech. And talk about ego stroking. I was so puffed up, I was afraid I wouldn't be able to get through the door.

"I'd like you to come back," I told him. And since I thought perhaps the tiniest apology on my part might be nice, I added, "I'm sorry too."

He smiled broadly. "Well, then. How about it? Is there a chance you'd like to see my etchings?"

I stood up from the table and took his hand. "Yes," I said. "I believe there is."

About the Author

Linda S Clayton lives in South Carolina with her husband and two English cocker spaniels.

0-595-28101-X

Printed in the United States
94989LV00003B/274-291/A